WHICH SIDE WAS SHE ON?

Margo was part French, and perhaps that accounted for her elegance and wit. She was part Laotian, which gave her her smoldering, exoctic beauty. And she was all woman, as Marc Dean found out the moment he touched her and his arousal systems went on "go."

The only question was: Had Margo surrendered to his sensual appeal, or was she the sexual weapon of an unknown enemy who was far more interested in Dean's death than his desires?

Where did Margo's loyalty lie? For the moment, Marc Dean really didn't care—just so long as her body was where he wanted it. . . .

READY, AIM, DIE

More SIGNET Adventure Stories

MARC DEAN
MERCENARY
READY, AIM, DIE

#6

PETER BUCK

A SIGNET BOOK
NEW AMERICAN LIBRARY
TIMES MIRROR

PUBLISHER'S NOTE

This novel is a work of fiction. Names, characters, places, and incidents are either the product of the author's imagination or are used fictitiously, and any resemblance to actual persons, living or dead, events, or locales is entirely coincidental.

NAL BOOKS ARE AVAILABLE AT QUANTITY DISCOUNTS WHEN USED TO PROMOTE PRODUCTS OR SERVICES. FOR INFORMATION PLEASE WRITE TO PREMIUM MARKETING DIVISION, THE NEW AMERICAN LIBRARY, INC., 1633 BROADWAY, NEW YORK, NEW YORK 10019.

The first chapter of this book appeared in *School for Slaughter,* the fifth volume of this series.

 SIGNET TRADEMARK REG. U.S. PAT. OFF. AND FOREIGN COUNTRIES REGISTERED TRADEMARK—MARCA REGISTRADA HECHO EN CHICAGO, U.S.A.

SIGNET, SIGNET CLASSICS, MENTOR, PLUME, MERIDIAN AND NAL BOOKS are published by The New American Library, Inc., 1633 Broadway, New York, New York 10019

First Printing, July, 1982

1 2 3 4 5 6 7 8 9

PRINTED IN THE UNITED STATES OF AMERICA

I

Assassination Arranged

ASSASSIN, noun, masculine (it. *assassino*, from archaic *hachchāchi*, a hashish smoker—1560). One who kills with premeditation a human being; one responsible for the death of another. *If one looks closely enough into the eyes of an assassin, one can no longer see anything that is human* (Louis Aragon).

—LEXIS, *The Larousse-Selection Dictionary*

Prologue

Communist planes had bombed the hill village that morning, but in the afternoon low clouds blew up from the west and rolled over the rim of the escarpment, so the Cuban and Libyan pilots in that sector were grounded. The planes were old—subsonic Mystére II jets that had been resold several times since the French quit Indochina and passed them off on some unsuspecting Central African republic late in the 1950's. But even if they had been flying, they would have found it hard to locate a worthwhile target, for most of the buildings—drystone and thatch alike—had collapsed. The narrow streets were choked with rubble, dust lay thickly over the neglected paddies, and the parched brown landscape beyond was deserted.

There was more dust above the winding dirt road that led down to the village from the pass: an irregular yellow haze moving slowly around the curves and then out across the plateau toward the abandoned terraces and the bomb craters. At the head of the dust column was a small Citroën Mehari utility. It bounced and lurched along the rutted track, slid around a final bend in a shower of loose shale, and stopped with a squeal of brakes at the edge of a dried-up riverbed. A single wooden span had carried the roadway over the gulch, but the splintered planks now lay scattered among the pebbles that hid the meager trickle of water moistening the rocks below. The shallow door of the Citroën opened. A tall, thin man uncoiled himself from the driver's seat and got out. Although the heat had now become humid and close, he wore a Western-style suit, complete with jacket and vest. He stared at the wrecked bridge for a moment and shook his head. "Jesus Christ!" he said aloud. "That's all I need!"

He turned and walked along the bare earth of the river-

3

bank, looking for a gap where he might be able to drive across. Behind him, the motor of the Citroën, which had been running unevenly, spluttered and stopped. The thin man cursed. He had seen a place lower down where the bank was less steep and a determined driver might possibly force a passage. He hurried back to the stalled vehicle.

The corrugated bodywork beneath the tattered canvas top had once been bright orange, but now the paint was dulled, the fenders were scratched and dented, and behind the cracked glass of the headlamps the reflectors were rusted and peeling. The license plates were unreadable beneath a veneer of mud, but the rear panel bore a rectangle of faded blue on which white lettering spelled out the words "P. RAMIREZ, PLOMBERIE-ZINGUERIE, VIENTIANE."

The thin man's name wasn't Ramirez, he was not by profession a plumber, and he had not come from a border town between Laos and Thailand. He was in fact American, and he had bought the Citroën for two hundred dollars, cash, from a Cambodian refugee in Luang Prabang five days previously. He was still unsure which party to the deal had cheated the other.

He lifted the canvas-and-mica dust flap above the door and eased himself into the threadbare driver's seat again. The back of his jacket was dark with sweat where he had leaned against the scruffy tergal covering. Pumping the accelerator pedal with his foot, he activated the starter. The engine wheezed, moving slowly, like a man with laryngitis clearing his throat. At the third attempt, it coughed and finally stuttered to life. He drove to the place where he figured the riverbed could be crossed, gunned the motor, banged the gearshift into second, and sent the Citroën careering down the stony bank.

They were halfway across when the front wheels hit a patch of soft gravel. The car stopped bouncing and slewed sideways. The bald tires slipped, spun; the wheels churned up the gravel and then sank to the axle. The overheated engine stalled once more.

The American opened the door, swung his long body out, and crunched wearily around to the front of the hood. Maybe if he could locate a couple of planks and slide them beneath the wheels . . . ? But the car had sunk

4

in so deeply that the drive shafts were resting on the stones. He swore again and shook his head—a lean-faced man with a prominent nose and lines of fatigue etched around his gray eyes. Finally he shrugged and scrambled over the trickle of muddy water to climb the far bank. There was no point wasting any more time down here: it would take a tractor or a team of oxen to drag the Citroën back onto hard ground. "I just hope," he muttered furiously, "that there's still some son of a bitch in this godforsaken hole who's willing to be bribed or black-mailed into action!"

It was only a hundred yards to the first broken houses. Between the shattered walls, the air was acrid with plaster dust, sour with the stench of death. The American took a cigarette from a crumpled pack and felt in his pockets for matches. He struck one and shielded the flame with cupped hands, gazing at the ruin of the village square as he sucked in smoke. Blast had ripped away the front of a two-story house, allowing the sagging joists to shower chairs, picture frames, smashed china, and a striped mattress into the street. Farther on, a cloud of flies buzzed over the entrails of a dog half-buried in a slant of rubble. Nothing else moved among the charred beams and fractured stonework: even the scrawny fowls that seemed to have the highest survival count in the East had vanished.

Inhaling deeply, the thin man shook out the match flame and strode on. But he saw nothing and heard nobody. Away to the north, local militia were said to be making a stand against Khmer Rouge troops advancing along a tributary of the Pa Sak River. Whether or not it was successful, the peasants in this part of the range were evidently taking no chances: the survivors of the bombardment had fled, and the only ox to be seen lay dead by an overturned cart outside a roofless Christian church.

Why should they have bombed the hell out of this isolated village anyway? the American wondered. Was some fugitive Laotian anti-Communist leader supposed to be hiding there? Had they been tipped off to an illusory arms cache? Was it expected to be a stronghold of capitalist imperialism because there had been a missionary settlement there before independence and the houses were built of stone? There was no way of knowing. The nearest

5

fighting, other than isolated patrol action, was twenty miles away. Most likely the raid was simply a mistake: the fliers had picked the wrong valley and unloaded their lethal cargo on the innocent. Local wars in Southeast Asia were like that.

He pitched away the stub of his cigarette and lit another. Through a gap in the scorched and bomb-scarred wall of the church he could see the dull gleam of gold behind the altar. There were bodies in there, like bundles of old clothes among the splintered chairs. Huge splashes of red stained the whitewashed stone.

The American rounded the corner of the building and halted in mid-stride. The narrow, mud-packed lane beyond was blocked by a battered Citroën Mehari utility with its hood propped open. Another body was draped over the front fender, the head and shoulders apparently resting on the motor. Apart from the fact that it had once been painted beige, the car could have been the twin of his own. "I'll be damned!" the thin man exclaimed.

A sudden spasm shook the body. It heaved backward, then straightened up and turned around to reveal itself as a very large black man of about forty, dressed in khaki shorts and an oil-smeared bush jacket. "English, by God!" he said. "Spoken with a curious accent, but the genuine native tongue nevertheless! You wouldn't happen to have a spare Citroën carburetor about you, I suppose?"

The thin man gave a snort of laughter. "Funny you should say that," he drawled. "Right now, there are precious few things I could lay my hands on . . . but as it happens, a Citroën carburetor is one of them!"

"You wouldn't be pulling my leg, would you? You wouldn't have a fellow on?" The black man's own accent was unmistakably English of the kind little heard since the halcyon days of flanneled fools before World War II. He was extremely tall, demonstrably muscular, and deep-voiced, with a smile that revealed a flash of white teeth.

"Certainly not," the American replied. "I'm driving a buggy like this, but the bitch is bogged down in the riverbed. Immobilized. About the only thing that still works is the goddamn carburetor." He shrugged. "Seems reasonable to make one serviceable automobile out of two wrecks. Take the bastard, it you can raise the tools to get

6

it off—on condition that you take me too, wherever you're headed."

"Done!" the black man said. "We'll shake on that, eh?" He held out a huge hand.

The American took it. "The name's Mettner," he said. "Jason Mettner of *Worldwide*, presently on Southeast Asian assignment as a war correspondent."

"A newspaperman! I might have known it! My name's Edmond Mazzari."

"Glad to know you, Ed. What are you doing in this neck of the woods? Writing up the parade too? Or are you prospecting for oil?"

"Er . . . not exactly, old lad. Matter of fact, I'm on sort of a police job."

"A *cop?*" Mettner laughed again. "What the hell did they send you out *here* for, in heaven's name? To direct the traffic?"

Mazzari looked vague. "Not exactly," he repeated. "More of a guard duty, really. Protect Red Ridinghood against the wolf."

"*Red* Ridinghood? You don't mean . . . ? Not the Khmer—?"

"No, no. Absolutely not. Boot on the other foot, actually. Figure of speech, old boy. No more than that. . . . Look, do you think we could go ahead with this carburetor show? Every single jet in this perisher is choked. You can't go a yard in this bally country at this time of year without the dust getting into everything."

"Sure. Bring the tools and I'll show you where my little darling died on me." Mettner turned to retrace his steps.

The express-train screech had hardly registered before he was blinded by an orange flash. The ground beneath their feet shook to a thunderous detonation, and a cloud of brown smoke billowed into the air on the far side of the church. Tiles and fragments of stone clattered to earth all around them.

"Jesus!" Mettner said. "That was . . ."

"ZIS-3. 76mm cannon. Must have the glasses trained on us somewhere along the jolly old ridge." Mazzari gestured toward the distant rock crest just visible over the rooftops. "Probably think they're breaking up a secret rendezvous."

"Yeah, but why should they—?"

"Dust again, old boy. Followed you across the plain, if you came in from the east. They must have waited to see what you were going to do." The big man sniffed. "Viet Cong or Malay gunners! They'd've scored a direct hit three minutes ago if it'd been a crew supplied by the johnnies who sold them the gun."

"The Soviets? You seem to know a lot about artillery for a cop."

"Professional experience, chum. Know the sound of the old 76mm. It's war-surplus stuff, designed as an antitank weapon, sold off cheap to the third-world small-timers. Very distinctive bang." Mazzari flung himself facedown on the packed earth as the whistle of another approaching shell seared the air.

Farther down the narrow street, the wall of a house leaned outward, separated into individual blocks of stone, and then crashed to the ground. The roof caved in and disappeared behind a pillar of dust. Mettner was on his hands and knees behind the Citroën. "That was too darned close for comfort, Ed," he said when the echoes of the explosion had died away. "You figure maybe those Malay gunners got spelled by their Russian friends?"

Mazzari was coughing. "Bloody dust!" he choked. "For three flaming days—" They lay flat as a third shellburst smashed a crater in the square beyond the church.

"As the song says," Mettner gasped, "let's you and I go down by the riverside. If we can wrench off that carb . . ."

"Don't be a bloody fool. Fatal. They'd see us and knock out the crate as soon as we got to her. There's a cellar under what's left of the old mission. I vote we nip in there and lie low until the panic's over. They don't have all that many rounds to waste, you know. If we vanished, they might think they'd got us . . . and it'll be dusk pretty soon; then we can get on with the job, and do it safely."

"Okay," Mettner agreed. "Just so long as we're not left with a carburetor but no car."

"That's a risk we'll have to take." Mazzari glanced at the Citroën. "But if they see us scooting across the square, it should draw their fire away from this corner anyway."

The newspaperman nodded and scrambled to his feet. "Let's go," he said.

Bombs dropped by the Communist planes had blown

out all the doors and windows of the old mission and set fire to the thatched huts surrounding it. But the main brick-and-stucco structure was still standing amid the charred timbers. There was a basement at one side with a flight of stone steps worn smooth by the passage of countless feet leading down to the cellar entrance. Before they descended, Mettner turned and looked over the savaged rooftops at the ridge. Even at this distance the twinkle of flame as the gun fired was visible against the dun cloud background. The shell burst harmlessly on a piece of waste ground. "Good-oh," Mazzari said approvingly. "That was a couple of hundred yards away from the car. They must have spotted us as we took off."

The cellar was cool and damp, but even here the air was thick with dust. "I'd hoped the good brothers might have used it as a wine cellar," Mettner said with regret, "but I see we scored zero there. Boy, what I'd do for a drink!"

"My dear chap!" Mazzari produced a flat fifth of Japanese saki from the pocket of his bush shirt. "Most remiss of me. 'Fraid it may be a bit above room temperature, but you're supposed to drink the stuff warm. Do help yourself."

Mettner unscrewed the cap and swallowed a mouthful of the tepid liquor. "Hey! Not *bad*!" he said when the smooth, fiery spirit had washed the dryness from his throat and spread through his veins. "Not quite as thirst-quenching as a mint julep or a stein of cold beer—but not bad!" He wiped the palm of his hand across the neck of the flask and handed it back to Mazzari. "How much longer do we have to wait for the monsoon to lay this fucking dust?" The dark, vaulted walls of the cellar trembled.

"Hundred and fifty yards, I should say," Mazzari observed. He drank. "Yes, it's good stuff, all right. I'd prefer a drop of Scotch or a cognac, but at least it's better than that rice—" He paused. The next explosion had been considerably nearer. A small stream of plaster pattered down from the roof of the cellar. "Bracketing us," he said. "That one was on the other side. They're not very big shells. Ordinary HE, something like a British six-pounder, perhaps. Unpleasant enough, though, if one happens to be caught in the blast area with one's pants down."

Mettner produced some wisecrack in reply. He knew that it had pleased him at the time, but he could never remember what it was. In the same way, the only thing that he recalled of the direct hit on the mission was the brightness of the flash. It seemed to him later on when he tried to fix the exact sequence of events in his mind that this flash had started at maximum brilliance . . . and then slowly brightened even further, brightened until its intensity was intolerable and he passed out from the pain behind his eyes. That of course might have been an illusion produced by the concussion. What was certain was that he regained consciousness in total darkness: the slits up near the vaulting that had allowed a dim light to filter down when they came in were now blocked with rubble. Something heavy lay across his chest. His mouth and nose were full of dust again. "Mazzari?" he called faintly. "Ed? Where's that fucking saki?"

"Still in the flask, old lad," a voice replied from somewhere in the blackness. "Bottle's intact, thank God, but I seem . . . that is to say . . . some bugger threw me under a train or something!" A match scraped. In the circle of light cast by the wavering flame, Mettner saw slivers of wood emerging from a slope of pulverized masonry, a buckled steel filing cabinet sitting incongruously at one side of the rubble, a single star gleaming in a triangle of night sky exposed by the fallen ceiling. Mazzari was struggling to sit up. The slabs of plaster pinning him down slid to the floor. He coughed, holding the match high as he searched for his companion.

Mettner had been hurled by the explosion halfway into a niche between two of the vaulted arches. He was lying on his back among the debris. There were no bones broken, but one end of a huge balk of timber supporting the floor above had dropped, falling across his hips and immobilizing him as effectively as a butterfly in a display case. "A fine thing," he said as Mazzari staggered across. "He knocks down half a building to avoid a short walk and a little work with a screwdriver!"

"Come out of that corner fighting, old bean, and I'll teach you about screwdrivers!" Mazzari grinned. "It wasn't me took a two-hour sleep to shake off the effects of an economy-size Indonesian shellburst." The match burned his fingers and he dropped it with a curse.

Mettner grunted and struck one of his own matches. Plaster dust still swirled in the wrecked cellar where Mazzari had walked. Somewhere overhead, a cool breeze moaned among the ruins. "Why the hell should the Khmer attack a tiny undefended village like this?" the American complained as Mazzari maneuvered himself under the beam before the match flame died. "I guess it *was* the Reds firing at us, huh? And their buddies who bombed the place this morning?"

"Absolutely." Mazzari was shifting his position in the dust. "The loyalist forces don't have any big-caliber anti-tank guns in this sector—not even outdated ZIS-3's. Most of the detachments are lucky to come up with half a dozen old Armalites stolen from stores when your lads were in Vietnam, and a couple of Jap bazookas. As to the village, they say it was the birthplace of Ngon Thek."

"The ex-guerrilla chief? The guy who was made Minister of Home Security when the king came to power? But he's in Bangkok, trying to drum up support from the Thais."

"They say that too. But intelligence reports in a civil war are more rumor than fact. You're a newshawk; you should know that."

"I guess they figured they might as well rub out the village anyway. That way they have a fifty-fifty chance of getting the guy. Unless they did it as a hate gesture, what the Nazis used to call a show of frightfulness." Mettner struck another match. Mazzari had managed to wedge one shoulder beneath a section of the slanting beam. He was immensely strong, but Mettner dared not think how much the beam weighed—fortunately he was not bearing its full weight himself—or how much rubble it was holding up. For a few moments there was no sound in the dark cellar but the straining of his breath. Then plaster and small pieces of debris showered to the floor as the massive timber balk moved slightly. Once more Mettner struck a match.

Through the coating of dust, the bunched muscles on Mazzari's bare calves gleamed like oiled teak. The veins on his neck were corded and the muscles of his great shoulders rippled against the bush shirt as it darkened with sweat. He inched toward the lower end of the beam and heaved afresh, thrusting up with one shoulder as he flexed his knees. The remainder of the rubble slid from the beam.

"Swell! . . . That's great, man. . . . Couple more inches, and I . . ." Mettner gasped, scraping his body along the ground, dragging it through between timber and floor. "And I'll make it . . . out from under . . . this goddamn tree!" Shoes clattered on the flagstones and he finally pulled himself free. "Thanks, Ed. Obliged . . ." he panted. And then groaned in the blackness as the blood began coursing back into his constricted lower limbs.

This time Mazzari struck the match. White dust covered the American from head to foot, and his pants and jacket were ripped at the knee and hip, but apart from severe bruising around his middle and a crimson gash in the brow of his clown's face, he was unhurt.

As soon as the circulation in his legs was restored, they finished the contents of the flask. Mazzari then helped him across the heaps of fallen masonry and began to look for the doorway. The shell had burst somewhere in the center of the building, destroying the upper story and collapsing part of the ground floor into the cellar. But the outer walls were still standing, and it was simple enough to clear away enough of the rubble to permit them to crawl through to the area and the undamaged stairway leading to freedom.

The wind had blown away the clouds. Above the blasted roofs and smoldering rafters of the village, stars shone brightly in a clear sky. They picked their way over the wreckage and went back to the church. Mazzari's Citroën was just as he had left it. "Thank Christ!" Mettner said. "They can't see us now. Let's tread on the gas and make it down to my jalopy as quick as whenever. Once those carbs are switched, I want out of here, but fast! You don't happen to have a flashlight in there, do you?"

Mazzari laughed. "Funny you should say that," he mimicked. "Right now there are precious few things I could lay my hands on . . . but, yes, as it happens, a flashlight *is* one of them." He reached into the rear of the utility and produced a small, flat torch.

"Great," Mettner said. "Bring the tools, and we're on our way."

It was an eerie task, dismantling the carburetor of the American's car in the dark, with only the thin beam of light escaping between the fingers of his hand to guide them. It was unlikely that the Communist gunners on the ridge would be keeping watch at night; they might even have withdrawn altogether, finding no resistance in the village while Mettner and Mazzari were buried beneath the mission. But there was always the risk that an unguarded light could bring an artillery barrage down on them, and they thought it more prudent to mask the beam—just in case a lookout was posted on the heights.

The nuts and bolts fixing the mechanism to the inlet manifold were reluctant to move. Screwdrivers and wrenches slipped and skidded in the obscurity, and soon both men were nursing bleeding knuckles. Apart from the chink of metal on metal and the smothered curses of one man or the other, there was no sound but the rustle of wind in dried grasses and a faint chuckle of water beneath the stones forming the riverbed. Mettner finally succeeded in disconnecting the fuel feed from the float chamber. Liquid splashed to the ground, and the thin aromatic stink of gasoline swamped the odors of defeat and corruption carried on the breeze. Soon afterward, the first of the bolts locating the blackplate loosened. "Thank Christ!" Mettner said for the second time. "Five more minutes and the bastard should be off. All we have to do then is sneak back to the village and play the whole scene over."

In the narrow lane behind the church they permitted themselves a wider beam of light. Mazzari, furthermore, had already started work on his carburetor before. Even so, it was another half-hour before they were successfully interchanged. "There you go," Mettner said, tightening the final joint in the fuel line. "I was on my way to do an eyewitnesser on the fighting in Pa Sak province. If it's not being indiscreet, what the hell kind of work brings a *policeman*—an African policeman—to this village?"

Mazzari was in the driving seat, fiddling with the controls. "Not actually a member of the constabulary," he said absently. "What I meant to convey—doing a job of poli*cing*. I say, would you mind awfully giving us a shove? There's a slope at the end of the street, and the battery's pretty wonky. I'd rather not risk exhausting it, and it'll be a while before she sucks up enough juice to fill the float chamber of the new carb. Quite apart from the noise that starter makes."

"You're not after Ngon Thek?"

"God, no. Absolutely not. Nothing to do with the chap. Nothing to do with this blasted village, if it comes to that. The car just happened to die on me here. No, I told you: kind of a bodyguard job."

"Okay. A bodyguard. Whose body? Here in Muong-Thang?"

"The fellow that signs the check. Look . . . I really think we should push on. I'd like to be quite a few miles away by the time the sun rises. Mind your knuckles on the tailgate handle."

Mettner grinned. "I guess I know when a guy's stalling me. If it's all that secret, why not just say, 'No comment'?" He moved around to the back of the Citroën. Leaned down to place his hands on the rear panel, and then suddenly straightened up. "Just a minute." he said. "Mazzari? Bodyguard? Writing out the check; paying for your 'police' work? *Mazzari!* I knew I'd heard that name before. We didn't meet, but surely you were on that terrorist job in Corsica last fall? You're a mercenary . . . you work for that guy Dean. Marc Dean. Isn't that right?"

"Hole in one, old boy," the voice from the front of the car said cheerfully. "Bravo! Not to say work *for*. We're all free-lances, but I've worked with the Colonel a number of times, yes."

"And you're working together here, now?"

"I'm afraid that's classified information," Mazzari said. "If you wouldn't mind giving her a bit of a heave . . ."

The car was light and the roadway relatively smooth. Even so, Mettner was drenched in sweat by the time he had pushed it the seventy or eighty yards to the top of the grade. The noise, when Mazzari let in the clutch and the motor caught, was ear-shattering after the silence of the deserted village. Since their return from the riverbed they had heard nothing but the distant hoot of a night bird and an occasional stealthy rustle as wreckage settled or rats moved among the dead.

"The headlamps are blinkered," Mazzari said. "Government orders in time of war an' all that. Should we take a chance and use 'em? Or would you rather play safe and do without? I think I could kind of feel my way by starlight—if you walked ahead with the torch."

"Take a chance," Mettner said. "I've had just about enough of this dump." He tossed the canvas holdall he had salvaged from his own car into the back and climbed in beside the big man. Mazzari shoved the lever into first, switched on the lights, and sent the Citroën grinding down the incline.

Mettner swung around in his seat and stared anxiously out the clouded perspex panel in back of the canvas top. But no gun flashes brightened the hard line of the escarpment bulked against the starry sky; no orange shellbursts charted their progress across the darkened countryside.

The road was rutted and at times rocky, the spread of light cast by the hooded lamps limited. For a long time they could average no more than fifteen miles per hour. But at least they spiraled down a scrub-covered hillside and passed through another village. This one was more typical of Indochina: mud walls and thatched roofs around a central market. It was undamaged, but the place looked as deserted as the first. Beyond it, nevertheless, the terrain altered dramatically. Now the track wound between steep, wooded hills corrugated by closely packed terraces where every available square foot of earth was cultivated. They had left the plateau and were driving down into the monsoon forest.

" 'Muong-Thang: a small buffer state between Thailand and the Khmer Republic, only recently granted autonomy,' " Mettner quoted scornfully. " 'The capital, Am-Phallang, population 65,000, is the only industrial center in what is largely an agricultural region,' it says in the *Worldwide* morgue." He sighed theatrically. "And do you suppose I'd be heading for that capital even for one night if it wasn't for . . . We *are* heading that way, aren't we?"

"If the route isn't cut," Mazzari said. "Since, like every other Southeast Asian country, they have Red trouble, one never knows." He negotiated a sharp curve and shifted into fourth gear for the first time in five miles. "If you're headed for Am-Phallang," he said casually, "how come you're up in this part of the country? Wouldn't it have been simpler just to fly there?"

"I was already in northern Laos," Mettner said. "Color-supplement special. Now that the war clouds have

15

withdrawn, how do these simple, lovable people rebuild their age-old traditional life in the shadow of the Electronic Age? Then the simple, lovable people of Muong-Thang, aided by certain left-wing neighbors, decided they wanted to chuck out their king. Rebellion and civil war." He shook his head. "Folks will do anything to get on television."

"So you decided to drive down and see what's cooking?"

"That's about the size of it. Come to that, if you're headed for Am-Phallang yourself, why didn't *you* fly there?"

"Airport people too heavily into security checks. It's important that I stay . . . er . . . incognito. Doing another color piece, are you?"

"Tell you the truth," said Mettner, "we got a tipoff that there's likely to be an assassination attempt, heavily financed from outside, on his royal majesty. Send Mettner, the man on the spot."

Mazzari laughed his deep, rumbling laugh. "Tell you the truth," he echoed, "on condition you promise not to use it—I'm here to squash that attempt!"

Less than a minute later—the road was arrowing through flat paddy fields that stretched away to a line of distant hills in the east—a battery of 88mm antitank guns opened fire on them.

1 Marc Dean

The girl's voice was as mellow as the recorded chimes preceding it. *"Pan-Asiatic Airlines announce the departure of their Flight PS-977 for Honolulu and Tokyo, with connections for Hanoi, Karachi, and Cairo. Will passengers with boarding passes please proceed to Gate 27 in the departure lounge. . . . This is the second and last call for Pan-Asiatic Flight PS-977. . . .*

Most of the international travelers heading west across the Pacific from San Francisco had already crowded into the lounge, clutching their plastic sacks of off-duty liquor and cigarettes. But a trickle of late arrivals was still hurrying up to the immigration desks, milling impatiently outside the security-check booths as they waited for the routine electronic scan for arms or explosives. Among them was a tall, husky man in his late thirties. He was pale-haired and his features were rugged. Six feet and around one-eighty, the passport-control officer noted automatically as he handed back the ID document. Name of Marcus Matthew Dean, born June 6, 1944, at Johnstown, New York. In the space left for profession were the words "Military Adviser."

The guy looked tough, all right, the officer thought, watching the lean, muscular figure stride toward the booths, but he didn't have too much of a military air about him.

He was wearing handmade British chukka boots with tan whipcord slacks, and there was a black turtleneck sweater beneath his sand-colored suede windbreaker. None of the items in his lightweight nylon grip bothered the cop with the Geiger counter, although in fact some of the things that made the device bleep—the barrel of an old-fashioned fountain pen, part of an electric-razor mechanism, certain components from a set of mathe-

17

matical instruments—could be assembled into a small spring gun firing a metal bolt that would knock a man out at anything from three to five yards.

On the far side of the booth two large, smooth-faced young civilians stepped forward. "Mr. Marcus Dean?" one inquired politely.

"Yes?" Dean frowned. "I'm in kind of a hurry. They already called my flight twice."

"Your passport, please."

Dean stared at the two men. Dark suits, white button-down shirts, sober neckties. "What the hell for?" he demanded. "I already showed—"

A leather folder snapped open. Inside was a card behind a cellophane window; a photo and a seal. "FBI?" Dean exclaimed. "What would you guys want with me?" He looked at them again. It figured. They were the kind of men you saw walking beside the President's automobile in motorcades.

The man with the folder took Dean's passport, flipped over the pages, glanced from the photo to Dean's face, and then slid the passport into his pocket. "If you would just step this way . . ." he said.

"I aim to make that plane," said Dean. They didn't exactly crowd him, there was no question of manhandling, but pressure was exerted in some subtle, professional way, and the three of them were walking toward a flush-fitting door set in the lounge wall at one side of the entrance to the men's room.

"Just tell me what this is all about," Dean said tightly. "That passport's one hundred percent in order, and you know it. My visit was strictly personal: a meeting with my ex-wife. You've got no call to—"

"You won't be kept long, Mr. Dean," the man with the folder said. His companion opened the door.

The room on the far side was about fifteen feet square. It had copper-screened fluorescent lighting in the ceiling. The walls were cream and the floor was covered in brown General Services Administration carpeting. Apart from three tubular chrome chairs and a gray steel desk, it was unfurnished. The top of the desk held a press-putton telephone and nothing else. Behind it stood a thin man with pale eyes and a prominent nose.

Dean walked two paces into the room and stopped dead. "Quinnel!" he exclaimed. "What the hell goes on? What are *you* doing here? What the fuck are you playing at?"

Hugh Quinnel was as tall as the other three men but otherwise as different physically as could be. His baggy tweed jacket hung loose on his spare frame. The cuffs of his out-of-style gray flannel pants ended at ankle height. Above and behind his bladelike nose an unruly tuft of hair fanned out on the crown of his head. He looked more like an overgrown schoolkid than a top undercover man, but he was in fact heavily into the CIA hierarchy; on several occasions—very unofficially, of course—he had worked with Dean on the combat leader's trickier missions. "All right, Dean," he said now. "Cool it. No need to blow your top."

"I need to make that goddamn plane," said Dean angrily. "And, just for kicks, I'd like to know by what right you haul me in here—"

"You'll make it."

"But they already called the final—"

"Look." Quinnel nodded toward the wall at one side of the door, where a one-way mirror permitted those in the office to survey the departure lounge unobserved. The FBI agent with the folder laid Dean's passport on the desk; his colleague had closed the door and leaned his broad shoulders against it. The honeyed voice intoning through the PA speakers announced: "*. . . positively the last call for Pan-Asiatic Flight PS-977. Will Mr. Marcus Dean please report at once to Gate 27. . . . Flight PS-977 boarding now for Honolulu and Tokyo. Will Mr. Dean please report . . .*"

"What did I tell you?" Dean was furious.

Quinnel simply pointed at the glass. Dean saw a tall, muscular man burst through the curtained exit from a security booth and hurry across the deserted lounge. The man had close-cropped blond hair. He was dressed in tan whipcord slacks, a black turtleneck sweater, and a sandcolored suede windbreaker. He was carrying a nylon grip identical to Dean's own. The Pan-Asiatic stewardess hustled him through the doors, hooked a cord across the exit, and followed him out of sight.

"There you are," said Quinnel. "You made the plane."

19

Dean stared at him.

Quinnel grinned, exposing large yellow teeth. " 'Kay," he said. "No need to worry. No need to get sore. If necessary, we'll fly you there in USA-1. Make a special trip. But first I want to have you meet a guy. He has a proposition that could interest you."

"But, for Pete's sake, what's the idea . . . ?" Dean gestured helplessly at the empty lounge.

"The ringer? You take the job, and it could be a good idea to make folks think you went to Cairo the way you planned. That guy will make your connection in Tokyo, go through the Egyptian immigration—and get lost. So, okay: Marc Dean hightailed it for the Middle East; folks won't tie him in with my friend's proposition."

"What folks?"

Quinnel shrugged, the loose jacket riding up on his bony shoulders. "Anyone who was interested in this guy's reasons for being here in the U.S.," he said vaguely.

"Of course, you couldn't have contacted me before? You couldn't have located me while I was here and avoided all this . . . this comic-strip routine? I've only been in town nine days."

Quinnel shook his head. "This thing only came up yesterday," he replied. "By the time the dragnet was out and we had you fingered, you'd already left your hotel on the way to the airport."

Dean sighed. "Okay," he said. "I'll buy it. Lay it on me."

The CIA man lowered himself into a chair behind the desk. "Take a seat," he said. "I guess that's all for now, fellows. Thanks for your help. Appreciate it." The FBI agents nodded briefly and left.

Dean sat. He was still annoyed, the way anyone is whose plans are unexpectedly changed, whose preconceived idea of the course of events during the next few hours is abruptly upset. Whether the alteration is advantageous or not, there remains always a residue of wistfulness, a subconscious—if illogical—regret for the routine that has been fouled up. On the other hand, he was in business to consider propositions, even unexpected ones—and few of those he received could be guessed in advance. If Quinnel was putting something his way, it would be churlish not to listen. And pointless to get mad at the man, however offbeat his approach . . . and despite the fact that he would certainly have at least one ulterior motive in suggesting Dean for the job.

"The king," Quinnel was saying. "We got word that the comrades are funding a high-powered scheme to write him out of the script."

"The king?"

"The All Highest Kao Dinh, King-Emperor of Muong-Thang. You know where that is?"

"Sure. It's the new buffer state between Thailand and the Khmer Republic, right? Kind of a long, thin triangle of country, reaching practically up to Laos. Do I score?"

Quinnel nodded. "Independent by UN vote a couple of years ago. The base of the triangle is a flat stretch of coastline, mostly monsoon delta, separating the Siamese from the Khmers. So it's useful as a balance between right and left, if you get my meaning. Especially as the king's party is a little way our side of center. You familiar with the reasoning that created the place a separate state?"

"No. But you're going to tell me, aren't you?" Dean invited.

Quinnel clasped his large hands on the empty desktop. The sleeves of his jacket were too short, exposing several inches of wrist. The pale flesh there and on the backs of the hands was downed with hair that was almost without color. "I'll keep the history lesson short," he rapped with his usual machine-gun delivery. "Main reasons for granting autonomy were, one, ethnic. Like over half the population have ties with the Annamites, on the other side of the Indochina peninsula. Two, religious. It seems the missionaries crowded the place out during the last century like Grand Central Station on a Friday night. Result: a society that's largely Christian, surrounded by Buddhists, Muslims, Marxists yet. Shows up even in the architecture, they tell me. Lot more stone houses among the wood and thatch. In the sticks, that is. Am-Phallang's like any other postwar city in Southeast Asia."

"You said 'largely Christian,'" Dean prompted. "I guess that means his majesty's crew vote that way, huh? But there's a sizable body of opposition from those other minorities?"

"Check. You know the region, don't you?"

"Some." The combat leader smiled faintly. His military

decorations had been won during the Tet offensive in Vietnam, on the other side of the peninsula. After a spell with the Peace Corps, he had returned to Indochina as an AID "pacification specialist" in 1972 and 1973. From secret bases deep in supposedly neutral Cambodia he had relayed information used by General Westmoreland in the saturation raids on the Ho Chi Minh Trail whose existence nobody would admit. He had revisited Cambodia once since it was transformed into the Khmer Republic—on a fact-finding mission for Amnesty International. "You could say I have a rough idea of the terrain," he added.

" 'Kay." Quinnel was immune to irony. "So you got the ruling clique, moderately right. And of course, like everywhere else, it's jobs for the boys: every post worth a good goddamn in the whole country is filled by one of the king's men. Which leaves a mess of dissidents who ganged up and looked for some help from the neighbors. In this case, the Khmers and Vietnam."

"The classic pattern," said Dean. "Don't tell me. The helpful neighbors, aided by 'volunteers' from such places as Cuba and Libya, backed up by Russian 'advisers' on modern hardware, have infiltrated half the country, the way the VC did during the war in South Vietnam?"

"You got it. They're in a virtual civil-war situation, the way it was some years ago in Angola."

"Yeah." Dean was reminiscent. "That strikes a chord too!"

"In this case," Quinnel said, "there are complications on account of the king and his number two are the real strong men of the party. The only strong men. If one or the other, or both of them, were wiped out . . . well, the whole scene would collapse. The Reds would almost certainly take over on the Vietnam pattern, like you say."

He pushed back his chair and rose to his feet, pacing the small room with jerky strides. "Mustn't happen," he said, shaking his schoolboy head. "Several reasons. Balance of power in the area. The threat to Thailand. Propaganda. More especially, loss of face for the administration: after all, it was the U.S. underwrote the regime." Quinnel blew out his cheeks and passed a hand over his unruly hair. "On the other hand, we dare not openly intervene or even appear to intervene. Again, several reasons.

22

The Pan-Asian Conference coming up next month; tacit solidarity with China against the Soviets—and don't forget, a successful assassination would be a feather in the Russian, not the Chinese, cap."

"I admire your choice of metaphor," Dean murmured.

Quinnel let that one go with the tide. "Lastly," he said, "I don't have to remind you: this is election year. After Vietnam, every son of a bitch connected with the White House or the Pentagon is shit-scared of coming within a million miles of an engagement in Southeast Asia."

Leaning back in his chair, Dean stretched out his feet and crossed his ankles. "Okay," he said. "And so?"

"So the assassination attempt has to be squashed . . . but not by us." Quinnel returned to the desk. "There's a guy here, name of Ngon Thek. He's the king's right-hand man, Minister of Home Security, President of the Assembly, and like that. Used to be a bigtime guerrilla chief, fighting for Kao Dinh before we sat him on his throne. He came here to ask our help, and we can't give it."

Dean's rugged features were alive with interest. "And you think . . . ?" he began.

Quinnel picked up the phone and stabbed a button. "Have our man come in," he barked. And then, to Dean: "I'd like for you to meet this character. He may have a job for you."

2 Hugh Quinnel

Ngon Thek was tall for a Southeast Asian, perhaps five feet, eight inches without his shoes. He was, in addition, wearing Western-style boots with two-inch heels to complement his beige tussore suit. His body, cadaverous and slightly hunched, still bore witness to the years of prison and privation, fighting as a guerrilla in the steaming jungles of Laos and Cambodia; the brown face was as seamed and wrinkled as a forgotten apple. He could have been any age from thirty-five to fifty.

Dean rose to shake hands and made his usual lightning inventory, taking stock of those exterior signs that helped him form an opinion when he was considering an offer from a potential employer. Expressionless, guarded eyes. A slightly arrogant flare to the wide nostrils. The smile a little tight, but a firm, dry handshake. Three rings—one of them a large square-cut emerald—and heavy gold cufflinks. The necktie was from Sulka and the suit must have been sculptured by a master hand to fit that tortured frame so well. A man of authority, all right, Dean decided. And a man who enjoyed using it.

"I will come straight to the point, Colonel," Ngon Thek said when the formalities had been completed and they were all three seated around the desk. (Dean did not hold, had never held, the rank of colonel, but his own innate authority was such that there seemed to be a tacit understanding among those who employed him or worked with him that any lower form of address would be an insult to his qualities as a combat leader. It was perhaps indicative of the man and his effect on others that he himself never used the term.)

He listened politely to a résumé of the political situation in Muong-Thang—largely a more wordy recap of what Quinnel had already told him—and noted with a

24

wry inner smile that it was in fact almost ten minutes before the point actually was reached. Before that, Ngon Thek said:

"Perhaps you will forgive me if I remind you of the extra complication, that our enemies are divided among themselves. We refer to our Cambodian neighbor still as the Khmer Republic. And indeed, despite the fact that it was internationally discredited and ousted from power three years ago because it was practicing genocide on its opponents, the Khmer Rouge remains the legal government of that unhappy country today. But the Khmer Rouge is supported by China. *Our* enemies, like the Vietnamese of Hanoi, are the tools of Soviet Russia. And the bitter struggle between these two brands of communism accounts for the fact that at this moment there are a quarter of a million Vietnamese troops fighting in what was once Cambodia, fighting to supplant the Maoist dictatorship with that of Brezhnev." He paused, his dark eyes staring piercingly into Dean's own, and then added: "It also accounts for the fact that there are a few Khmer Rouge among the Soviet-backed Cubans and Libyans aiding our own rebels. It was getting too hot for them at home . . . and the pickings are expected to be easier on our side of the border."

Dean nodded briefly. "Noted," he said.

Before Ngon Thek could continue, Quinnel rose to his feet and stretched his arms above his head. "I guess you guys don't need me anymore." He yawned. "Now that I've made the connection, I'll leave you to it. If you need me, I'm staying at the Astra—but I'd rather not know. It's better you should organize what you have to organize in secret, okay?"

Nodding again, Dean raised a farewell hand—wondering cynically, as he watched the lanky CIA man springheel out the door, just where the bug would be hidden.

It was concealed, not very originally, in the base of the desk phone. But then, it was unlikely that anyone, even if he were suspicious, would be stripping down the fixtures and fittings in an FBI interview room at an international airport.

Quinnel started the tape spools turning as soon as he reached the monitor room high up in another part of the building. Ngon Thek's thin, nasal, almost expressionless voice was speaking of assassination.

Behind the recording deck, a small, lean, gray man with a military bearing and a clipped mustache sat at another gray steel desk with a notebook and a ball-point. The notebook was open at the first page, which was still blank. "Be okay, sir, I think," Quinnel said. "Pretty sure Dean will take the hook, from what I know of him."

The man behind the desk nodded. He was listening to the relay and he didn't believe in wasting words. His name, on the rare occasions that he chose to use it, was A. A. Mackenzie. The initials stood for Alexander Archibald, but if there was any Scottish ancestry implied by those multisyllables, it no longer showed in his voice, which was as clipped and precise and neutral as his mustache.

Mackenzie was Quinnel's immediate superior, a CIA regional director outposted in New York. Like a well-organized spider general, installed at the center of an orderly web, he customarily officered his international intrigues from his base, seldom leaving the bureau that was concealed in an old brownstone facing the United Nations Building across the East River. Quinnel had been forced to pull out all the stops in his efforts to persuade Mackenzie to fly to the Coast, but he had finally managed to convince his chief of the urgency and importance of Ngon Thek's plea. Now Mackenzie was eager to know whether the mercenary leader could be talked into the job that the United States dared not touch.

"You're absolutely certain there's a contract out for the king?" Dean's amplified voice was asking.

"A . . . contract?"

"That there are plans to assassinate him."

"Ah. Yes, certainly. There will be an attempt, directed against the emperor—possibly against myself as well. That is undisputed," Ngon Thek replied. *"The double agents who have furnished the information have proved too reliable in the past for us to risk doubting them now."*

"But they can't tell you when or how?"

"That is so. Not so far. They may never be able to do so: they are not well enough into the rebel organization to learn of their plans in detail. This is a task which I hope you will feel able to accept."

Dean said, *"What exactly are you suggesting, sir?"*

"I would like you," the Indochinese replied, *"working quite openly as—if you will forgive the term—as a mercenary, to be employed as a palace guard. With a picked body of men of your own choice. With the specific aim of seeking out these putative assassins and . . . ah . . . eliminating them before they can strike."*

For a while the speakers were silent. Perhaps Dean was considering the offer. Perhaps he was weighing the pros and cons. Maybe he was just gazing into space, trying to make up his mind. The tape spools continued noiselessly revolving. Mackenzie, who had been taking notes, sat immobile, his ball-point poised above the paper. Quinnel stared out the window: in the distance, magnified by the layer of smog veiling the city, an orange sun sank toward the ocean beyond the Golden Gate. *"Well, Colonel?"* Ngon Thek's voice queried at last. *"I need hardly add that you can name virtually any fee you like. We are most anxious for you to accept the commission."*

"It sounds an interesting challenge," said Dean. *"I'll do what I can."*

"What did I tell you!" Quinnel crowed enthusiastically in the monitor room. "If anyone can pull it off, he can!"

After a brief discussion on the financial aspect, Ngon Thek said, *"Should we return to my hotel to finalize the details, do you think? It will be more comfortable . . . and we can hardly plan travel schedules here in this empty room."*

"Sure," Dean said. *"It will be more private, too."*

"Bastard!" Quinnel exclaimed, catching the know-all, slightly mocking note in the mercenary leader's voice.

"There's only one thing. As you know, I was on my way to Egypt. I had business there and in Tokyo. But my young son was due to fly out and join me for an educational trip in a couple of weeks. You know—a ten-day Nile cruise taking in Abu Simbl, Karnak, Aswan, and all that."

"Just so." Ngon Thek sounded puzzled.

"What I mean," Dean explained, *"I came over here to discuss his schooling with his mother—my ex-wife. She was visiting relatives on the Coast. But she's gone back east now. If you don't mind, I'd like to stop off and cable her before we leave."*

27

"My dear Colonel! Take as long as you like. I have a motor outside. I will wait for you there."

Dean went to the Western Union desk and composed a long cable addressed to Samantha Hurok—his former wife's unmarried name—at a village near Orleans, Massachusetts. Through circumstances beyond his control, the message stated, he was obliged to postpone seven-year-old Patrick's trip for a short while. Would she please apologize to the boy, cancel his plane reservation, and hold his ticket until Dean got in touch with her again. He hoped that would be very soon.

He checked the wordage, paid for the cable, and went to look for Ngon Thek's Cadillac.

The Western Union operator carried the completed form through to the telex room. Quinnel and Mackenzie were standing by one of the machines. Quinnel held out a huge hand and took the cable. He glanced once at the message and then tore the form across, and across again, dropping the fragments into a waste bin.

Mackenzie was looking dubious. "He already left for Tokyo, Karachi, and Cairo," Quinnel said. "Nobody, but nobody, must know that he didn't make that trip."

3 Sean Hammer

He had left a leg behind, escaping from Russian missiles across the freezing waters of the Baltic. But for a cripple he moved amazingly fast, using both hands and the remaining foot to propel himself from kitchenette to living room, and from there out to the hallway, swinging from chair to desk and from desk to sofa with the agility of a monkey. There was something almost simian about his face, too. As he lowered himself with a final thrust of his powerful arms to an easy chair beside the telephone console, light from the north window cast his craggy features into relief: the long, seamed upper lip, the nutcracker mouth and jaw, a narrow, lined forehead, and wicked little eyes. He was a short man, not heavily built, but he looked as durable as granite.

Before the instrument had rung four times he had scooped the handset from its cradle, barking into the mouthpiece: "Hammer here. Who is this, please?" And then, the Northern Irish accent becoming more pronounced: "Marc! The hard man himself! Sure, it's quare and happy I am to be hearin' that familiar ould voice of yours. Now, what would you be wantin' with a one-legged ex-con on a bright day like this?"

Sean Hammer was the son of Ulster immigrant parents. His father had been a New York cop and his mother a felling hand in a series of sweatshops off Seventh Avenue. Hammer himself was a Vietnam veteran. In forty-three years of hard living he had also worked as a long-distance truck driver, an unarmed combat instructor with the Selous Scouts in Rhodesia, and, more recently, as Marc Dean's most valued friend and trusted lieutenant. The ex-con tag came almost by mistake. It was something of a private joke, deriving from a short spell in Leavenworth occasioned by the death of an oversize Swedish seaman who had attacked Hammer with a knife during a barroom brawl in Galveston.

"I have a job for you, Sean," Dean said now, explaining briefly—without naming the country—what the mission involved.

"Well, isn't that the best piece of news I've heard in a long, long time!" said Hammer. "And me with me pockets emptier than a Salvation Army hall at collection time."

"Have you been backing losers again? Or curvy blonds who need a stake so they can make themselves a little tiny screen test?"

"Ah, come off it, Marc!" Hammer protested. "You know I quit that kind of caper years back. And wasn't I down Kentucky way, well ahead of the odds in a week's play, when the jock pulled a fast one and an animal well tipped for a win didn't come in but third. Sure it's a crooked bloody racket, but . . . the turf."

"What happened to the jock?" Dean sounded amused.

"I heard tell he met with an accident," said Hammer. "It's not a game to be mixed up with seriously. But this job of yours, now—how would it be for the spondulicks?"

"The what?"

"The emolument. The loot. The lolly. What a Frenchman would term his *honoraires*."

"Oh. Satisfactory. Unless you've changed your mind since the last time."

"Forgive my vulgarity, Colonel, but that is to say . . . ?"

"Two and a half down. The same at the end of the operation. Certified check, lodged with a Swiss bank of your choice."

"You're talking in thousands of dollars? Dollars U.S.?"

"Certainly. That five thou covers ten days' work, including travel—which will be paid for separately. Each additional day after that nets you an extra five hundred bucks. Okay?"

"Okay indeed. Now, why do you not come right over, and we'll split a fifth of John Jameson to seal the bargain and celebrate?"

"For one thing," Dean said, "because I'm . . . well, to be honest, I don't have cab fare."

"The Dear help us!" Hammer exclaimed piously. "Is it that bad now? So come on over and I'll square the cabbie meself."

Dean laughed. "I'm in San Francisco, you dope! And I have to stay here, fixing the details. Then, tomorrow, I make it to . . . where we're heading. Now here's what I want you to do."

"I'm listening," said Hammer. "Pour it on."

"This is a job for a small, ultrareliable detail. I'd like for you to contact Novotny, Wassermann, and Alf Daler. They should all be stateside someplace. I already cabled you an advance. You'll find airline tickets for the four of you waiting at La Guardia. When you land here, you'll be met and given instructions, papers, and tickets for your onward flight."

"You don't want Ed in on this one? Sure, he's ultrareliable if any man is."

"I'll raise Mazzari myself," Dean said. "I'm not one hundred percent certain of the guidelines on this job. I'm going to tell him to make his way to the target area overland. No apparent connection with us. It may be useful at that to have a free agent working undercover: the rest of us, after all, will be slap in the limelight, official bodyguards to Himself. So far as a sixth guy is concerned officially, I plan to use Kurt Schneider—if I can tempt him away from whatever part of Germany he's building boats in now."

"Okay," Hammer said. "And the hardware?"

"For once, we pay it no mind. The gentleman employing us assures me that we'll find everything we need when we get there."

After a few other, more explicit instructions, Dean rang off. Sean Hammer drew the phone book toward him and began to make his calls. The apartment—a shabby but well-organized bachelor pad—was on the fourteenth floor of a run-down building in the East Fifties. As he dialed and talked and made notes and dialed again, the sun withdrew behind the cliffs of Manhattan and the light faded from the stone canyons of the city. By the time darkness fell and the lights of automobiles were garlanding the streets below, his task was completed and the three mercs Dean had wanted were lined up. The first of these, Emil Novotny, was a naturalized Pole, a wiry man of medium height who looked a little like Moshe Dayan without the black eyepatch. Novotny was an explosives expert. He had once been a quarryman in Colorado, and apart from a number of exploits with Dean, he had no military experience. But he was tough as hell and he had a quality that Dean prized above all others: he never gave up.

A New Yorker, Abe Wassermann was something of a dual personality. With shell-rim glasses, a cigar, and an immaculate mohair suit, he personified the owner—slightly overweight—of a prosperous tailoring business in the garment district. He was in fact the owner of a successful business in that district. Yet in combat gear, wearing a battered fatigue cap with an Armalite rifle slung across his back, he looked like nothing so much as a character from the old Sergeant Bilko TV series. In action, Wassermann scorned the Armalite, preferring the more accurate, long-distance, express products from the Husqvarna, Mannlicher, or Winchester catalogs. For Wassermann, astonishingly, was a crack shot, a world-class marksman capable of winning the King's Prize at Bisley—or, more usefully to Dean, picking off an officer or knocking a sniper out of a tree at one thousand yards.

Alfred Daler was perhaps the most bizarre member of that unconventional quartet. He was a thin, gray, balding man with unremarkable features and wrists of steel. Although he had worked many times with Dean, he remained something of a mystery even to the mercenary chief. He claimed to be Norwegian (and in fact he had a Norwegian passport bearing his photo and the name Alfred Jørgen Daler), but there were rumors that the passport had once been British, that he had been a serving officer with that country's oddly named Special Air Service—which has nothing to do with aviation, being a specialized riot-control formation. There was, however, no trace of anyone named Daler in the official records of that organization, and the man himself was giving nothing away. What was certain was that all the European languages he knew—and he spoke many, all of them badly—were pronounced with an unmistakable cockney accent.

Dean didn't care a damn what Daler's background was. He was perfectly content to leave him as the enigma he clearly wished—or needed—to be. The important thing was that Daler was much tougher than he looked. And he was one hundred percent reliable.

Typically, he was the only one of the three to question Sean Hammer on the terms of the contract Dean was offering.

"Two and two," the Ulsterman said. "With an extra five hundred a day after the first ten."

"In writing?"

"If you want it that way. Though of course it can't be specific. You'd have to take that up with himself, once you get to Frisco. But the down payment will be waiting for you here."

"The end money in a certified check, lodged with a Swiss bank before we start?"

"Sure."

"To be paid to a person of my choice if I shouldn't—"

"If a guy croaks, the Colonel always pays out to dependents," Hammer interrupted. "You know that."

"All right, cock," Daler said cheerfully. "I just like to have the details laid on the line."

When he had finished telephoning, Hammer swung himself back into his bedroom and strapped on his artificial leg. For a man who moved so swiftly without it, he had a curiously stiff gait once the lightweight prosthetic limb was in place. This was because the perforated aluminum casing concealed a number of items that would have confounded a customs inspector, had he chosen to insist that Hammer remove the device.

The idea had come to him when he was convalescing after the amputation in a Stockholm hospital. It would, he thought, be an ideal way of spiriting certain merchandise past security checks. The bleeping of the Geiger counters would naturally be attributed to the metal of the false leg itself. It could, in addition, prove a lifesaver in the kind of tight corner where you had been captured and disarmed and were threatened with prison or execution.

Once out of hospital, he had arranged, with Dean's help, a conference between himself, an orthopedic surgeon, and Gaston Jammot, the inventor and gunsmith in Belgium who supplied Dean with the hardware for most of his operations.

After this meeting and several subsequent encounters

for testing and modification, the weight of the original prosthetic was increased by several pounds. There was, for example, just above the ankle articulation, a cylindrical transistorized transmitter/receiver hidden inside the lower part of the calf. What appeared to be boltheads were in reality tuners and control knobs for this secret radio. Higher up, securely clipped to the inside of the shin, the components of a Dural-framed burp gun competed for space with a plastic grenade, a CS gas aerosol, and a lightweight commando knife furnished with lock-picking accessories. For longer-range work, the calf section could be detached from ankle and knee joints and screwed as a shoulder stock to the gun, which fired high-velocity .22-caliber rounds, on the principle of the U.S. Army's AR-5 paratroop survival rifle. . . . .

Hammer had gotten used to the weight of the leg now, although it imposed on him a pronounced limp, and to avoid a confusion of balance and equilibrium in what should be a quasi-automatic action, he carried the full complement of goodies whenever and wherever he walked, even if it was only to the corner saloon for a drink with buddies.

He rode down in the elevator now and stumped along to the bar after he had eaten a quick dinner in the Italian restaurant across the street. Wassermann and Novotny were in town and he had arranged to meet them for a preliminary discussion right away. Daler, blocked in Detroit on some obscure operation involving the importation of foreign automobiles, would be unable to join them until the following day. But it was necessary for Hammer to tell his fellow mercs as much as he knew about the mission before they went to collect their tickets at La Guardia: once at the field, Dean had insisted, they were to travel as four separate passengers, none of them appearing to know any of the others.

"An' that," Hammer told Novotny and Wassermann when they were seated in a booth with drinks before them, "goes double once we leave the Coast for wherever-it-is. For the Dear knows, in this bloody game, what man has you in his sights or when the shootin' starts!"

4 Marc Dean

The shooting—at least figuratively speaking—started sooner than any of them expected.

Hammer and his three companions had arrived in Muong-Thang on a short-haul Boeing jet flying via Shanghai, Hong Kong, and Manila, less than seventy-two hours after Dean had first called the Ulsterman. An intercontinental strip capable of taking the largest jumbos was under construction fifteen miles north of Am-Phallang, but the field had still to be completed, and for the moment traffic was restricted to those planes which could safely land on the shorter runways of the old French airport on the outskirts of the city.

Kurt Schneider, blond, bearded, and equable of temperament, a seasoned navigator and a tenacious fighter, had already arrived from Germany. Edmond Mazzari, in some kind of vehicle, was supposed to be on his way south through Bangladesh, Burma, and Thailand. The first thing to do now that his "official" six-man squad was present, Dean decided, was report to Ngon Thek at the Ministry of Home Security, and then install themselves in the royal palace and meet the man they were there to protect.

Dean had already organized the use of a Toyota Land Cruiser—a tall utility that looked like a cross between a Range Rover and an outsize Jeep. They flung in the overnight cases they had brought (uniforms were to be provided from the royal armory) and climbed aboard.

It was a hot afternoon, with a great deal of humidity in the air and a dun-colored overcast veiling the sky. Rickshaws, tri-shaws, and pedal cycles added to the hazards of driving among the odd mixture of modern American and ancient, beat-up French cars. Between the stained, cracked walls of postwar concrete apartment buildings, the wide avenues were nevertheless surprisingly free of pedestrians for an Oriental city. Nearer the center of town, when palm trees and pagodas had begun to appear behind the high walls separating the temples of commerce, it was even possible to cross an intersection on the green light without running into a throng of gesticulating locals.

The mercs were on good form; they always were at the start of a mission. Schneider, who was driving the Land Cruiser, whistled the tune of "Lilli Marlene" as he jerked at the gearshift and spun the wheel. "You know something?" Novotny said. "These folks here are missing out: I don't see no pickups and no delivery trucks on the street. How can anyone live without he has a nineteen-year-old grand prix ace at the wheel of a panel truck to swear at?"

"Markets are the answer," said Dean. "This is a delta town. Most of the inhabitants live on houseboats or thatched huts on stilts beside the canals. There's no need for stores selling food: the waterways are crowded with guys selling everything you want from sampans."

"Sampans?" Wassermann repeated. "I thought that was a movie term: you know—like a camera movement in Goldwyn pictures."

Over the collective groan that greeted this remark, Hammer said, "If we're here as an official bodyguard, it don't seem we can count on too much home help: I haven't seen a single fuckin' flatfoot since we left the plane!"

"Most of them have been sent north to stiffen the fighting front against the rebels," Dean said. "Those that are still here are sitting at home making plans."

There was a chorus of voices from which a single announcement—Wassermann's again—emerged. "I tell you it's true. It was in Saigon. This ambassador, anxious he should make a good impression at his first diplomatic party there, he finds he has nothing with him but heavy garments from the north of Europe. So he takes a Savile Row tuxedo and he goes to a local tailor and he says: 'Look, make me a suit exactly like this, but in shantung silk, okay? I don't mind what I pay, but it has to be fast: I need that suit the day after tomorrow.' And, right enough, the suit is delivered forty-eight hours later, on the dot. It fits all right; not brilliant, but all right. The tux, on the other hand, it looked like it had been fed twice through an olive mill already. And you know what those bastards had done?" Wassermann's face was pink with indignation. "They unpicked every single goddamn seam in that tuxedo suit, and they used the pieces as patterns and they cut their shantung to the same size. And then they tried to hand-sew that tuxedo back the way it was before! Can you imagine!"

"Sounds just like Seventh Avenue," Daler teased.

"Now just a minute . . ."

"All right, you guys, cool it," Dean cut in. "Time for the funnies later, when we're bedded down in our quarters, okay?"

He paused to watch a white Mercedes-Benz coupé forge past them with a snarl of twin exhausts. It was driven by a small dark man in a white suit, whose face was masked by wraparound sunglasses. *"Grüss Gott!"* Schneider exclaimed, tramping on the brake pedal as the big sports car carved up the Toyota and then slowed suddenly, passing a driveway with a triple blast of its airhorns. "Some people they should not be allowed . . ." He shook his head, shifting the Land Cruiser to a lower gear.

All of them had been thrown forward by the abrupt deceleration. Only Dean, leaning forward between the two front seats, saw the old black Peugeot sedan shoot out of the entry ahead of them and balk Schneider for a second time as they approached an intersection. Two men in the rear of the French car seemed to be having some difficulty closing the offside door.

"You know how it is," he said to Schneider. "You get guys suddenly run into money, and they . . ." He paused fractionally and then yelled: "Watch out!" seeing the heavy, squat package fall from the open rear door of the Peugeot and spin toward them as the sedan raced ahead.

He jammed his arm between the front seats and seized the handbrake lever, hauling on it with all his strength.

The humidity in the air had left the roadway greasy. The four-wheel-drive Toyota, with two wheels suddenly locked, tried to pull up in a straight line; but Schneider, half-turning his head in astonishment, moved the steering, and the utility skated across the macadam with a screech of tires. The back end broke away. Schneider overcorrected, and the Toyota—with Dean still wrenching

37

grim-faced at the lever—turned completely around. It shot backward across the street, clipped the curb, and then rebounded into a pedestrian refuge, narrowly missing a rickshaw and a Citroën cab before it slammed against a post and tipped over on its side.

The crash was drowned in the thunderclap of the explosion, which blasted a ten-foot crater in the roadway where they would have been if Dean had not grabbed the handbrake. Miraculously, nobody was hurt.

They scrambled to their feet and extricated themselves from the wreck. Traffic—fortunately it had been light—was stalled all over the street. People were running toward the cloud of yellow smoke blanketing the intersection. In the distance a whistle shrilled.

"All right," Dean panted. "Grab your baggage and split. We'll separate and take rickshaws to the ministry when we're a block or more away." And then, picking fragments of toughened glass from his hair as the crowd of chattering locals surged toward them: "Welcome to Muong-Thang!" he called.

5 Jason Mettner

All this happened, of course, some time before me and Ed Mazzari hit town. The plastic bomb that nearly put Dean and his crew below ground—Novotny said later that it was a minimum-fuse baby fueled with Dialacton—was bouncing out of the Peugeot sedan just about the time we were hightailing it for the mission building in the deserted hill village. I never did find out what they called that place.

Okay, next morning, like I said, the Reds or whoever start throwing 88mm shells at us like rice at your grandpa's wedding (the road ran through paddy fields too, so don't tag me a mixed-metaphor man). That's the rub with these damned wars in Southeast Asia: you can be accredited to their side, you can be wearing official passes the way Göring wore medals—you can even be sporting their *own* medals, for Christ's sake!—and they can still sling a knife or press the trigger of an AK-47 like you just dishonored their sister. I mean, just because you happen to be there and they happen to be there. You soon learn to walk kind of casual, not staring right or left, the hands held well away from the body and always visible. Above all, you don't point at anything; some marksman hidden in that direction might think you spotted him and open up to shut your mouth. Trouble is, they can't easily tell friend from foe even among themselves: nobody wears any uniform; out in the sticks all the guys wear these black pajama suits and the gals hide beneath those hats that look like clam shells—and half of them are guerrillas anyway, or they were when I was last in the neighborhood, covering the Cambodian frame-up. In any case, Viet Minh, Viet Cong, Khmer Rouge, Annamite, Cochin Chinese—how the hell do you tell them apart when they're up to their neck in water in a paddy field

39

preparing to blow you to pieces with a mortar made from the exhaust tailpipe of a Chevrolet?

Mazzari and me were in the sticks, all right. Half a mile ahead there was another village on the edge of a low bluff. Apart from that, there were just ten million miles of rice fields between us and the forest covering those mountains.

I said village. There *had* been a village. There wasn't a living tree or bush above or below the bluff; just charred stumps, splinters white as bone, and drifts of leaves that had been blown off, lying like green snow. The houses were all smashed. Behind the ruined walls we could see figures moving. Sometimes they would drop down and start firing rifles or SMG's; sometimes they would scatter and there would be flame and brown smoke as mortar shells burst. We couldn't see what they were firing at or where the shells came from.

We couldn't see who was firing those 88's, either. It could have been the folks in the village or the guys they were fighting. Whoever it was, they figured us for the enemy. The first shell burst fifty yards behind Mazzari's Citroën. The second blew a hole in the roadway about the size of a Boeing 747. It was near enough for the blast to suck out the windshield and rip the soft top to ribbons. The road ran along an embankment and the crater was too steep to drive through. Mazzari jammed on the brakes and we both dived for the bank, rolling down into the mud at the edge of the paddy in a shower of small stones.

Just in time, for the third one was smack on target. There are something like 3,200 moving parts in a modern automobile. Most of that Citroën's got claustrophobia and made it across the shell hole on their own. Something heavy thunked into the mud beside us and rolled to a stop by Mazzari's knee.

A Citroën carburetor.

"Yours, old man, I think," Mazzari said.

"I told you those screws weren't tight enough," I said. "Now we'll have to walk back for the other car." It wasn't one of my best, but conditions were against the kind that scintillate.

We scrambled up and began to run along the foot of the embankment. The firing must have been from the other side of the road, because nothing was thrown at us as we went. Beyond the village, the road curved around the bluff and we got a different slant on the scene. A canal ran through our paddy and at least one of the mortars was being operated from a clump of bushes on the far side of the water.

It had been a small battle, a skirmish, almost private. But now suddenly it was bigger. Tracer flashed; the thudding of mortars was louder; the ground shook; above the rim of the embankment we could see men—more men than we had thought—in firing positions among the rubble on top of the bluff.

Wherever they were, the 88's had now cottoned on to the positions beyond the canal. Shells exploded and a fire started in among the bush, sending a column of black smoke straight up into the sky. The sky was blue, but blue like a watercolor painted with a dirty brush. The heat was enough to plaster your shirt to your back even when you weren't moving.

Mazzari and me moved. Thirty yards away among the stalks of rice, a bomb sent up a fountain of mud and water. And then the Q and A of machine-gun fire grew quicker . . . and louder. Slugs thwacked into the bank all around us with a noise like Roscoe Tanner serving aces. There was a shallow firing position someone had once dug up near the lip of the embankment. I made the depression only slightly faster than the speed of light and threw myself in. There was already a big black guy there. "Would you mind moving your head?" I snarled. "I can't see the screen."

The shellfire and the clatter of automatic arms rose to a crescendo. And then all at once everyone seemed to tire of the fun and quit. Maybe those 88mm boys *had* handed over to the Russkies and taken all the mortars out. We crawled to the top of the bank and peered over.

Some guy was gunning a truck motor beyond the pall of smoke that hid the ruins on top of the bluff. Down below, a little boy about six years old was squatting in the dust with two girls even younger playing some elaborate private game with a small pile of stones. They looked like they had been there forever. "Poor little sods," Mazzari said in that dude voice of his. "They've never known anything else. Bullets and bombs and shells passing overhead—for them it's no more than traffic at the end of the street for the kids in our cities."

"Only not so dangerous," I said.

He grinned. Big teeth, very white. "Cynics are always sentimental at heart," he said. "Come on: let's take a shufti at the other side of the road."

We ran across. The shooting was only sporadic now— single shots punctuated by an occasional short burst from an SMG. None of them seemed to be aimed at us. Before we reached the bluff, an old man on a bicycle rode very slowly out of the smoke and disappeared among a grove of trees still standing some way beyond the village. He had a straggly white beard and he was holding a large black umbrella over his head. "You see what I mean?" I said.

Not far from the children a dead man lay by an empty barber's chair. Flies were still settling on the fresh blood clotted beneath his jaw, but his boots and his gun had already been taken. Along a trail in back of the bluff the refugees had begun to file. They were leading pigs and oxen, pushing handcarts, carrying baskets of meat and fruit strung from the ends of long poles. On either side the wounded squirmed and jerked among the shattered trees.

Mazzari shook his head. "Crazy country, crazy war," he said. "None of it makes any sense really, does it? I mean, what the hell do these people think they're fighting *for*? Do they even know who they're fighting *against*?"

"Brother, you ain't seen nothing yet," I told him. "Down south, where we're headed, they have—or they used to have—a religion that was a mixture of Buddhism, Confucianism, and Christianity. It's a region where the missionaries didn't have it all their own way. There's a local pope; Victor Hugo is a saint; the priests wear pith helmets—and there's a gang of lady cardinals that wear ivory silk pants! Caodai, they call it."

"Very droll," Mazzari said. "I'm afraid I don't quite . . . ?"

"The joke," I said, "apart from the French colonial influence, is that the Caodaists tell you God loves the truth. And if you ask which one, they say that all truths are reconciled in their faith and that truth is love. In a country where every son of a bitch has been fighting his neighbor for more than thirty years, I figure that for this week's big laugh."

"Ecumenical!" said Mazzari. "Where did this great new faith come from?"

"It was invented by a civil servant from Cochin China," I said.

We had been following the refugees along the track. Now it curled back to the road on top of the embankment. Below us, water buffalo stood knee-deep in the irrigated fields. The truck motor we had heard had grown louder. It roared down behind us, scattering the crowd—an old half-track still with U.S. Army markings. Lurching off the trail, one of the caterpillars picked up a legless corpse, emaciated, yellow as dust, and stiff as a plank. For a few yards the desiccated cadaver was batted back and forth between the guide wheels, and then it was spewed out to slide down the bank as the half-track accelerated away. None of the refugees took any notice. None of them tried to hitch a ride on the truck. Maybe it was on a round trip to the next undamaged village to pick up a fresh supply of ammunition. Or a fresh supply of bodies to combat the Russian 88's and then lie beside the road near the kids who played with stones.

We felt kind of vulnerable, the West African ex-sergeant and me, walking south among those folks whose homes had been destroyed. Mazzari was over six feet tall, and broad with it; although I was thin as a rake, I was almost the same height. But few of the Thais, the Khmers, the Hoas, the Laotians, and the Vietnamese make more than five-feet-six, and many of them are several inches shorter than that. We must have looked about as conspicuous as delphiniums in a bed of lobelia.

It wasn't far to the next village, not more than six or seven hundred miles as the crow flies. Although any crow dopey enough to try to fly through air that heavy would need liquid-oxygen fuel and an afterburner even to leave the runway. And that forest on the far side of the paddies—where the Reds were supposed to hang out until dark, when they came out with the vampire bats—the forest seemed no nearer as we staggered through the damp heat and the sun forced its way down toward the horizon. Finally, however, we made it—and I found myself in the

43

first undamaged village I'd seen since I crossed the border near Battambang.

There were colored lanterns strung across the main drag, *samisen* music tinkled somewhere in the background, and the market canals were crammed with sampans plying between the stilt houses.

In among the bright lights at dusk, even sitting down drinking some kind of fermented fruit juice outside an inn, we were as noticeable as we had been with the refugees. All the guys were dressed in their neat pajama suits and the women wore black silk trousers with tight quilted jackets, slit up the sides, in flower patterns of pink and mauve. But we looked like something the Bowery bums didn't want to know. My camera was still slung over my shoulder, my papers and my billfold were stuffed into my hip pocket, but my vest and jacket had been in the Citroën, my valise was probably in orbit, my pants were ripped at the knee, and my shirt looked like it was rehearsing for a commando raid. Mazzari wasn't much better: his cheek was grazed, there was caked blood on his face, and his clothes were covered in dried mud. He still had a neat little Berretta .32-caliber automatic tucked into the waistband of his short pants, though.

We ate some savory rice and then Mazzari transformed himself into a forage master. For ten U.S. dollars he obtained a room for the night equipped with two mattresses, and a couple of Raleigh bicycles. "It seems almost like bloody robbery," he said.

"It probably was," I told him, "as soon as you said what you wanted. Don't worry: there'll be enough deaths before dawn for the suppliers to be able to steal two more and replace them."

Dawn was the interminable crowing of a hundred million roosters, the barking of dogs, the squawk of chickens for sale in wicker coops, and a shrill chatter of bargaining voices that made sleep impossible. We were on our way before the sun peered over the rim of the rice fields and turned the pale green eastern sky blue.

Apart from the ring of silent spectators around us while we ate and the football crowd we attracted washing at a primitive pump, nobody seemed to take much notice of us at the village. The bush telegraph must have been working overtime just the same.

We had been riding just over an hour. The sun had staggered up into the sky, which was now the color of dishwater. It was hotter and damper than it had been the day before. Nobody had passed us in either direction. The flooded paddies still stretched away forever, and the water buffalo hadn't moved. You get the picture: the teeming millions of this colorful and picturesque subcontinent busy about their varied and fascinating tasks.

We were approaching a village—it was the third so far, but this one was built among trees on top of a mountain range that must have been all of twelve feet high. "Do you think we can make that grade?" I asked Mazzari. "It must be nearly two degrees."

"Keep your eyes skinned, old lad," he said. "I don't see any children around in this one. Usually, in this part of the world, that means trouble."

"Just so long as I don't get vertigo looking all the way down into those fields," I replied. He was right, though. The dusty trail at the entrance to the village was deserted. In the other two there'd been so many kids the dogs had been forced to take second place.

The wood-and-thatch houses hadn't been touched by the civil war here. There was even a pink-washed church with the all-seeing eye of God painted over the door. But no people. The place was deserted as a ball park when the team is playing away. Until we rode around a bend in the road at the top of a gentle slope that led down to an embankment crossing the paddies again.

There were three of them, standing in the shade of a jacaranda. As we came in sight, they walked slowly out until they were in the center of the dusty trail, barring our way. They wore camouflaged battle fatigues and netted helmets, and they were carrying machine pistols—Uzis, FN's, wartime Schmeissers, you tell me. All I knew was that they carried thirty-round box magazines and they looked as if they knew how to use them.

"All right," Mazzari said quietly, "just leave this to me. Don't look at them. Don't say anything. Just sit tight."

"Wh-what gives?" I croaked, hoping my voice was not more than an octave higher than usual.

"The bikes. Around here they're almost as valuable as dollars."

"And the . . . riders?"

"Probably aim to kill us. It's much the easiest way. No complaints, no inquest, no comeback. We're not worth torturing because we don't know anything. We're not rich enough to ransom."

I swallowed, squeezing both brakes so that I coasted to a halt with Mazzari a few feet in front of the gunmen. They were quite short and their brown faces were totally without expression. The one in the middle raised the barrel of his machine pistol and jerked it brusquely toward the side of the road. The gesture was unmistakable. We dismounted, laid down the machines . . . and you know who made it to the roadside.

One of the goons slung his weapon, raised up the bikes, and began wheeling them toward the tree. The leader hustled us to an adobe wall surrounding some kind of yard while the third man stood off to cover us.

We faced the wall, leaning forward to take the weight on hands held high above our heads in the classic search position. My mouth was dry, and all I could think of was the fact that Mazzari's bastard hip flask was empty. Was this to be the final curtain? The darkness forever in a few short seconds? For what? For nothing at all—a bicycle that I would gladly have given away for a drink of water on a day of clammy heat. Surely death wouldn't, couldn't, come in so trivial a fashion? It couldn't be true! And then—sudden cold wave of panic—it *was* true! It was (Mettner's farewell crack?) too true to be good. . . .

Experienced hands patted my weaponless body, slid billfold and papers from my hip pocket. And it was then that Mazzari showed what it meant to be a soldier of fortune, showed up the difference between professional and amateur.

I still don't know exactly what happened. He had maneuvered his position in such a way that the guy doing the frisking was between him and the man with the gun. There was a sudden flurry of action, and he had spun around, knocking the gun barrel aside and swinging the searcher in front of him. The gun went off, scarring the surface of the road . . . and the man who was covering the leader pressed his trigger involuntarily, hosing the boss man with lead.

Even then, I hadn't realized Mazzari's ferocious strength. He dived forward, picked the dead man up by the heels, and whirled him around his head like a bola, felling the guy who'd shot him as easily as a sapling tidied away by lumberjacks. I shall never forget the sound of those two heads thunking together: it was like a kid bursting an air-filled paper sack.

Before those two guys hit the ground, my West African savior had whipped the Berretta from the waistband above his hip pocket and drilled the third man between the eyes while he was still wondering which of us to plug first. The goon folded forward some, sat down suddenly in the dust, and than leaned over sideways, kind of tired, and lay still.

It was quite a performance, I'm telling you. I was still standing there with my mouth hanging open, the hands pressed against the adobe wall above my head.

Mazzari dropped the automatic into the side pocket of his bush jacket. He picked up two of the machine pistols, slung one across his back, and handed me the other. He righted the bikes where the third man had let them fall. "Shall we go?" he said.

I was holding my machine steady with one hand and shoving my other arm through the gun's cartridge-filled bandolier. I jerked my head at the corpses in the road. "What about them?"

Mazzari shrugged. "Leave them where they are, old son. That's the way they'd have left us. Only we don't rob the bodies."

We remounted the bikes and rode away. I don't know how many people had watched our private drama: there could have been hundreds hidden among the trees or behind the blank walls of those houses; but I'd hazard a guess that the old bush telegraph had been clattering again, because nobody came near us all the way to Am-Phallang. In fact, they tended to scatter every time we approached a village.

It was a little before dusk when we rode across the wooden canal bridge that led to the outskirts of the capital. It was as hot as it had been at midday, and the humidity was so oppressive that it was like breathing pea soup. "If they want to knock off their bloody king," Mazzari said, "they'll have to do it soon, before the monsoon starts, or they won't even be able to see the bugger, there's so much dampness in the air."

We passed the rotted, discolored concrete blocks that crooked French entrepreneurs had made millions out of in the early fifties, skirted a factory area heavy with the odor of vulcanized rubber, and pedaled through a shantytown suburb where the workers really lived. There was a residential quarter with big white mansions behind palm trees and pillared porticoes, and then we were approaching the administrative sector where the multinationals gnawed their fingernails in air-conditioned silence and watched the Dow Jones index on teletype machines between dry martinis. With rubber and tea and rice to worry over, they were more concerned about the monsoon arriving on time than the number of people killed in an inconvenient civil war. Just so long as there were enough coolies left alive to gather in the crop.

Beyond the old Monastery of the Sacred Moonstone (the last time I'd been here, it was housing the assembly line for a brand of German sewing machine) we could see the tiered pagodas of the royal palace at the far end of a wide avenue, but Mazzari turned through an ornate gateway and dismounted in the courtyard of a Caodaist temple. Before we could contact Dean, it seemed we had to make it with a go-between someplace in here.

The inside of the place was a cross between Disneyland in Technicolor and the set for a television commercial advertising Turkish Delight. Bronze Buddhas and Taoist deities jostled for position with metal Christs in the niches above an Oriental bestiary of sacred snakes, cows, and dragons. Above the altar, a brightly enameled Virgin cradled something that looked like an effigy of Winston Churchill against her Christian Dior ensemble.

"Kind of spooky, what!" Mazzari murmured.

"You should have seen it before the war," I said. "They had an army of twenty-five thousand men in Cambodia, to make sure the government carried out the Caodai concept of political truth and love and brotherhood. The Khmer Rouge massacred most of them, but they still function on a limited scale in this country." I looked up into the cavernous space beneath the bell tower, where a line of ocular windows in stained glass repeated the all-seeing-eye motif. There were doves flapping around and creaking their wings up there, but I didn't see

48

any olive branch. "What are we doing here?" I hissed. "Waiting our turn to pray?"

Mazzari didn't reply directly. "Sit down and wait there like a good chap," he said. "I shan't be long."

He walked across and stood at the entrance to a small side chapel, an arresting figure in the dim light, rather more impressive than any of the deities around the walls. After a while I heard the slap-slap of sandals on the mosaic floor, and a priest appeared out of the shadows and shook Mazzari's hand. His head was shaved and he was wearing a black soutane. He looked like any priest from any church—except for the cigarette jutting from the corner of his mouth. He ushered Mazzari into the chapel and for a while I listened to the sound of their distorted voices trying to lose themselves up among the echoes beneath the roof.

I stared at the statues around the walls. Unless you counted the arms, it was difficult to tell the Christs from the Buddhas. If the priests could smoke, I wondered, was it okay for their flock to do the same? Or was it like a movie theater in France and you had to wait for the intermission? There was a single limp Chesterfield in a pack crumpled in my hip pocket, and I could sense that it wanted out. I looked around hopefully—after all, the place had once been French—but finally decided against it. No ashtrays.

I sighed and shifted my position on the wooden bench. A whole day's cycling had taken toll of my leg muscles. I tilted back my head, massaged my neck, and found myself once more regarding the all-seeing ocular windows beneath the bell tower. Apparently God's eye was green. Perhaps he was jealous of Buddha.

It seemed a long time before Mazzari emerged alone from the chapel. "It's all fixed," he said. "Dean and five other blokes are here quite openly as bodyguards to the king. The Colonel doesn't want anyone to suss out the connection between him and me, but it's reasonable—and believable—that a newspaperman would want to interview foreign mercenaries hired for such an unusual job. So that's what I'm going to pretend to be . . . and then he can fill me in on the orders of the day. You can breeze along too, if you like: as you've been here before, it'll help to strengthen the bally cover."

49

"Swell," I said. "Thank you very much." And then, as I picked up my machine pistol and followed him out of the temple: "Apart from St. Victor Hugo, the Caodaists have a gang of resident prophets, you know. Which one presided over the little shrine where you just did your stuff? Marshall McLuhan? Truman Capote?"

"We can go and see Dean right away," Mazzari said. "It's all laid on."

The royal palace was something Cecil B. De Mille would have rejected out of hand as too ostentatious. There were twelve sentries on the gate. They wore pretty smart uniforms, too—a general effect not unlike the personal bodyguard of Montcalm during the siege of Quebec, with detail touches borrowed from the doorman at the Hotel Negresco in Nice. But the company of soldiers drilling in the courtyard beyond were in olive-drab combat gear and they looked kind of impressive as they marched and countermarched.

Mazzari's ecclesiastical friend must have had some pull, for the sentries leaped to attention as we approached, and we weren't even asked to show our ID papers. The way we looked, I guess it would have been difficult to mistake us for anyone else.

Some kind of majordomo led us past the seven-tiered pagoda where the military were housed, through beaten gold gates in a high wall, and then past a formal garden with tropical trees and fountains to the flight of steps leading to the palace entrance. There were stone tigers guarding the foot of the stairs, and again on either side of the line of metal-studded doors above. ("The Tiger of Muong-Thang, that's the traditional style and title of the emperors here," I told Mazzari. "Wacko!" he said).

I can't begin to describe the outside of the palace. Bands of brilliant mosaic, carved sandstone frescoes, delicate wrought-iron work over the pointed-arch window embrasures, onion domes, towers, minarets yet, they had them all. The place looked like the Taj Mahal in color.

Inside there was a marble-floored lobby the size of a ball park. Wooden settles, carved into the shapes of dragons and tigers again, stood roughly where first, second, and third base would be. Otherwise the great room was empty.

The majordomo went away and we were left wondering

whether it would be dancing girls or a firing squad who came in next. "I think they keep the Cadillacs outside the rear entrance," Mazzari whispered.

Pretty soon the majordomo came back and beckoned us to follow him. We went through two more chambers as large and empty as the first. Then we were joined by a couple of guys with swords who looked like stunt men out of an early kung-fu movie. The five of us approached another pair of soldiers, and finally we were shown into the royal antechamber. This was something else again. Inlaid furniture, lacquered stuff, carved chinoiserie and Japanese screens, tigerskin rugs and silk hangings on the walls—this was the background for his majesty, who lay on a divan scattered with cushions covered in cloth-of-gold.

He rose to his feet as we came in—and that gave me, at any rate, another surprise. The guy was tall for a Thai, or whatever he was, not much wider than a two-car garage, with a hairless face and an expression on it as mean and ornery as anything I've ever seen. He looked as though he could have gone the distance with Man Mountain Dean without getting out of breath. Until he smiled, that is.

And as soon as he smiled, the face was transformed. It became almost genial. Almost. But I couldn't help thinking of that line, "the smile on the face of the tiger."

"Gentlemen," he said, bowing at least a millimeter in our direction, "we are overjoyed to receive members of the Western press in our humble quarters." It sounded like "Shentlemer" and "Welssten prenss," but I let it pass: it was something that the guy spoke English at all. Mazzari and me made suitable noises expressing pleasure and gratitude, and then he said: "And to what do I owe the pleasure of this visit, sirs?"

That was par for the course, and I came up with the obvious answer. There were rumors circulating that the Communist hordes ravaging his country had dared to mount an operation aimed at the elimination of his august self; it was said that his Minister of Home Security had been obliged to seek specialist help from outside to combat this menace; in the light of increasing violence throughout the world, such a bold step would be of great interest to our readers; and like that.

"The press in the emergent countries of Africa, too,

51

would be especially interested in the courageous example set by Muong-Thang," Mazzari added swiftly.

Kao Dinh inclined his imperial head. "Mr. Mettner, I know," he said affably, "represents the American newsmagazine *Worldwide*. To what organ are you, sir, attached and accredited?"

"*The Accra Examiner, Ghana Today* and *Dahomey News and Views*," Mazzari said unblushingly. "A syndicated column."

"Just so." The king-emperor adjusted a fold of his black-and-scarlet robe. "You will realize, of course, dear sirs, that we cannot reveal the details of precautions taken to safeguard our person, nor the precise measures adopted by our new protectors to winnow out and eliminate those who presume to threaten the life of our royal selves. However"—he made a graceful gesture toward the northeast corner of the antechamber—"our trusted Minister of Home Security, the Honorable Ngon Thek, and Colonel Marc Dean, who is in command of the specialists charged with our well-being, will doubtless between them be able to furnish you with a generalized picture of the situation. The Honorable Ngon Thek, in addition, can provide colorful information on the complementary activities of our own security services."

I turned and looked northeast. At the far end of a hundred-yard dash, I could make out two figures, both standing: a thin, skeletal guy with a face the texture of a walnut shell, and Dean himself. He was sporting a very nice line in tailored combat gear, forest green, with four broad gold stripes on the shoulder straps of the bloused top. I nodded as though I'd never set eyes on him before, and Mazzari followed suit.

We asked a lot of damn-fool questions, pretended to take notes, and made a date with the Honorable Minister for a conducted tour of the city security system the following day. After that we bowed ourselves out, and our grateful thanks to your Supreme Highness. Dean was deputed to escort us to the exit.

" 'Our royal selves' is good," I said, "even if he is wide enough for two.

"He's okay really," Dean said. "He's begun to believe his own publicity, that's all."

I nodded again and clammed up, because the walk to

the gates was the only chance we had to get the lowdown on the questions we had really come to ask.

Dean's six-man team was working in pairs, it seemed—two guys on duty actually making with the bodyguard bit and staying close to the king; two resting; and two on call. Alternate watches, twenty-four hours per day.

That was the official picture. In fact it was the two men off duty who would be doing the important work, quartering the city incognito, eyes and ears open for any hint, any lead that could finger a group, an organization or an individual likely to be involved in an assassination attempt . . . and any rumors about when that attempt could be. If and when they hit paydirt, the group as a whole would strike. Until then Mazzari was to stay undercover, retaining the newshawk front and liaising with the others twice a day. Neither the king nor the minister was to be wised up on Mazzari's true identity.

And me? "This time," Dean told me—was it with a certain reluctance?—"this time you can help instead of hinder. If you stick around with Ed, it will strengthen his cover. And since the damned town is crawling with as much gossip as Casablanca in World War Two, your nose for news could maybe help put us on the scent." He favored me with a wintry smile. "You might even get a story out of it."

"Exclusive?"

"Exclusive. So far as any inside information is concerned. Obviously I can't muzzle the whole world's press if there *is* an assassination attempt, or keep it off the air if they make it and the guy croaks."

"It's a deal," I said. "As of now, meet Mettner the acting unpaid mercenary, stoolpigeon, and spy."

We shook hands. Dean instructed us to make contact twice a day, either with him or one of his men, at the Teahouse of the Fragrant Blossoms, just off the city's central square. There was also an emergency routine in case something big broke between meetings.

Mazzari and me went to pick up the machine pistols we'd checked in at the guardhouse, and then we walked out past the twelve sentries to recuperate our bicycles.

They had, of course, been stolen.

6 Sean Hammer

The Teahouse of the Fragrant Blossoms boasted a small garden. In the center of this was a sinuous ornamental pond crossed by a wooden bridge, and around the water, white-painted tables and chairs had been set among the almond, cherry, lotus, and frangipani flowers that were supposed to justify the establishment's name. Insofar as there was a fashionable meeting place in Am-Phallang, this was it. The wives of those minor consular officials the major powers had consigned to Muong-Thang could gather there without blemishing their reputations; local profiteers could show off their concubines; foreign correspondents used the somber interior almost as a club; traders and planters drowned their economic sorrows among the reflected lilies in the pond; and senior officers in Kao Dinh's army drank there in the evening. For the refreshments obtainable were not restricted to jasmine tea and Oriental sweetmeats. If the garden in fact was something like a cross between the Anne de Sévigny tearoom in the Champs Elysées and the old American bar at the Hotel Aletti in Algiers, the place as a whole stirred memories of Munich beer gardens as well as Shepherd's Hotel in Cairo.

"Okay, okay," Jason Mettner protested when Dean had explained all this to him. "So the joint's cosmopolitan. What do you want me to do: stand up and cheer?"

"Sit down and listen, smart-ass," Dean told him. "Like I said at the palace yesterday. With all the gossip going in this town, and enough of us on the lookout, something's bound to come up in the way of a lead sometime."

"I go for a guy he should be specific, I really do," said Abe Wassermann, who was the other off-duty merc that afternoon. "You will be expecting us maybe to make a round of the city's opium dens, all expenses paid, in the hope of a tipoff from one of the addicts?"

"You could do worse," Dean said. "If your money's the right color and you know the right words, you could even do that here."

"You're joking!" Wassermann looked across at the Chinese proprietor and his slender wife, who stood smiling beneath the pagoda awning between the teahouse and the garden. "You mean to say that Han Yin and Mrs. Han . . . ?"

"Certainly." Dean was amused. "Up the stairway in back of the bar. It's not a crime here, you know."

"Don't tell me," Wassermann said. "Some of your best friends . . ."

"Some of my best contacts. It was up there last night that I heard tell of a certain Mr. Theng, an import-export merchant with a godown on the main canal. I suspect that he's the local Mr. Big in the dope racket, and his imports come mainly from the poppy fields of Pakistan. Nevertheless, I have a date with him tomorrow. Mr. Theng, I am told, will also export anything—even information—if the price is right."

It was not, however, through the mysterious Mr. Theng that Dean's first lead finally arrived. The break came that same evening, when the teahouse and the garden were at their fullest. Dean had returned to spell the mercs at the palace. Hammer and Novotny were the off-duty men. Novotny was sitting with Mettner at one of the sidewalk cafés that were a carryover from the French, by the government buildings beyond the fountains in the square. The little Ulsterman was with Mazzari in the teahouse bar.

The place was crowded and noisy, more boisterous than it ever was in the afternoon, and rattan chairs had been pushed back against the bamboo walls to make room for the closely packed drinkers. "By God," Hammer exclaimed suddenly, a tankard of beer halted halfway to his mouth, "if that isn't your man Furneux over there!" He nodded toward a chunky, hard-faced character hinged forward over an outsize rye-and-dry at the far end of the bar.

Mazzari looked over and nodded in his turn. "Hole in one, old lad," he said. "I wonder what the devil he's doing here?"

"Me too," Hammer said. "I'll not be the better of it,

but I guess I'd better buy the fucker a drink and try to find out."

Furneux was a Canadian, a French-Canadian from Quebec. He was also a mercenary. He had worked with Marc Dean once, on a madcap adventure in West Africa—but experience had shown that he suffered from the three defects that the combat leader could not tolerate at any price: he was a racist; he was a moaner; he was the first to take cover when the shooting started . . . and the first to brag after it stopped. When the mission was successfully completed, Dean swore never to use the man again.

"Me," said Mazzari, "I'd better split. In this town, I'm supposed to be a newspaperman, nothing whatever to do with you chaps. And Furneux knows perfectly well that I *am* connected with you. I'll join Emil and Mettner across the road and see you later." He finished his drink and made for the door.

Hammer threaded his way through the crowd and limped up to the bar. He figured it would be more . . . More what? More stylish? Yes, more stylish. more professional, to allow himself to be recognized rather than blundering straight in the deep end with a big hello.

It was clear that Furneux was very drunk. The network of tiny veins on either side of his nose was flushed, his forehead was glistening, and his eyelids drooped. Fortunately, Hammer recalled, he always had been a loudmouth, so the pumping shouldn't be too hard a job now.

Just the same, it was not until two drinks later that the Canadian's bleary eyes focused on him and the familiar, overhearty voice cried out, "Jeez! If it ain't the chief Mick himself! I never expected to see you here, Hammer: what the fuck are you doin' in this neck of the woods?"

"Hi, there, Furneux," said Hammer, doing his best to sound equally surprised. "I could ask you the same. I just finished a private job for a group of planters up in Malaysia there. Some of the locals getting above themselves. You know. An' I figured maybe—since I was in this part of the world anyway—there might be pickin's around here. Where there's fighting there's usually loot to be picked up, eh? I guess that's why you're here too?"

The Canadian's features arranged themselves in a cunning expression. "Listen," he said, leaning forward until his liquored breath played on Hammer's face, "anyone he's real smart, he don't have to mess with the shootin' himself. He can leave that to the gooks—and the wogs and dagos the Reds send to help them. A smart guy, he fixes it so he stays in the background, organizing. You understand what I mean?"

"Sure I understand," Hammer said. "Your glass is empty: what'll you have?"

"Rye-and-dry," Furneux mumbled. "Set 'em up, Jack. Same again . . . and keep your fuckin' thumb outta the measure this time, huh? It's my friend here that's pickin' up the tab, and he's on the ball."

The bartender's face remained inscrutable. He refilled Hammer's tankard and placed another glass in front of Furneux. Hammer said, "Well, here's to you, but." He raised his glass and drank. "It's the clever ones row themselves into the kind of billet you have, all right. By what you say, you got yourself a good one?"

"I ain't complainin'," Furneux said.

Hammer took a long pull at his beer and marshaled his thoughts. It seemed clear from what the man had said already that he was in some way connected with the rebels—the derogatory reference to Arabs and/or Cubans tended to prove that. But exactly what the connection was, it might be hard to discover. "Would there," he said carefully, "be anny way a feller who's not afraid to press a trigger could carve himself a wee slice outta this?"

Furneux drooped still farther over his drink. Discipline and discretion, those two traits so essential to a mercenary, were obviously warring with his desire to make himself out a big shot. "Search me," he said finally, breathing heavily into the rye. "How would I know?"

Hammer said nothing.

"I tell you what, though." Furneux's need to boast was winning over what remained of his caution. "No dice so far as my detail's concerned. You have to be known personally to . . . well, to the guy writes the check. But if you wanna do yourself a bit of good . . ." The cunning smile was turning into a leer. "Why not try the old bastard runs the pottery at Phra Kao?"

"The old pottery?"

"The one in the monastery. The old frog's been there a hundred years." Furneux began to sing to himself; some of the liquor slopped over his wrist as he raised his glass to his mouth. It was evident that he wasn't going to stay lucid much longer.

"Mention your name?" Hammer said ingratiatingly, trying to memorize what the drunk had said.

"Why the hell not?" The Canadian shook with raucous laughter. "You won't get anyplace without you do!" Abruptly he folded his arms on the bar and rested his forehead against them. He didn't even notice Hammer go.

Hammer in fact went only as far as the square. Flags and banners and lanterns from some local fete were strung across the roadway between the streetlamps, but traffic in the administrative center was light at this time. Most of Am-Phallang's night life was concentrated along the waterfront a couple of blocks away: every now and then he could hear snatches of laughter and music, and the sound of many voices. He crossed over to the ornamental fountains, where colored lights played red and green and blue on jets of water between shining stone dragons and tigers. Two tri-shaws skated past, heading for the riverside. A large black sedan sped around in the opposite direction, its tires hissing where gusts of wind had blown spray across the wet macadam.

The Ulsterman sat on the rim of a basin surrounding one of the fountains, resting his artificial leg along the concrete lip. He leaned forward, as a man might retying a shoelace or pulling up a sock. In reality, he was manipulating the controls of the radio concealed in the casing just above the ankle joint.

"It's all right," he said quietly into the perforations of the shin, "you can talk back when I've made me report, for there's nobody here but meself and the tigers—and the sound of the water will mask our voices unless some person will sit directly beside me."

"*Phra Kao?*" Dean repeated when Hammer had wised him up on the unexpected meeting with the Canadian merc. "*That's an area just this side of the Khmer border, up in the northeast. And it's not more than a half-hour's drive from the frontier with Laos. It could be a promising lead, Sean.*"

"I would hope," Hammer said. "I think the man was flustered enough not to realize how much he was giving away. He's in with the Reds, all right—and some other fellers too, from what he said. But what he meant, talking of potteries and monasteries, I do not know."

"We'll find out; we'll go there right away." The voice emanating from the tiny speaker was suddenly dubious. *"What I don't get, Sean . . ."*

"Yes?"

"There's something here doesn't quite stack up. Edmond's undercover, okay. But the rest of us—shit, the whole world knows we're here, and why. That was part of the idea, to make it public. I'm not too sure myself, but Ngon Thek believed it might act as some kind of deterrent, publicizing the fact that pros had been employed. The opposition were even expecting us, witness the bomb attempt on our Toyota the day the boys arrived." Dean paused. Hammer could almost see him shake his head. Then he added: *"Yet here's this guy Furneux, not a good one, but a pro just the same—a pro working for the opposition, by his own admission—and apparently he's never heard of us being here, he's astonished to see you, and he swallows a story that you just 'happen' to be in town on the lookout for a job. Don't you think that's . . . well, odd?"*

"Maybe he just hit town," Hammer said. "From this Phra Kao dump. Especially if, like you say, it's out in the sticks."

"Yeah," Dean said. *"I guess that must be it."* But he didn't sound entirely convinced. He said: *"Anyway, before we go up there, I'll try to check it out with this Mr. Theng tomorrow. If I'm loaded with enough U.S. dollars, maybe I can persuade him to export a little information about this monastery—and about friend Furneux too."*

Hammer was still leaning forward, returning the various controls to zero, when the two men rushed him.

The splashing of the fountains had drowned the sound of their approaching footsteps, and it was only in the last few yards, when they began to run and their feet struck hard on the pavement, that he looked up. He saw nothing but two dark silhouettes, huge figures against the overhead lights, with outstretched arms. And then he was pushed violently sideways and fell into the water brimming the basin.

He had no time to react, to wonder, even to register surprise, before his two ankles were seized, the true and the false, and his legs were hoisted high into the air and twisted, so that he was facedown in the water.

He choked, gasping for breath, arching his back in an attempt to raise his head above the surface. But steely fingers closed in a viselike grip over the back of his neck, forcing his head down, holding it under.

Hammer's chest heaved; his lungs expanded, screaming for air. The mouth opened involuntarily underwater, sucking inward. Water flooded the lungs, and he choked again.

The water was less than eighteen inches deep, but it does not take long to drown a man when he has no chance of breathing air at all. It is a matter of only seconds if the attack is a surprise and the lungs empty to start with.

Hammer's arms threshed this way and that, seeking a hold. His flailing hands encountered nothing but air and water. His ankles were still held firmly high in the air; the ferocious clamp on his neck was not relaxed. He could feel the blood thundering behind his eyes. An iron band tightened around his chest. And for a short while the world receded, and everything became faint and distant and extraordinarily slow.

Then he was astonishingly on his hands and knees, vomiting water. The pavement was cold and hard beneath his bones. A voice—a dark, low, liquid voice—said somewhere above him, "Thank Christ—I think he's going to be all right."

Mazzari.

Mazzari? He spun around and sat up, his head still swimming. Mazzari and Jason Mettner crouched above him, their faces anxious. "We couldn't catch them," Mettner said. "They saw us coming and ran."

"How . . . ?" Hammer croaked. "How did you . . . ?"

"We were drinking at the French café up the street there," Mazzari said. "We thought we'd call by the teahouse and collect you. And on the way, crossing the square, we saw . . ."

Hammer coughed up some more water. "The Dear knows you just made it in time," he said weakly. "One leg I can manage without, but both me lungs, in full workin' condition, I need all the time!"

7 Marc Dean

Mr. Theng's godown proved to be a ramshackle complex at the end of a stretch of waste ground bordering the canal on the western side of the city. It had originally been a large, single-story, individual warehouse with a corrugated iron roof, but a collection of lean-to buildings had been added one by one, and now the place was an L-shaped testament to the increasing prosperity of its owner, an extraordinary agglomeration of cane furniture and bales of cloth, of French *chiffoniers* and Chinese cabinets and monkish refectory tables. The annexes which had been built on as the trade increased framed an open-air scrapyard, mainly composed of the wrecks of American automobiles. Dean wondered, making his way to the office, how many of them had lost their tailpipes to rebel mortar crews.

Mr. Theng was a Cochin Chinese, a bland and ageless man wearing a cinnamon shantung suit and a green necktie. He received Dean in a surprisingly luxurious room hidden behind a mountain of galvanized bathtubs, marble-topped café tables, and fiber suitcases roped together in dozens. Dean stared around the room with interest. It was a complete anomaly: a deep-pile, off-white wall-to-wall carpet, black hide armchairs, a modernistic Italian desk made of some hard marbled synthetic that glittered beneath a futurist ceiling light. There were no pictures, but the wall behind the desk was covered by a collection of nineteenth-century pendulum clocks—perhaps fifteen or twenty of them—whose stealthy ticking supplied a mechanical obbligato to the sibilants of Mr. Theng's greeting.

"Do you care to smoke, Colonel Dean?" he asked when the preliminary courtesies had been exchanged, waving a languid hand at a row of ivory opium pipes on a carved stand.

"It is kind of you, but I have yet to acquire the taste," Dean said in the Thai language. "I should, however, be desolated if you were to deny yourself that pleasure on my account."

"My pleasure," said Mr. Theng politely, "is already at its zenith, since you honor my house with your visit."

Dean permitted his mind to wander as the ritual exchange of Oriental pleasantries ran its ceremonial course. He knew that, until the late seventies, 80 percent of the world's heroin supply had come from the "golden triangle" formed by Burma, Laos, and Thailand—but that since then the huge opium crops and illicit refineries of Pakistan's northwest frontier provinces had reduced the Southeast Asians' share of the market. He knew that they were more than anxious to recover that share—and why. Refined heroin cost from $2,500 to $5,000 a pound in the countries where it was produced; on the open market of the West, it fetched between $20,000 and $100,000. With such huge profits available, the original suppliers wanted to climb back aboard. With the additional advantage that such profits derived from a product with so little bulk, it was to be expected that a small country like Muong-Thang wanted a piece. It was hardly surprising that growers and dealers and pushers and middlemen were familiar with the underworld—from penniless addicts who would kill for a fix to the crime barons who had added dope to the gambling, prostitution, and protection rackets that they controlled.

It was likely that a man like Mr. Theng knew something about the professional assassins in his own manor.

Once his host had discreetly steered the subject of conversation to the reasons for his own presence in Am-Phallang, Dean was no longer obliged to make his approach circuitously. It was an open secret that a bodyguard of "roundeyes" had been employed because of a feared assassination attempt. "In order that our task may be made more simple," he said cautiously, "there are those who would make available certain sums of money in return for information."

"Indeed?" said Mr. Theng.

"It has in fact been suggested that a man of your eminence in the business world might conceivably know of someone—a person of lesser stature, of course—who would in turn perhaps have contacts able to discover some of the things we wished to know. To avoid embarrassment and the possible identification of informants who might wish to remain anonymous, a further suggestion was made that the sums in question should be paid directly to you, for you to . . . disburse . . . as you saw fit."

Mr. Theng nodded. "It is conceivable that I might be able to assist in some small way," he admitted. "Nothing, of course, is certain . . . but it is certainly conceivable."

Dean acknowledged the elegance of the paradox with an inclination of his head. He said, "As surely as anything can be stated, I can assure you that your government would be grateful."

"*The* government," said Mr. Theng, expressly renouncing the possessive form, "relies for its continued existence on the support of your country. It would have no autonomous state to govern had it not been for the influence of your country at the UN. In exchange, the American government requires among other things that a strict control be exercised on the export from Muong-Thang of certain commodities in which I have an interest."

Dean said nothing.

"To be precise"—pale eyebrows lifted fractionally on the bland face across the desk—"the federal Narcotics Bureau have exerted pressure in such a way that the activities of the customs officials here are rapidly becoming insupportable. Insupportable."

Dean cleared his throat. "I have no mandate," he said, "to bargain in terms of . . . ah . . . concessions on the part of the authorities here. I am empowered only—you will forgive me if I put the matter in our crude Western way?—to offer money for information. In any case, I am not sure that the government—"

"Of course not!" Astonishingly for an Oriental, Mr. Theng interrupted. "Under the present circumstances, they could offer nothing; they have no freedom of maneuver. That is understood. But when order has been restored . . . We are used to employing patience in this part of the world; we take the long-term view, as you say.

A word from someone such as yourself into the right ear . . ."

The deeper implications were left unsaid. Dean promised to say the required word. Mr. Theng clapped his hands twice, and a Thai youth brought in an ornate tea set on a silver tray. While the infusion was being prepared and poured, the conversation became general once more. It was not until several cups of the fragrant, almost colorless drink had been consumed that the purpose of Dean's visit was referred to again. "Some while ago," Mr. Theng said carelessly, "I believe you mentioned, in a particular context, certain sums of money. How precisely could these be expressed?"

"In thousands of United States dollars," Dean said.

"Just so." Mr. Theng flicked a nonexistent speck of dust from the polished top of his desk. "Preceded by . . . ?" he asked.

"A single figure in the first instance. Double figures if an assassin or assassins should be identified and . . . immobilized."

Mr. Theng nodded. He drew a deep breath. And then, with the air of a man introducing a new subject, he said, "The annual review and march-past of infantry and armored formations at the royal palace in ten days' time should be a colorful event, do you not think, Colonel Dean?"

"Immensely," Dean said dryly.

"One supposes, nevertheless, that you and your men will be too busy fulfilling your prophylactic role to enjoy the spectacle."

"Doubtless."

Mr. Theng picked a tea leaf from his lower lip. "A pity," he said. "The ceremony will be well worth watching. This year in particular, I am told, it will repay the most minute attention."

"Indeed, there is something about parades that compels our . . . watchfulness," Dean rejoined. "But interest in a foreign country—one can, when off duty, regard oneself almost as a tourist, after all—interest in a foreign country does not begin and end with the splendor of its military."

"No?" For the first time, his host looked puzzled.

"As important, surely, is the impact of its culture? The work of its artists and artisans—poets and painters, sculptors and singers, weavers and workers in ceramic. They tell me, for instance, that the Phra Kao pottery is well worth a visit."

Mr. Theng was suddenly very quiet. The multiple ticking of his clocks appeared by contrast to increase in volume. He curled the fingers of both hands and inspected his long, pale, clean nails. Finally he said expressionlessly, "The aged Frenchman, yes. He attempts to combine the virtues of the Japanese Cha-No-Yu masters with the techniques of the best Soong craftsmen. But one cannot reproduce Ying-Ching or Tz'ou Chou glazes with the clays we have in this country."

"Perhaps not. Would you advise me nevertheless to go?"

"It is not *advisable* for anyone to go there. The monastery is very near the frontier; it is a route much favored by clandestine immigrants, guerrillas who come to aid the rebels. It is a dangerous region for foreigners to frequent."

"Even so . . . you think it might interest me? The pottery seems, despite the dangers, to have survived."

"Oh, yes." For the first time since Dean had raised the subject, Mr. Theng looked up. "It is possible that you would find it interesting. Anything is possible . . . even if nothing is certain."

Shortly afterward, Dean took his leave. The question of money was not raised again. "It is most kind of you to have received me," he said. "I thank you for your hospitality . . . and your help."

"Your welcome visit has transformed an otherwise dull day into one to remember," said his host courteously.

Hammer was waiting a block away in another of the palace Toyotas. "He as good as told me straight off the bat that the attempt will be made during the march-past in ten days' time," Dean said as they drove back to the palace. "What we have to do now is case the joint like crazy."

Hammer shifted down to negotiate a flood of tri-shaws pouring from a side street. "Case the joint? What kind of talk is that?" He swore, swerved around a sports car making an unexpected—and unsignaled—left turn, and then stamped on the brakes as a bus with several dozen people clinging to the rear platform stopped suddenly in front of

66

him. "You've been reading those pulp magazines again, Marc!" he accused.

"We have to survey that parade ground," Dean said, "like we were planning to rub out his excellency ourselves. And when we've discovered the places it could be done from, we have to keep them covered night and day until the killers show. In the meantime, we also have to find strategic points from which *we* can zap the killers as they draw a bead on the king."

"Why don't we just wait for them in *their* hiding places, and take them as they come in?" Hammer asked.

"Because they could have a backup, a reserve operation set up," his leader explained. "We dare not act until the very last moment, until they're certain their primary plan is in orbit. Otherwise, if they suspect anything has screwed up, they could bring that backup into play and we'd be fucked."

"What about your man Furneux's bloody pottery?"

"Cagey. Theng seemed almost sore when I mentioned it. I don't know if he was mad because he didn't want us to know about it for some reason or whether he was hoping to tell us about it later—and ask for more money on account of the information."

"How about his loot anyway? Did you make plans?"

Dean shook his head. "That wouldn't be smart. Not with an inscrutable Oriental. It would be indiscreet; he could lose face. Arrangements will be made so that a suitable sum finds its way into one of his accounts. He'll know what it's for."

"But you don't do anything so coarse, so frightfully vulgar, as haggling or actually talking terms?"

"You better not let Edmond hear you talk that way," Dean chuckled. "A Mick taking the Mickey, as Furneux would say. No—on the surface we're simply asking Theng's advice. Man to man, boss to boss. Five grand, ten grand, a bagatelle like that can be left to lesser men: in any case, it's just to cover expenses, in case his minions have to soil their hands offering bribes to the rabble."

"Got it," Hammer said. "Hey! Would you look at that!"

Dean looked. "What of it?" A white sports car had shot out of a side street one hundred yards ahead of them and was speeding toward the central square.

"That's the bugger carved me up a coupla minutes ago," Hammer said. "And isn't it the same fuckin' jalopy cut in on us a moment before them guys heaved the bomb at us on the way from the airport?"

Dean stared again. The car was a Mercedes-Benz coupé. So far as he could see through its rear window, the driver was a small man. "You could be right, Sean," he said slowly. "Watch out for Peugeot sedans with one door open!" He peered through the windshield, but the car, threading its way through a mass of tri-shaws, bicycles, and taxicabs circling the square, was lost to sight before he could make out the figures on the license plate. And nobody made any kind of attack on them as they returned to their palace quarters.

"Maybe it's just a tail," Dean said. "But I wonder . . . ?"

He found the girl standing by the arched window when he returned to his room after dinner that night. She was small and slender and she held herself very straight. The quilted cheongsam she wore was embroidered with scarlet hibiscus flowers on a midnight-blue background shot through with gold. Her straight, black, glossy hair was cut short with bangs across the forehead. Beneath the dark fringe, her almond eyes were made up in the Western fashion.

She swung around as Dean came into the room. "If you are interested in visiting Phra Kao," she said, "I can take you there—safely—tomorrow."

8 Jean-Paul Albi

Her name was Golden Dawn—or that at least was the Western equivalent of the unpronounceable Indochinese diphthongs that she uttered when Dean posed the question. Her voice was light and rather high, deepening suddenly and unexpectedly when she laughed, which, like many Eastern women, she did easily and often. She was unlike any girl he had ever known; he found her entirely fascinating.

"How did you know . . . who told you I wanted to go to the monastery?" he asked when he had gotten over his astonishment.

"Friends tell me," she replied. "You do want?"

"Yes, but . . . I understand it could be dangerous."

"It is my uncle," she said simply. "He teaches the potters—both sides know me. I can go freely." Her breasts, he saw, small by European standards, were nevertheless more pronounced than most Thai and Cambodian women's. They were firm and rounded, thrusting out the quilted garment just enough to be provocative.

"I would be most interested," Dean said warily. "I have been told that the pottery—"

"There are other things," she cut in. "You will come tomorrow morning?"

"Sure. That would be swell. You want me to pick you up someplace?"

"Pick me . . . ?"

"Call for you. Collect you. Pass by wherever you live with an automobile."

Golden Dawn shook her small dark head. "I will come here," she said firmly. "In the lane behind the stables. As the sun rises. I will bring bicycles."

"Bicycles!"

"But yes. It is no more than thirty-five miles, all flat.

Riding bicycles, for those with guns a long way off, with far-looking glasses, we are no more than the local peoples. Safe from each side. But a car, especially a strange car, can be an enemy to everyone, and the guns shall fire. Also, I am very well known in the villages: if we ride, they will see there too that it is all right."

"Okay, honey," Dean said with a sigh. "Bicycles it is."

The following morning, leaving Hammer and Daler to keep watch on the king, Schneider and Novotny on call, and Wassermann to help Mazzari and Mettner do the legwork, Dean made his way to the royal stables at dawn. The girl was already there. She was wearing black silk trousers with a shorter, printed top, and her flowerlike face looked as fresh as though she had just come out of a beautician's parlor.

The bicycles were lightweight sports-racing machines, with dropped handlebars and very narrow tires. Despite Dean's misgivings, they traveled fast across the fertile estuarine plain north of the city, passing through a dozen villages, where the inhabitants scarcely paused to look at them, and they were in the frontier region near the monastery before eight o'clock.

It was an area of waterways and canals, where the settlements—less frequent now in the border zone—huddled together on wooden piers a few feet above the surface, with skiffs and sampans moored to projecting boardwalks that surrounded the huts. Long lines of tropical trees— palms and papayas, magnolia and hibiscus and banana— separated the villages from the unending rice fields; and then, farther away still, where the teak forests rose toward the mountains of the interior, the plantations of maize and tea.

The monastery was built on a spit of land at the junction of a canal and a tributary of the Mun River. At the wider end of the spit there was a deep irrigation ditch crossed by a bamboo bridge, so that the place was effectively a triangular island with an area of ten or eleven acres. The main structure was severe and rectangular, five stories high, with lines of narrow oblong windows piercing the ocher walls beneath a shallow slate roof. Dean thought, when first he saw it rising bleakly above the fronded palms, that it looked more like a transplant from Tibet than a Southeast Asian building. But once they had crossed the bridge, the impression vanished: there were thatched outhouses surrounding the central pile, and even a miniature pagoda among the trees, as if the monks who had once been installed there had allowed a liberty of worship in their community, saffron robes among the black and brown.

There were no monks there now, Christian or Buddhist. Dean felt curiously vulnerable, wheeling his bicycle across the narrow bridge behind the girl. He had discarded his palace uniform in favor of jeans, sneakers, and a sweatshirt, and he was unarmed. If, as he imagined (Golden Dawn refused to say), the visit had been arranged by Mr. Theng, it was a service against payment to be made and therefore he had nothing to fear, at least for the moment. What he did not know, of course, was the amount of control, if any, that Theng exercised over those now inhabiting the monastery. But whether it was total or only partial, he figured it could do nothing but provoke suspicion if he came with the evidence of force about him.

No guard stood at the inner end of the bamboo bridge, which was odd in a region constantly changing hands between the king's men and rebels assisted by guerrillas filtering over the border. One of the villages they passed had been subjected recently to some kind of raid: nothing was left of the stilted wooden houses but charred embers and blackened beams floating in the canal. There were bodies there too, gray and bloated in the sluggish water beneath the stench of ashes and corruption. The girl had made no comment as they rode past.

Even if the potters were nonwarlike, Dean thought, it was strange that their domain shouldn't even have a lookout. And then, as they stepped along a rutted track winding toward the monastery, he saw movement off to his right. It was barely perceptible: a stirring of spearhead leaves in a bamboo thicket that screened a row of pipal trees and tamarind. Yet there was no wind, and it was unlikely that an animal would be rooting so vigorously among the close-packed canes.

Seconds later, glancing swiftly to the other side, he glimpsed a shadowy figure, and then another, flitting between the trunks of palms a hundred yards away. Was it his imagination, or were they holding machine pistols? Imagination or not, it was clear that they were being observed . . . and followed. No shots were fired, and nobody challenged them, but the sweat was standing on Dean's forehead and the hairs still prickled the nape of his neck when he walked out into the open space before the monastery.

The burst of color was an extraordianry contrast after the olive and gray and sulfur yellow of the plain. A group of low buildings surrounding the clearing was like houses of fire—a blaze that seemed brighter and more vivid even than the flames ravaging the sacked villages that found themselves in the path of war. The roofs and walls were consumed and almost obliterated by masses of crimson and salmon-pink bougainvillea, licked by the fiery tongues of bignonia, whose orange trailers were themselves swallowed up by furnaces of scarlet canna and hibiscus flowers. Below the sugar-white, rococo, pyramid tiers of the miniature pagoda, vermilion, green, and golden jungle fowl scratched in the dust like small enameled toys. And beyond these, the real furnaces, the domed kilns of the pottery with their vertical flues, were built out from the wall of the ancient building.

A man stood in the center of the courtyard. He was dressed in faded blue denims and a white undershirt. His face was craggy, with small eyes set in a network of wrinkles, and his white hair was crimped naturally into a series of parallel ridges.

He waited until they had come up to him, and then said in a dry, husky voice, "Jean-Paul Albi. What can I do for you?" He did not offer his hand.

"Mr. Dean is interested in the pots," Golden Dawn said, making no other introduction and no greeting of her own.

"Is that so? A strange part of the world—and a long way to come—to indulge such an interest!" The old man's near-contempt was barely concealed.

"Since I am in the country on business anyway," said Dean—it was not credible that Albi would be unaware of his function—"I ventured to ask if I might pass by, not only to view the pottery but also to ask about your community, and how you manage to survive in the middle of so many warring factions. Our friend kindly offered to show me the way." He nodded toward the girl, who was wheeling the two bicycles in the direction of a low wall.

Dean had spoken in French. "You speak the language well," Albi said in a more conciliatory tone. "Come, then, if you wish, and I will show you what we do." He led the way to an adobe outhouse where Annamite students in plain cotton shifts were busy about half a dozen potter's wheels, shaping and kneading and molding the wet clay with deft fingers as it rose from the spinning disks. Dean saw the workbenches where the different local glazes were painted onto finished pots before they were "cooked" in the furnaces. He was shown the woodburning kilns with their forced-draft ducts and their stacking shelves. He heard about oxidation and coloring agents and modeling tools and the hypocaust. In the lofty, cool interior of the monastery, he saw little sign of occupation: most of the Annamites seemed to be camping on the stone floor of what had once been a huge refectory. The tables and benches were long gone, but the rectangular sandstone flags were strewn with sleeping bags, palliasses, and small piles of clothes and personal belongings.

On the second floor, several of the rooms were used as stores for the pottery's product. Rows and rows of near-identical vases and jars stood on wooden shelves echeloned up toward the vaulted ceiling. Most of them were simple, bellied shapes, about twelve inches high. All were covered with a gray-green celadon glaze and decorated with a stylized bird shape in a muddy brown. Around the base of each pot there was a contrasting band of ultramarine two inches deep.

Dean listened to the old Frenchman's commentary with a part of his mind only. Apart from the half-seen military figures among the trees, there were other things here that made him vaguely uneasy. He couldn't define even to himself exactly what it was that struck false notes, but there was certainly something. As his keen gaze swept over every surface, searching for hints and clues, any anachronism or anomaly, the dry voice beside him continued its tireless monologue. "During the sixteenth century in Korea, the Ri dynasty produced a white porcelain that was exceptionally hard. . . . What we call an *argile vitrifiable* tends to melt and lose its shape at anything over 1350 degrees Celsius. . . . Now, if we had the ball-clays of Florida or Carolina in your country . . . No European potteries have ever equaled the Soong, T'ang, or Ming

73

glazes . . . a blue obtained with feldspar and cobalt nitrate . . . Meissen, Dresden, and Sévres in the world of ceramics . . ."

The meandering explanation abruptly ceased. They had arrived at the great winding staircase that spiraled up and down at the far end of the second floor. The upper stories, Albi said, were all closed off, had indeed been unused since the monks left during the war against the French in the fifties. He gestured with his left hand, and Dean saw the wooden partition boarding off the top of the next flight. "Only rats up there," Albi said, "the ones that didn't leave the sinking ship!"

"Not only the rats, surely?" Dean said.

"Pardon?"

"There were others who stayed with the ship."

"You mean me? This . . . work here? If you can call it that."

"Monsieur Albi, if the question is not impertinent, why did you not leave Indochina with the majority of your countrymen when the French pulled out in 1956?"

"My dear young man"—the potter uttered a short, coughing laugh—"I have been here since 1929! Where would I have gone? What could I have done?"

"There are artisan potters in France and other places."

"I know the materials, the minerals and clays and ashes, available locally. I could not support the idea of starting over with different ones. In any case . . ." He shrugged. "Wherever you go, whatever you do, any little success you may have—someone will spoil it, someone will take it away, something will louse it up. *À quoi ça sert*? What is the use?" Again that Gallic heave of the shoulders. "Nothing at all. *Absolument rien du tout.*"

At the foot of the staircase, Albi led the combat chief out into a second, inner courtyard where, beneath the low arches of a colonnade, another group of students were packing finished jars into wooden crates lined with straw.

"During the Han dynasty in China, Colonel Dean, glazing experiments were made using a formula combining sand with the oxides of copper and lead. But it seems that we here can take at least some of the credit for the ensuing cheap, low-temperature enamels—for it was from Annam and Cambodia between the years 200 and 300 that

74

the technique of blending a Liu Li glass mixture with sodium chloride or common salt . . ."

Albi paused in mid-flow. A brown-skinned youth of about seventeen had stumbled and lurched against a packing case. The jar he was carrying slipped from his hands and smashed to pieces on the flagstones at his feet. *"Espèce de petit con,"* Albi shouted, *tu fais encore une fois une chose pareille et je te casserai la gueule!"*

Dean stared. The man was white with rage, his anger altogether excessive in regard to the boy's fault. He had been clumsy, he had broken a pot—but it wasn't an "art" object; it was one of hundreds similar. Surely such fury was a little extreme?

Catching Dean's eye, Albi shook his head. "Excuse me," he said. "All the crates are booked on the same boat. This was a special consignment and now it will be one short . . . and we don't have another *cuisson*—the kilns are not ready to work—until tomorrow. Because of this young fool's carelessness, the whole shipment will now be delayed two days." He stirred the fragments of pottery with his foot, where grains of crystal white lay scattered among the splinters of reddish earthenware. "As you see, we still use salt today," he said. "Too much of it in this case, and it makes the finished product brittle." He ground the powder with his heel and led Dean back to the clearing on the other side of the building.

The sun was now high above the feathered tops of the palms, and the close heat beat back from the adobe walls of the outhouses and shimmered above the dusty ground. Soon the premonsoon haze would turn the sky the color of pewter, but for the moment it remained cloudless and blue. Above the hanging blaze of flowers, linked Buddhas surrounding the blinding white spire of the pagoda stared empty-eyed into the azure distance.

"Which are your main export markets today?" Dean asked as they walked out into the glare.

"Indonesia, Pakistan, the bazaars of Bombay and Rangoon. A smaller proportion to the Middle East," Albi replied. "It is simple cottage-industry material, not the kind of thing that gets shown in Western galleries."

"Even so, the amount of trade must be considerable—judging from what I have seen today. You don't find that the . . . uh . . . disturbances around here affect your work?"

"We have no interest in politics. My students are Annamites, from the other side of the peninsula. In any case, since Prince Souphanouvong threw in his lot with the Pathet Lao, we have been virtually surrounded by the left: Vietnam, Cambodia, and the Khmers to the east, as well as Laos to the north. So far, they have done us no harm, and unless the monastery is seized and used as a stronghold by one side or the other in the present conflict, I see no reason to fear that this state of affairs will not continue."

Dean thought for a moment of mentioning the armed men he had seen among the trees, but decided against it: if the enigmatic old Frenchman was a party to their presence, he wasn't going to admit it, or he would have said something before now; if he was unaware of their existence, it seemed pointless to alarm him—and anyway, Dean could do nothing about it.

"It has been most interesting," he said, "and I thank you for sparing me the time. It was of course due to our mutual friend Furneux that I heard of your work in the first place."

"Furneux?"

"A French-Canadian. In the same business as myself. We had the impression that perhaps he was employed . . . But never mind. At least we assumed that you knew each other quite well."

"I never heard of the man," Albi said curtly. He nodded once and then turned to walk back toward the kilns.

The girl was sitting in the shade of a tamarind, trying to coax one of the gilded jungle fowl to peck seeds from her hand. She rose quickly to her feet and went to fetch the bicycles when she saw that Dean was ready to go.

The visit was hardly a success from the point of view of information gained, he reflected as they pushed the machines back over the bridge. Apart from the elusiveness of Albi himself, there were a number of things, moreover, that required a specific explanation.

Foremost among these was the fact that Dean had noticed, half-hidden beneath a sleeping bag in the refectory, a lightweight suit of camouflaged jungle combat gear.

9 Golden Dawn

The ambush was carefully planned. Dean and the girl had been riding for a quarter of an hour—just time enough to become convinced that they were out of the danger zone. They were about five miles south of the monastery, and the dust road, bordered on either side by the deep-rutted tracks of bullock carts, arrowed straight as a die across the rice fields ahead.

There was a low bluff, surmounted by a clump of palms and the burned-out ruins of a watchtower, a hundred yards away on their left. To the right, on the far side of a stretch of scrub, the river curled slowly toward the sea.

Dean looked at the sky. As sediment dulls a glass of wine, the bright blue had been tarnished by the noonday haze, and now in the oppressive heat parts of this dun overcast were separating out into cloud masses that threatened to pile up into a hammerhead over the distant city. "I'm not too familiar with this particular corner," Dean said, "but anyplace else those clouds would spell rain to me. Would that be possible here today?"

"Oh, yes," Golden Dawn replied, laughing, "it is possible. A sudden heavy shower. The monsoon is only ten days or two weeks away."

"That's great," Dean complained. "Damned near thirty miles to go, and not an oilskin or a bus shelter—"

The sentence was never finished. The front wheel of the bike buckled beneath him and he was thrown head-first into the roadway. Instinctively he kept rolling, his hands and knees smarting from the sting of the gravel, as the echoes of the burst of submachine-gun fire lost themselves over the flat land.

In gunnery schools, students are always told that, with any weapon that commands a rapid rate of fire, it is virtually only the first shot that is accurate, the recoil effect jerking up the barrel and sending subsequent rounds high. The marksman who had fired at Dean and the girl from the ruins of the watchtower had learned this lesson—but he had overcompensated and aimed too low, which was why Dean's bicycle had collapsed instead of its rider.

Still rolling, he saw that the girl too was down, tangled up with her machine on the lip of the embankment carrying the road. He leaped to his feet and reached her in a single bound. Scooping her up in his arms, he flung himself down the far slope.

They landed amid the sun-dried ruts of the bullock track in a shower of small stones. A second burst of gunfire scuffed up the road surface and raised a cloud of dust along the rim of the embankment above them. "Quick!" Dean gasped. "In among the scrub . . . the river . . ."

"You don't have any . . . ?" Golden Dawn seemed more excited than alarmed.

"No," Dean rapped. "I'm unarmed. Run, before they come down and cross the road." He seized her hand and plunged in among the bushes.

From somewhere behind them they heard a shout. A long way off, an impatient driver was gunning a truck motor. They separated, zigzagging through the dried leaves and rattling, whippy branches as more shots rang out behind them—at least two gunmen, if not three, Dean thought, thanking his lucky stars that they were out of effective SMG range. Over fifty or sixty yards, he knew, a soldier would be lucky to bring down a moving target. Even so, some of the slugs were uncomfortably close: more than one was near enough to stir the waist-high leaves at his side.

It was just over a hundred yards to the water's edge. As they burst through the final screen of bushes, Dean saw that there was a logjam stretching halfway across the broad river. Huge rafts of teak, floating down from the forest to the sawmills outside the city, were piling up one behind the other on account of some obstruction downstream.

Swiftly he glanced behind. There were three gunmen. They were small men, rushing breast-high through the scrub. At that distance their faces were anonymous, their combat fatigues unrecognizable. They could have been rebels, they could have been Red mercenaries from over the border, they could have been Kao Dinh's men, trigger-happy at the sight of strangers. They could, for that matter, have been simple bandits, ready to use the civil war as an excuse to plunder the first travelers to come along.

Dean wasn't going to wait to find out. He took a running jump and leaped three yards onto the nearest raft. Golden Dawn plunged into the water and waded out to him. He hauled her up and they started to run out along the slippery logs. Their pursuers were only a few feet short of the riverbank.

It was difficult for Dean and the girl to keep their balance, hastening across the rafts: the convex surface of each balk of timber was wet, and apart from the rolling displacement caused by their pounding feet, each log was subject to movement by the water as its center of gravity shifted with the fugitives' passage. As soon as Dean saw that the ambushers were following them out across the jam, he rushed to the edge of the raft they were on and pulled the girl down beside him. "Can you swim underwater?" he panted.

She nodded.

"Good. We'll go in here, then. Cut across beneath the corner of each raft so you don't get trapped below the surface—but bring up your head only long enough to gulp in the air you need when you're in the open water between rafts." He smiled suddenly, the flesh around the blue eyes crinkling and the stern lines of his face softening into the rakish, devil-may-care expression that so many women were unable to resist. "See you on the other side," he said.

They disappeared beneath the surface as the gunmen opened fire once more.

Dean lost the cracking stammer of the SMG's in the gurgle of water closing over his head. The water was brackish, thick, opaque with the mud held in suspension—and surprisingly cold. There was also an unexpectedly strong current, flowing much faster than the immobilized rafts in the logjam would suggest. He struck out beneath the next raft, swimming with the current and conserving his strength.

He had hoped that the channel of open water between

each log platform would signal itself as the light filtered down below the surface, but the river was so muddy that no rays could penetrate its depths. He swam in total darkness, gauging when to come up for air by the number of strokes he had made. It was more hazardous—and a lot more difficult—than using a shaft of light. He hoped the girl was making out all right.

The first time, he judged it correctly, surfacing in a narrow alley between two rafts. He breathed deeply once, twice, and then filled his lungs with air and dived again.

The next time, he never knew exactly how, he made an error: instead of bursting out into the daylight, his head struck the underside of a raft as he came up. Was he too far left, right, or was it simply that he hadn't swum far enough? Eyes searching for the slightest paling of the darkness, he kicked out afresh.

And again when he tried to surface the back of his head jarred against wood.

For an instant Dean was near to panic. Had the raft moved downstream? How had he miscalculated? Which way should he go? The thought of that great mass of logs above him—and the relatively small proportion of the jam occupied by the channels between each raft—provoked a sudden onslaught of claustrophobia that threatened to engulf him. His lungs were bursting; he could hear the blood hammering behind his eyes. In seconds, perhaps only tenths of a second, he would be unable to control the involuntary contraction of his muscles any longer: his lungs would suck in water, and that would be the end.

Summoning the last reserves of his strength, he forced himself to make one final effort, striking out at random to his right . . . and this time, barely perceptible in the murk, there *was* a lightening of the darkness. He shot to the surface, his agonized mouth dragging in the air that his body craved.

But the gasping breath drew the attention of his pursuers: from startlingly near at hand there was a burst of gunfire. Bullets thwacked into the water and gouged splinters from the nearest log. Once again Dean dived.

He made the next channel without incident, and the next. By the time he reached the outer limit of the logjam, his breathing was back to normal.

Between the last raft and the farther bank of the river there was fifty yards of open water. For the moment he seemed to have escaped the attention of the gunmen, but how was he going to cross that reach without drawing their fire again? He rolled over onto his back and stared at the sky. It was as dark as the river water. The storm clouds that had been building up over Am-Phallang were now almost directly overhead.

He glanced along the assembly of rafts . . . and suddenly stiffened. A hundred yards downstream, a group of loggers sat in a sampan that was covered by a canvas awning stretched over hoops. Ninety yards nearer, one of Dean's pursuers stood at the edge of the jam, looking down into the water.

Clearly, it would be impossible to reach the far bank while he was there. And Dean was sure that he couldn't swim fifty yards underwater without surfacing at least once for air.

Characteristically, he decided to make use of the problem and turn it to his own advantage. Once more he looked left and right along the floating logs. There was no sign of Golden Dawn.

Dean uttered a choking gasp, and then—as the guerrilla started and looked his way—took a deep breath and submerged. He pushed himself just under the edge of the raft and waited until the shuddering of the wood, as the man ran up, transmitted itself to his shoulders. A shadow fell across the murky water surface.

Dean slid out from beneath the logs, rose out of the water, and seized an ankle of the watcher above in a single smooth movement. Before the man had a chance to react, he jerked violently and sank back into the river, still holding on to the ankle.

Pulled off balance, the gunman dropped his weapon, gave a startled cry, and plunged into the water.

Dean was waiting for him as he surfaced, open-mouthed, gasping for air. He launched himself forward, placed both hands on the guerrilla's shoulders, and shoved down with all his strength.

The man sank beneath the surface.

Before the first bubbles broke, Dean had brought up his knees, braced his feet against the struggling body, and then—straightening his legs suddenly—pushed it farther down and underneath the log platform.

He waited, panting slightly, treading water.

For perhaps fifteen or twenty seconds nothing happened. Then there was a commotion just below the surface a little way to his left. Swirls and eddies slapped wavelets against the wood. The top of the guerrilla's head, his agonized face, emerged from the water.

Dean surged tigerishly toward him. The man struggled feebly, choking, but he was no match for the combat leader. Remorselessly, he was forced under once more. As he fought, more weakly now, in the muddy depths of the river, Dean grasped the edge of the raft and supported his weight on his arms. Again he found the drowning gunman with his feet . . . and this time he thrust him deep down and far out under the logs.

For the second time he waited. A quarter of a minute passed, half a minute, forty-five seconds. Nothing disturbed the lazy flow of the current jostling the logs under the lowering sky.

When it was evident that there would be no coming up for the third time for his victim, Dean swam hurriedly back to the spot where the man had dropped his weapon. It was an Uzi submaching gun, balanced precariously on the edge of the raft. He hauled himself half out of the water and grabbed the gun. The other two guerrillas had been at the far end of the jam, questioning the loggers in their sampan, but they had started to run back across the balks of floating teak when they heard their companion fall into the water. The whole episode had taken less than two minutes, yet they were now no more than thirty or forty yards away. Supporting his weight on his elbows, Dean sighted the gun as best he could and squeezed the trigger.

After half a dozen shots, the hammer clicked uselessly: the magazine was expended. But the two men had already thrown themselves flat behind a supplementary log balanced on top of one of the rafts. In turn, they fired snap shots in Dean's direction from the safety of their refuge, but the slugs plowed harmlessly into the wood yards away from him. At the same time, as abruptly as a curtain falling across a stage, the heavens opened and a squall of torrential rain swept over the river. It snaked across the water like a whiplash, pock-marking the dun surface and then bouncing high off the logs, blotting out the view of the far bank in solid, drenching sheets.

The surviving guerrillas stumbled to their feet and ran back toward the embankment, the road, and the shelter of their ruin. They had lost one man and one SMG and gained a pair of smashed bicycles. Dean hoped they figured it for a fair deal.

He struck out for the farther shore, swimming mostly submerged to escape the stinging assault of the rain on his head and shoulders. As he forged ahead, he worried again about the girl. He had seen no sign of her since they first lowered themselves into the water. Now that he no longer had to contend with the attackers, he could devote all of his mental energy to self-reproach: could she swim well enough to judge when to emerge from beneath the rafts? There was no way of telling. Had she been gunned down by their assailants or trapped under the logs? It was impossible to say. Should he have stayed with her, swum by her side, tried to tow her with some kind of lifesaver's technique? It would have been suicide for both of them to have attempted it: their only hope was to try to make it going their separate ways.

By the time he waded ashore on the opposite bank, he was really alarmed. The girl was sitting waiting for him, trying to shelter beneath the broad leaves of a clump of wild bananas. Her dark hair was plastered to her skull; the black silk trousers and the lightweight top clung to her fragile body like a second skin. But she still looked to Dean like a million dollars. Or perhaps (it was only rarely that he permitted himself, even mentally, a pun) the yen would be a more apposite currency to quote.

"Well, you sure gave me a hard time for a couple of minutes there," he said. "For a moment I thought they'd zapped you. You could have yelled out to tell me hello or something!"

"I watch," she said simply. "You were very good, very quick, very strong. I like this."

He grinned down at her. "Anytime. Seats at half-price up until noon; matinees every Saturday." And then, as she looked bewildered: "C'mon, honey, let's get out of here."

He pulled her to her feet and they set off through the

blinding rain. A raised pathway led across the interminable paddy toward a line of trees that marked some kind of road.

Within a few yards they found that the path had become a quagmire. The rain lanced mercilessly down on them, stinging their faces, lashing across their shoulders. It was almost impossible to see; their feet stuck in the clayey mud.

"The hell with this," Dean gasped after a while. "What say we make it over there and sit this one out, huh?"

At one side of the rice field, he could just discern the remains of a gutted farm. The main buildings, standing among the splintered stumps of trees, looked as though they had been blasted by mortar bombs and then set on fire, but there was a small thatched hut off to one side that appeared to be relatively undamaged, and they ran for this.

Beyond the open doorway there was nothing but a beaten earth floor. The back of the hut was quite dry nevertheless; they were thankful to be in out of the downpour.

Dean shook himself like a wet dog. He tried to wring the water out of his hair. It was nonsense, considering that he had been immersed in the river, but somehow the drenching rain seemed to have made him wetter than ever. Golden Dawn stood looking up at him in the gloom of the windowless hut. The sodden shirt had become virtually transparent; molded to her small, taut breasts, it looked as though she was naked with colored flowers tattooed over her skin. Dean saw with a sudden dryness of the throat that the delicate material was pricked out in the center of two blooms by the thrust of her nipples. All at once he felt desire rising in him, sharp as a flame.

The girl laughed her husky laugh. "It is good in here," she said. "Now we can fuck."

Dean stared at her, amazed. "*What* did you say?"

"I think you are hearing what I say," she replied.

"Do you know what you're saying?"

She laughed again. "Try me," she said.

And then they were together, body to wet body, with his arms tightening around her and the drumming of the rain on the palm roof forgotten as their tongues met in the scalding intimacy of eager mouths. An age later he stood back and peeled the flowered top down off her shoulders. Her skin was the color of old ivory and the breasts were exquisite, the areolas surrounding the swollen nipples purplish in the dim light. "Jesus, honey," he said, "you're so . . . you're just the most . . . Oh, Christ, baby: I want you! And I want you now!"

Golden Dawn laughed once more. She reached out and plucked the waterlogged sweatshirt from the waistband of his pants. She unbuckled the belt at his waist. She sank to her knees and stripped the wet jeans down the hard, muscled length of his thighs. "In this country," she whispered, "there are men who are strong. But it is not easy to find a man who is strong and also big. You are strong and you are big too, and this is what I like."

Dean's hands, large hands tough as the teak logs they had crossed, hands which could nevertheless be as gentle as a child's, closed softly over the back of her wet head. "Oh, baby!" he said.

They made love hungrily, fiercely, on the bare earth floor, the girl's resilient body arching up to meet his powerful thrusts. Later, when the pounding of their hearts had slowed and their breathing had quietened, they saw that the rain had stopped as suddenly as it had begun, and the sun was shining outside the door.

Dean rose to his feet and spread their soaked garments over a thorn bush to dry. A few yards away there was some kind of dwarf willow. All the leaves had been blown off during the shelling of the farm, and now raindrops clung to the frail tracery of branches, glittering against the fresh blue of the sky like an untold number of diamonds in the bright light.

"I'd make you a necklace," he told the girl, "but they're the kind money can't buy. Unless you prefer the ones they tell you are a girl's best friend."

"Those you cannot buy are the best kind," said Golden Dawn. She nuzzled her dark head into the hollow of his shoulder, folding her slender form around his lean hardness. Somewhere outside, a coppersmith bird was repeating its monotonous ringing cry, and beyond the wet earth quietly steaming in the heat they could hear the distant voices of the loggers in their sampan. "As to a girl's best friend," she said, "I have my own ideas about this."

Three times, on their way back to the capital, they

were given a ride on bullock carts. Once, an army truck took them almost ten miles. But it was dusk before they finally crossed the canal bridge on the outskirts of town.

They had of course made two more stops on the way—in a deserted but undamaged watchtower, and among densely packed trees beside a stream that ran into the river. "With a skin as delicate as yours," Dean told the girl, "it's bad for you to stay in the sun too long."

10 Jason Mettner

To tell you the truth, I wondered sometimes what the hell I was doing in there with those boys.

I mean, I'd been roped in to do legwork for a gang of mercenaries on the promise of an exclusive. But an exclusive what? If the guys earned their money and put a stop to an assassination attempt, it would be the exclusive non-story of the year . . . and your friendly foreign correspondent would have helped to make it that way.

Terrorists knocking off a king—that would be a front-pager worldwide, no doubt about it. But killers who were *stopped* making a hit? A death that didn't happen? That would be the one that got away, all right! An inch and a quarter, single column, below the Cook County junior pool championship on page 37. I guess you know the famous story about the competition to see which paper could come up with the dullest headline—won hands down by *The Times* of London with "Small Earthquake in Chile: Not many Dead." Well, if Marc Dean and his merry men were to merit the bread they were being paid, the contest would have to be restaged, with my "exclusive" shortlisted and a hot tip to be first past the post.

Just the same, it was kind of stimulating, hanging in with those characters. Never a dull moment after we pulled Hammer out of the fountain and chased away the jokers who were trying to persuade him to drink more water than was good for him. I'd known Hammer before, of course; and by the time we reached Am-Phallang, I reckon I knew Ed Mazzari pretty well—and liked him pretty well too. But the others were new territory. Schneider was a mite heavy going, serious, solemn, the seafaring type, reliable as hell. Novotny slayed me with his command of the less printable vernacular used in his adopted country. Wassermann was all New York, as New York as

Arthur Kober. I'm a Chicago man myself, but you have to admit they make you laugh. That leaves Daler. Daler was the mystery man of the team. You know that already; you know that even Dean knew damned little about the guy. All I knew was that Daler was constantly surprising me: he had so many unsuspected talents it made you sick to your stomach!

Those first days in the city, we just ligged around. Mazzari and me were together most of the time. I mean like he was still making with the newshawk routine. Son of a bitch was doing it so damned well I figured on asking him for a few tips on how to get the most out of guys and dames, interviewing them! Sometimes one of the other mercs would stick around with us; sometimes two. Every now and then the off-duty ones would go off on their jack. Dean didn't want to make it too obvious that me and Ed were part of the same team, although it was reasonable that any newspaperman in town would want to keep his ear to the ground: rumors of the assassination threat had gotten around, the way things do, and the brand-new foreign-devil bodyguard, all spruced up in its nice green uniform, was an obvious angle for anyone who wanted inside stuff to cover. There were in any case several other specialist writers already installed: loudmouthed Hal Schenk from *The Chicago Globe,* a French guy from *Paris-Match,* Reuters' man from Bangkok, a TV crew, and a couple of photographers. You know.

It's kind of a funny feeling, when you're in my racket, putting in a lot of legwork . . . and not knowing what the hell you're looking for. Our briefing was as nonspecific as a politician at a press conference. Keep asking, keep listening, keep moving—and any hint or whisper or ghost of a suggestion that hit men are moving into town, any off-color mention of the military march-past, follow it up like hell. And be ready to duck.

The day Dean went up to see the old guy who ran the pottery school, I was doing the rounds with Ed and Wassermann. The drill was that Mazzari and me would act like we were rivals, each trying to pump Abe for whatever he had. And each trying to row in anyone else, at whatever dump we were at, in the hope of launching some fruitful line of gossip off the pad.

I'd done opium joints and dosshouses the day before

with Daler—had been knocked out by the ease with which he had gotten in with the bosses, treading on nobody's toes. But we'd drawn a total blank. Zero. Today it was to be teahouses and sidewalk cafés—with a touch of light relief at the waterfront bars before Abe went back to the palace to spell whoever was with his majesty.

We'd done Fragrant Blossoms and Lotus Pool and the Propitious Moon. It was hot as hell. The sidewalks were melting and the air was like a steambath. I couldn't understand how the Muong-Thang women could look so cool in that humidity. Some of them wore cheongsams; some favored the slit-side, patterned top with black silk pants; others were swathed in bright wraparound ankle-length skirts with thin, pale shirts. Most of them carried parasols.

I don't know if you've watched gals from that part of the world walking in the street. They don't walk: they glide, they progress, they transmit themselves from A to B without apparent locomotion. When the traffic lights tell you *Walk* at a busy intersection, it's like a breeze suddenly scattered all the petals from a bed of multicolored flowers (and don't think I won't use a more polished version of that next time the proprietor asks me for a situationer on the exotic Orient; it's down in my notebook already).

Abe Wassermann summed it up more succinctly perhaps. "Them broads," he announced, "they walk like there wasn't an ass among the lot of them. A man he should come this far only to discover the local girls they don't sling their cans!"

"My dear fellow!" Mazzari begins. "If the matchless elegance of these pretty butterflies doesn't strike you …"

He stops. That breeze in among the petals and butterflies suddenly blew up a storm. Dollar-sized raindrops are pock-marking the sidewalk, the sky's the color of liver sausage, and everybody's hightailing it to the nearest shelter.

We are quite near the royal palace. No sidewalk cafés. It's either in under the wedding-cake pinnacles of a Buddhist temple or up the steps of the Am-Phallang Hilton. Since we want to keep our shoes on our feet, we take the Hilton. Wassermann pauses to shake his fist at a monk in a yellow robe who's begging outside the temple, and we pile on up and into the hotel lobby.

There's the usual crowd inside: automobile salesmen, air hostesses, cardsharps, record executives, oil-rig maintenance engineers, PR girls, rich widows with young Italians, television glamour boys whose names have been linked with Princess Margaret—just a typical cross section of our capitalist aristocracy. We go through to the American bar.

An American bar can be identified anyplace outside the United States by the following criteria: (1) it will be twice as expensive as any other bar in the same establishment; (2) there will be a wall-to-wall carpet covered with a tasteful pattern of cigarette burns; (3) you have to tip the barkeep. From my own experience, I would add, (4) you will find at one end of it, shooting off his mouth, Hal Schenk of *The Chicago Globe*.

He was certainly there in this one, thumb hooked over the rim of his beer tankard, which he held down at arm's length in the approved Brit fashion, the heel of one suede chukka boot resting on the brass footrail. With him was this Canadian merc, Furneux.

Mazzari brushed aside a couple of Gulf sheikhs and an Armenian carpet dealer to make room for us at the bar. We stayed there, the back turned and the head down, for as long as we could without being recognized. This is what we heard:

Furneux: "It's only the dumb ones, Mr. Schenk, who stay in the business fighting for their pay. There's smarter ways of pulling it in, after all. Backroom stuff. Organization. Import-export."

Schenk: "Import-export?"

Furneux: "Of people, Mr. Schenk. Paks into the U.K., Red Chinks into Taiwan, PLO wogs across the Israeli frontier, comrades out of East Germany, Carlos to . . . Well, never mind about him."

Schenk: "Is that your particular racket?"

Furneux: "I'm a mercenary, sir, a soldier of fortune. I guess you could also call me a kind of cabdriver; I'm in the transport business. People call me up and tell me where they wanna go, and I take them there. I get paid for it. That's mercenary, ain't it?"

Schenk: "In fact you're a smuggler—only the contraband, the merchandise you ferry across the frontier, eats and sleeps and shits instead of being packed in oiled silk sachets, is that it?"

The bartender was approaching us. I fed a cigarette into my mouth and thumbed a lighter into flame. It was a mistake. Something about the way I moved attracted Schenk's attention, tipped him off, and he recognized me. "For Jesus' sake!" he bellowed. "Mettner! What the hell are you doing here? Trying to horn in on my story?"

"Fuck your story," I said. "You know we don't touch porn. My colleague and I came in for a drink: this is the only place in town where they take American Express."

"Hey, black boy," Schenk said to Mazzari, "who do you represent in this neck of the woods? *Ebony? The Chicago Defender?*"

Mazzari turned to Furneux. "Who's your South African friend?" he asked politely.

That was our second mistake. Because Furneux might have been flying high as a kite—he usually was—but he knew Mazzari, he'd worked with him once, and he knew Wassermann. "That's no newspaper guy," he said thickly. "That's another of Dean's sidekicks—both of them are. He must be working undercover for HRH."

"Well, whaddya know . . ." Schenk began.

But Furneux must have realized that maybe he was talking out of turn, here, there, and everyplace. He turned to go, swaying slightly, and tapped Mazzari on the chest. "You're wastin' your time, Ed," he said. "Wastin' your fuckin' time. You all are: you'll never smell those guys out." He lurched out of the bar and vanished among the crowd in the lobby.

Schenk's small eyes narrowed. He looked real mean. It didn't require any acting ability. "Well, thanks for scaring off my contact," he said nastily. "What I call professional etiquette."

I made the only reply possible, a custom-built phrase tailored for Schenk. "Aw, piss off, Hal!" I said.

We went up to the rooftop restaurant for lunch. It was still raining, after all. The place was on the fifteenth floor, and from the windows you could look down over the palace wall and across the parade ground to the pagoda. "You know what?" Wassermann said. "If I was a hit man and had a contract to knock off the king, the roof of this dump is the first place I'd case. Especially for a march-past."

We looked at him. "Hey," I said, "maybe you got something there, at that!"

Then Mazzari said, "*One* of the places you'd case, Abe."

"Come again?"

"Our drunken friend made a couple of boobs," Mazzari explained. "For one thing, he let on that there's something to waste our time about—in other words, there *is* some scheme afoot and he knows about it. Secondly, if you remember, he said something like, 'You'll never smell out *those guys*.' Plural."

"Yeah," Wassermann said slowly. "That's right. You mean there ain't one hit man involved, but several?"

"Exactly. And judging from all the boasting in front of that dear little newspaperman, I'd say that Furneux is the chap who's being paid to spirit them into the country."

"So we have to look, not for just one place it should suit a sniper, but several?"

Mazzari nodded. "You're the marksman, Abe. Maybe you should sniff about a bit, make out a list—your own short list of Reliable Roofs for Rubbing Out Royalty, or Heights for Hitting His Imperial Highness."

"After the coffee already," said Wassermann. "And, like I say, we'll start right here—if we can get up there unseen."

Getting up there was no problem. We probably looked like maintenance men anyway. You go through a door marked "No Entry," make a short passageway leading to a door marked "Private," and then take a third door carrying the legend "No Exit." After that it's just concrete emergency stairs to the top.

Wassermann was right, too. There were stacks up there from some kind of heating plant, a rectangular housing the size of an apartment building to conceal the air-conditioning vents, one or two slanting skylights, and a two-foot-high parapet all the way around. "Perfect," Wassermann said. "Elbows on the coping, or steady yourself against one of those stacks, you're home and dry."

"What would you say the range was?" Mazzari asked. "If the saluting base is at the far side of the parade ground, that is. Four hundred?"

"More. By me it should be four-sixty, seventy, at least."

"Too far for an Armalite?"

"Certainly too far. The Armalite has a muzzle velocity of three-two-eight-zero feet per second, but the maximum range is 433 yards—and that's not to be one hundred percent sure you hit a vital spot."

"A Kalashnikov AKM?"

Wassermann shook his head. "A heavier round, but one thousand FPS slower at the muzzle. Maximum accurate range, four hundred. No, the only assault rifle capable at this range would be the Belgian FN, Model FAL. This one is good for 650 yards, but I wouldn't think they're lying very thick on the ground in this part of the world. More likely a Heckler and Koch or even the Indian Ishapore rifle." Again the florid head shook. "No damned good."

"What would you use yourself?" I asked.

Wassermann pinched his lower lip with a fat forefinger and thumb. "With a telescopic sight," he said at length, "to place a round between the rows of medals on a guy's chest, myself I should most likely choose a sporting rifle. A Mannlicher, some kind of Winchester Express, a Husqvarna even. Something with a positive knockdown power."

"Would the Red assassins have access to such a gun?" I said.

He shrugged. "You tell me. Depends on how professional they are—and where they come from."

"Right you are," Mazzari said briskly. "We found the first likely place. Now, what about—?"

"I don't think so," Wassermann interrupted.

"You don't think what, old boy?"

"I don't think we found a likely place."

"But you said . . . ?"

"I said I should *choose* such a place. But do you think any police chief, even a police chief in a town like this, would leave such an obvious ambush site unguarded? When there have been explicit threats made against the king, and the Colonel knows the march-past will be the likely target? I would guess there will be cops lining this roof ten deep—and any other place overlooking the parade ground—on the day of the review."

My coinhabitant of bombed cellars sighed. "We'll have

93

to keep an eye on it just the same. Mistakes can be made."

"Oh, sure."

"Where would you expect to find your sharpshooters, then?"

Wassermann walked to the parapet and scanned the town laid out below. I expected a zoom shot at any moment, homing on a window of the palace guardhouse. Interior, early afternoon. The orderly room. An Officer and a Clerk sit writing at separate desks. Enter a Wily Oriental. W. O.: *How long do you think you can carry on this ludicrous charade, sahib, when half the country is up in arms against your tyrannical rule?* Officer (shouts): *Ve ask ze questions!*

Wassermann said, "The temple we saw when we came in: there's a bell tower. That warehouse—a godown isn't it?—on the far side of the palace grounds. Maybe someplace inside the grounds: the security ain't the strictest. At least not yet."

"Check," said Mazzari. "I vote we nip back to the royal mews now and report our findings to the boss man."

"You're out of your mind, Ed!" Wassermann protested. "You forget: you're supposed to be a journalist yet. You can't come in there without you have a special invite. You been listening to too many French-Canadians recently."

"By George, I did forget for a moment!" Mazzari was laughing. "Off you go, then, all on your nelly. My colleague and I will retire to our hostelry to sink a stoup of ale."

The hostelry was behind the Teahouse of the Fragrant Blossoms, not far from the central square. It was okay. The beer was cold, and they had those big horizontal fans that hung down from the ceiling in each bedroom. For reasons too subtle for my Midwestern mind to comprehend, it was called the Hotel Samoa.

Wassermann told us later that Dean had been pleased with the dope we'd dug up, and he'd agreed with our deductions. "There's something screwball about this deal," he told Abe. "I don't know what it is, but something smells. There are too many things don't stack up, you know what I mean?"

Wassermann said he knew what Dean meant. He didn't, but he figured Dean was going to tell him anyway.

Dean said, "Mr. Theng promised, for a consideration, to put us on the right track. He's done so, as far as it goes. But so has that bum Furneux, twice. And he's supposed to be on the other side, or at least that's how I read him. Then there's the pattern of these attacks on us: the bomb thrown at the Toyota, the assault on Hammer, the ambush I ran into with the girl. It doesn't make sense."

Wassermann said nothing. He felt safer that way.

"I mean," Dean said, "it doesn't make sense that none of them were followed up. They could have been—one or the other of us is in a target situation ten times a day—but they weren't. Why not? Either someone wants us out of the way, or they don't."

"Yeah," Wassermann ventured. "Sure."

"Then there's something screwy about the girl's uncle, the old French guy up at that pottery: he's just too vague to be true. It's my hunch that place is in some way connected with the comrades who filter across the border—and I figure Furneux plans to bring in his assassins there or near there. Albi was a little too quick off the mark denying that he knew the guy. So you know what I aim to do, Abe?"

Wassermann shook his head.

"I'm going back up there secretly. At night. I'm going to take Kurt Schneider, and we'll go by the river . . . and we'll hang in there eavesdropping, and we'll damned well stay until we find out how—and why—the bloody place ticks!"

"A hunch is no use if you don't back it," Wassermann said.

11 Marc Dean

The Most Exalted King-Emperor Kao Dinh, Tiger of Muong-Thang, was wearing a white sharkskin suit with a turban in which there glittered a single ruby the size of a quarter. He was also—although he had been educated in Rangoon and Battambang—wearing an Etonian tie.

Dean, Sean Hammer, and the lined, cadaverous Ngon Thek were talking to him in a small but luxuriously appointed office at the rear of the palace. Kao Dinh stood, hands clasped behind his burly back, looking out the window at a formal garden planted with zinnias, gallia, and dimorphotheca in the national colors of red, bronze, and mauve. "In view of your findings, Colonel," he said over his shoulder, "do you think that perhaps I should cancel the march-past or postpone it to another date?"

"No," Dean said frankly. "I don't. If you do that, the killers will set up an alternative plan, and we won't know when or where. As it is, at least we know time and place—and this gives us the best chance of all to catch these characters red-handed and put them out of the way for good."

"You are right, of course. It will be good propaganda, if the people are shown at first hand how base are our enemies, that they would even stoop to the commission of violence upon our royal selves. And if the assassins could be shown to be foreign, financed from abroad, that would be even better: it would show the world whom we are really fighting in this so-called civil war that is in reality an invasion."

"I doubt not you'll find them foreign, all right," Hammer said.

"So much the better." Kao Dinh turned back into the room. Behind him, peacocks spread their tails on the graveled walks and a flock of parakeets swooped in front of a pavilion screened by Japanese honeysuckle. "Minister, what are the police precautions to be during our parade?"

"Roadblocks checking the identity of all people entering the city, Excellency," Ngon Thek replied. "All buildings overlooking the parade ground to be searched and then sealed off. Those suspected of leftist sympathies to be held in protective custody. Secret police in plain clothes to be seeded through the crowds. Double-checking of passes for those permitted to watch the march-past—with armed rooftop spotters strategically placed in collaboration with Colonel Dean. Every available man will be detailed to line the streets in the neighborhood of the palace."

"Every *available* man," the king repeated. "By this I mean every man not essentially engaged on other duties."

"But surely, Excellency, the protection of your royal—"

"Yes, yes. It is of paramount importance," Kao Dinh said testily. "Nevertheless, the men on customs duty must not be required to desert their posts. On a national holiday, with a special parade and many thousands of extra people flocking into the city to watch, the narcotics smugglers could well consider it a suitable time to try to move their product. For this reason, I wish the men on this detail to keep specially alert. Is that understood?"

Ngon Thek bowed and said nothing, his parchment face expressionless.

"The modern equipment—the hardware, I believe you call it—on show during this parade comes from the United States," Kao Dinh said to Dean. "Without their *appui*, we could not exist. But it is not just because the Narcotics Bureau has . . . tied strings, do you say? . . . to the supplies that we wish to stamp out this trade. We wish our country to be accepted as a modern democracy, not as some backward ex-colony only fit to grow opium and tend goats. And to achieve this aim, we must obey democracy's rules. Is that not so?"

"Yes, sir. Of course," said Dean. "Most . . . er . . . wise."

"The Afyon province of Turkey is said to produce the world's best raw opium; the hardened gum from the poppy seedcap contains up to eighteen percent of morphine base—and that is what brings the traffickers their profit. I now understand that illegal fields in the northeast of our country are producing a yield of fifteen to sixteen percent, and that the . . . material . . . smuggled in from Afghanistan is almost as rich."

Staring at the short, wide, muscular little man, Dean was suddenly aware that he was speaking not for effect but from conviction, that cleansing of the drug stigma from his country was to him as important as, if not more important than, his own safety. And with the realization came a change of context. From being an anachronistic, slightly absurd figure, Kao Dinh gained stature and presence to the point where his sincerity commanded both attention and respect.

"Anyone with a smattering of first-year chemistry can turn opium into morphine base in a backyard shack," he continued. "But it's bulky still, and not too profitable. To make the real money, they need to go one step further and transform the morphine base into pure heroin. But that is a different story altogether. For this they must have up-to-date laboratories, with highly qualified chemists both skillfull and patient. The process takes several days and, in its final stages, is highly dangerous: toxic and inflammable vapors are given off; the least spark could provoke an explosion."

"You figure there are people doing that here?" Dean asked.

"It would be the logical thing to do: one or more of these 'factories' in the hills somewhere upcountry. Then, reduced to manageable proportions, the drug will be easier—and more profitable—to 'export.' In the Middle East, they feed oiled silk packages to camels, and then administer laxatives to the beasts once they have crossed the frontier. Here, it is not so easy, but you see why I insist that the customs men remain on guard during the festivities? The opium harvest is at the end of March; by the time the double refinement has been carried out and the product separated and packaged, I would expect it to be sent away about now—just before the monsoon season."

Dean nodded. "You know where we are going tonight, sir," he said. "Should we hear anything connected with this traffic, we shall of course inform you at once."

"Good. I shall in any case await your report with interest, my dear Colonel." Kao Dinh turned back to Ngon

Thek. "You tell me, Minister, that you plan to operate roadblocks at all entrances to the city on the day of the parade. It has not, I suppose, occurred to you that any putative assassin or assassins might have thought of that and installed themselves here well before that day?"

"The blocks are already in operation, Highness," Ngon Thek replied.

Novotny and Daler patrolled outside the king's private apartments that evening. Hammer and Wassermann remained on call. Dean himself went with Kurt Schneider to the riverside dock where the German merc had rented a power boat from Paris-based shipping agents who still operated out of Am-Phallang. It was a French-built Arcoa 900—a five-berth cruiser with very little top hamper, a fiberglass hull, and twin 125 Couach diesels. The craft was 27 feet long and only 10 feet wide, easily maneuverable for river work, Schneider said. It was, in addition, extremely quiet.

They cast off an hour after dusk, threaded their way through the sampans, and then left the waterfront neon behind as they burbled upstream past the logjam where Dean had almost drowned.

Sometime later, Dean laid a hand on Schneider's arm and murmured, "Throttle right back now, Kurt—we should be nearing the place where we have to cut the motors."

The surface of the river, muddy and leaden in daylight, was now silvered by the light of a three-quarter moon. On either side, the rice fields stretched away into the distance, where lines of trees stood on their shadows like cardboard cutouts in the milky light. Farther away still, the wooded hills humped serrated sugarloaf outlines into the night sky.

Dean recognized the knoll with the ruined watchtower where he had been ambushed. Five minutes later, he pressed the German's arm again, and the boat nosed silently in to the bank. Schneider hitched a rope around a wooden pier that retained a length of rotten planking designed to protect the bank when the river was in flood. For a while the two men remained silent. They could hear nothing but the lazy gurgle of slow-flowing water, a rustle of wind in the dry grasses above their heads, and, far off, the insistent, repeated cry of some night bird. At last

Dean nodded, satisfied. "Let's go," he whispered. "It shouldn't be more than three or four hundred yards upstream."

They unshipped the rubber dinghy from the stern of the launch and began paddling slowly against the current, keeping well in toward the bank where the shadow cast by the moon was dense. Kao Dinh's comprehensive armory had provided each of Dean's men with an American Colt Commando submachine gun, half a dozen plastic grenades that could be slung to a cartridge belt, and a Browning GP-35 automatic pistol. British EM-2 precision rifles were to be available for picking off the assassins when their firing positions had been discovered. For their night sortie, Dean and Schneider had each taken a Browning, with a single Colt Commando between them for covering fire, if that became necessary. The SMG was fitted with a telescopic butt, a flash-hider, and a Trilux infrared night sight.

The junction between the river and the canal was farther away than the combat leader had imagined, and it was a full half-hour before Schneider was able to steer the dinghy into the dike linking the two that made the spit into an island.

The sloping banks were covered with a thick growth of mangrove, and behind this there was a palisade of bamboo reaching as far as the bridge that Dean and Golden Dawn had crossed the previous day. Fearful of making an unexpected noise that could alert any guards—if indeed the figures he had seen on his first visit had been guards, and not intruders like himself—Dean led the way through the gnarled complex of roots and branches as carefully as a man walking on eggs. Beyond the rank slant of marsh vegetation there was still the cane thicket to contend with, but here the breeze they had noticed earlier blew to their advantage: the dry stalks rubbing together beneath a light clatter of leaves effectively masked the sounds of their advance. Even so, another hour had passed before they parted the final screen of bamboo and looked at the trees beyond which the monastery was built.

In this enclosed area, the moon seemed brighter than ever. The clearing was tiger-striped with shadow, barred black and silver in the wan light. Nothing moved on the bare earth between the trees and the gaunt facade of the building. But faintly on the night air, from the far side of the monastery where the outhouses and the pottery kilns were located, they could hear a hum of voices.

Dean handed his companion the submachine gun, laid a finger on his lips, and tiptoed away through the trees, circling the clearing where the shadows were deepest. Schneider followed ten yards behind.

There was very little undergrowth; even beneath the spreading branches of teak and acajou, the tufted fronds of palm, there were patches of bright moonlight to be crossed. Dean advanced in a series of quick dashes, halting after each spurt to hide behind the widest trunk he could find, checking that their progress was still unobserved.

They were a little more than halfway around when they saw the first sign of life. Schneider had just joined his leader on the farther side of a particularly wide swath of light. As Dean tensed for the next run, there was a sudden and unmistakable chink of metal, the scrape of a booted foot. Like puppets controlled by the same string, the two men ducked and froze. To experienced guerrilla fighters, the sounds could mean only one thing: somewhere nearby, a sentry was standing; he had just shifted his equipment, perhaps grounded a gun, or transferred a sling from one shoulder to another.

It took them some time to locate the man. Only when he moved again could they pinpoint his position aurally, and then they saw that he was standing close to the wall that ran along behind the kilns, which had just come into their line of vision. At first he was no more than a darker blur that separated itself from the dense shadow. Then, as he shifted his position once more, there was a tiny gleam of reflected light, a buckle maybe, or a D-ring snaring an errant ray from the brightly illuminated clearing.

Dean put his lips close to Schneider's ear. "We can't possibly get around him or take him by surprise with forty yards of moonlight to cross," he whispered. "If he has orders to shoot, we'd be dead before we made ten feet. If not, he could alert the whole damned place before we silenced him."

"What do you plan to do, Cap?"

"Go farther back in the trees. Make a noise that will draw him over there. Don't make it too definite, and don't show yourself, or he could shoot. Rustle a branch or move a stone or something; anything to decoy him out of that shadow. I'll jump him as he comes over."

Schneider nodded and glided away into the shadows himself.

Two minutes later there was a soft thump from somewhere behind Dean. It was followed by the clatter of a stone and a shower of small pebbles spilling to the ground. By the wall, the foot scraped, the metal chinked once more; there was a heavy click as some weapon was cocked. Dean could almost see the sentry tensing, straining to see, eyes squinting in an attempt to pierce the darkness beyond the moonlit clearing.

A second thump, a little louder—but no stones falling this time. The man by the wall moved. His figure sprang into sharp relief as he emerged from the shadow and strode swiftly across the clearing toward the trees. A short, wiry man. Combat boots, steel helmet, what looked like an Uzi SMG held at the ready.

Dean edged around the bole of a tree to keep out of sight as the guard approached. The man stole forward between the trees, treading softly on the baked earth. Ghostlike, Dean padded after him.

The steel helmet posed a problem. The brim was too low to permit a fast rabbit punch aimed at the nape of the neck with the edge of a hand. On the other hand, a frontal attack would surely result in at least a shout, a cry of alarm, before the sentry could be dealt with.

Dean was a physical-fitness freak; he believed in the disciplined control of the body by the mind. But—unfashionably in the 1980's—he scorned kung-fu, karate, and most Oriental fighting techniques as a waste of time and energy. "All that huffing and puffing and stamping about," he had many times told mercenaries under his leadership, "just saps your reserves. Any man skilled in the dirtier tricks of unarmed combat should be able to lay one of those shouting characters waste in thirty seconds flat." The sole exception he made was for the original judo method—"because there you're using *his* energy and turning it against himself."

But judo, he thought, approaching the sentry's unsuspecting back, was going to be of no use now: it presup-

102

posed a frontal attack, and that was out. His assault would therefore have to be basic . . . and fast.

He drew back a fist and dealt the man a paralyzing blow in the area of the left kidney. The guard went momentarily rigid, like the victim of a 250-volt electrical discharge. His cry of agony and alarm was choked in his throat as Dean's forearm whipped around and locked beneath his chin. Dean's free hand streaked over the man's shoulder to grasp his own wrist, reinforcing the lock across his throat. He kneed the base of the guard's spine, bending him backward like a bow. At the same time, Kurt Schneider rose upright from behind a thorn bush, hauled off, and punched the man hard in the pit of the stomach.

The blow carried all the German's stocky weight behind it. The guard uttered a strangled gurgle. His two knees jackknifed upward involuntarily, as if to protect his savaged abdominal muscles. And then, as Dean released his grip, he dropped gasping to the ground and writhed helplessly at their feet with his lungs groaning for air.

Dean tipped his helmet forward and tapped him expertly behind the ear with the butt of his Browning. The guard went limp.

"That should keep him quiet for all the time we need," Dean murmured. "What the hell was that noise you made, Kurt?"

Schneider grinned in the moonlight. "An old stone wall, Cap, that turned into a kind of bank. I dislodged a rock and a gang of earth, sent them tumbling down among the mangroves."

"Good for you, buddy!" Dean clapped him on the shoulder. "Now we must get next to those voices and see what cooks." He picked up the Uzi and threw it as far as he could into the bushes that grew in back of the wood, and they continued their silent circuit of the glade.

They passed the massed bignonia and bougainvillea and canna—their fiery blooms turned mauve in the light of the moon—and stopped when they could look along the facades of the pottery shacks. Here there was no shadow, and every detail of door and window and shutter was etched against the illuminated adobe walls. Artificial light was visible nevertheless behind the shutters of the laboratory where the glazes were colored—and, to Dean's astonishment, thin threads of light showed from behind the blanked-off windows of the unused fourth and fifth floors high up in the bleak face of the monastery itself.

The voices—it sounded as though there were at least half a dozen people—were coming from the glaze lab. Next to it, the door of a shed housing some of the potter's wheels hung invitingly open. "I've been in there," Dean whispered. "If we could sneak into that shack, I'll bet we could hear damn near every word they say. Those walls are kind of thin."

"Sure, Cap," Schneider replied. "But look there." He gestured toward the far corner of the main building.

Another guard stood at the angle of the wall. He was dressed exactly like the man they had already taken care of, but he was so immobile, staring out into the trees on the opposite side of the clearing, that Dean's eyes had not yet registered his presence.

"You figure we could slip across there quiet enough for this man not to hear?" Schneider queried.

Dean shook his head. "Too risky. If we dislodged a stone halfway across and the guy turned around, it'd be curtains. Same thing if he's supposed to be on guard outside the shack where they're talking, and just stepped out for a minute. We could be trapped maybe until daylight if he came back while we were in there. End of story."

"You want me to work my way around and pull the same routine back in the trees while you zap him from behind?"

"I don't know." Dean was dubious. "But one thing's for sure, Kurt: with sentries dressed and armed like that, this is no simple goddamn pottery school for Annamite students they're running here."

He stared out at the second guard, weighing the chances of a successful second attack on the lines of the first. As he watched, the man suddenly moved. He glanced at a watch strapped to his wrist, unslung his Uzi, and strode away toward the track that led to the bridge.

"Okay," Dean muttered. "That looks like they have a regular beat to tread. Let's hope he's not due to rendezvous with the other guy. And that there are only two of them."

"We go across now?"

"Uh-uh. My objection still stands. But at least there's a

chance to get there unobserved while the guy's away. I'm going on over myself and pick up whatever I can; you stay right here—"

"But, Cap—"

"That's an order, Kurt. You stay here and keep watch. I'll leave you the Colt. If I have to come out shooting, cover me. Okay?"

"Whatever you say, sir."

"Right. See you." Dean handed over the SMG, took a final look around the clearing, and sped across to the pottery hut.

He slipped through the open door and crouched down in the darkness, breathing in the sour, damp clay odor and a smell of machine oil from a mechanical grindstone he remembered seeing in back of the shed.

He had been right. The voices were loud and clear. He could hear every word. There was, moreover, a split in one of the planks forming the dividing wall. If he closed one eye and brought the other as near as possible to the crack, he could see straight into the lab where the meeting was taking place.

Seven men were seated around a heavy, unpolished teak table. They were drinking some kind of colorless liquor from a stone jar that was passed around from time to time. The air above their heads was layered with cigarette smoke.

In view of the information given him by Wassermann, Dean was hardly surprised to see Furneux among them. The Frenchman, Jean-Paul Albi, sat at the head of the table. On one side of him were three men unknown to Dean—two officers in battle dress who could have been Cambodians or Thais, and a third man whose features were Slavic. Furneux sat opposite with two other men whom Dean did know. And it was the sight of these that made him catch his breath.

One, a tall, thin, seamed Central American known as Ramon, had been chief instructor at a Corsican school for terrorists that Dean had been instrumental in destroying. The other was a huge man from southern China. His name was Chan. He was a graduate of the Corsican school, probably the world's finest snap-shot marksman, and—next to Carlos—possibly its best-known urban guerrilla. His dossier at Interpol credited him with at least fifteen personal assassinations, added to complicity in a number of outrages which had cost the lives of many hundreds of innocent people.

". . . now that plans are complete for the introduction of our riflemen to their safe houses in the city," Albi was saying, "I feel that it might be useful to run over our strategy—purely from the global point of view—for the benefit of our friends here." He nodded toward the two Cambodian-Thais.

Furneux held his glass out toward the liquor jar. He was smiling. "Go ahead J-P," he said. "They won't be able to pick no holes in the scheme."

"Well, I thought perhaps . . . ?" Albi raised inquiring eyebrows at the far end of the table.

Ramon said, "It is very simple, a matter of scrupulous planning to cover, and double-cover, every eventuality. What the Americans term a fail-safe situation, where if any one component proves faulty, there is always a backup arranged to take its place: an alternative arrangement, equally efficient and ready to go."

"Specifically?" the Slav asked.

"Specifically, the five marksmen will be lodged, well in advance of the arrival of crowds and the police cordons, in the places we have chosen—the bell tower, the warehouse, the Hilton roof, and the other two locations that you know. Agents have already been infiltrated among the screened guests who will be near the saluting base. Their task will be to organize the diversion we have discussed, to distract the attention of police and public at the appropriate time."

"And that will be?"

"As in the execution of Anwar Sadat, during the passage of the armor, at the rear of the procession. The noise will at least partially mask the sound of the shots; hopefully, it might help to delay any police or military reaction—which would of course greatly help our people during the subsequent *coup d'état*, when every second could count."

"The godown, the bell tower, perhaps the other two locations, very well. But the Hilton roof—surely the police themselves will be posting men there?" the Slav objected. "Especially since there have already been rumors of an assassination. The place will be searched, as will all points

106

overlooking the parade ground. Even if our men can be smuggled in long before the security measures are in force, they still cannot fire from a roof lined with police-men."

Ramon brushed the ends of his heavy mustache outward with the tips of his fingers. "We also have agents infiltrated into suitable ranks of the police," he said.

One of the officers asked a question in Thai. "He asks," Jean-Paul Albi translated, "what steps have been taken to neutralize the mercenary Dean and the body-guard he commands."

It was Furneux who replied. "Don't let him worry about that." He chuckled. "First of all, no bodyguard ain't gonna be able to do much when the shootin' comes from way outside the palace, right? I mean, they're gonna be in there, right next to his flamin' majesty, ain't they? Second of all, I got special plans for those guys anyway: they may not even make the parade at all."

"Very well. We will leave that to you and your specialized squad," said Albi. "We can, I suppose, be one hundred percent sure that one or more of these riflemen will succeed in making a fatal hit?"

Chan spoke for the first time, his face expressionless. "Naturally they will succeed," he said. "I shall be among them."

"I told you, these guys are whing-ding experts," Furneux said, still smiling. He seemed to find the whole conversation amusing. "Shoot a cigarette out of a guy's mouth at fifty feet; plug the red spot on the ace of hearts at seventy-five."

"We are talking about 450 *yards*," the Slav said coldly.

"Sure. With high-precision rifles. I was talking about pistols, but what I said holds good over the long-distance stuff too. You'll see."

"I hope so. We cannot afford to make mistakes."

Chan said, "There will be no mistakes."

"Very well." Ramon took up the conversation again. "Chan and our two friends here will move into the city tomorrow morning and pick up their weapons later at the godown. The other two will land from the *Arethusa* the following day and rendezvous as arranged." He looked at the Slav. "Are there any more questions?"

Before the man could reply, a volley of automatic fire,

shockingly loud in the stillness, erupted from the clearing outside.

Dean leaped to the doorway, his Browning in his hand.

He could see Schneider half-concealed behind the trunk of a tree. Flame belching from the muzzle of the Colt Commando was invisible within the flash-hider, but moonlight glinted on the brass of the spent shells as they were ejected from the breech. He was firing toward the corner of the monastery where they had seen the second guard. "Colonel!" he yelled. "Split now, while I keep this guy's head down; there's another bastard on the way."

He ducked back to avoid a rattle of answering fire that spat from the corner of the building, and then stepped out to hose a long burst from side to side of the glade while Dean sprinted across the moonlit ground into the shadow of the trees.

"Where's the second man?" Dean panted. He looked back toward the outhouses, where a confused shouting had broken out in the lab where the meeting was taking place. "We have to get out of here before the people in there decide to join the fight."

"Behind the bushes . . . where the track from the bridge comes out," Schneider replied.

As he spoke, crimson flashes stabbed the gloom from the sector he had indicated. At the same time, the guard sheltering behind the angle of the monastery opened fire again. Bullets splattered against the boles of trees and ripped through the branches above the two mercs. "Cover me," Dean rapped, preparing to move off toward the second man.

"Magazine's empty, Cap. Shall I—?"

"No. Go back the way we came. I'll join you."

Accustomed to obey orders without question, the German sped away into the darkness. Dean expended the Browning's magazine in three bursts and felt in his pocket for a fresh clip. The range was too great for the automatic to be effective, but the noise should keep the guards pinned down while he made his escape.

For a moment there was silence. He could sense movement in the shadows near the pottery kilns, but the men who emerged from the meeting wouldn't know yet what they were up against—or in which direction their own guards were firing. Dean loosed off a few shots from the new magazine and then dodged away through the trees after Schneider. He was thirty yards off when the first random burst of firing broke out from the kilns, and halfway around the perimeter of the clearing before he heard the sounds of pursuit. Ten minutes later, he joined Schneider on the far side of the bamboo thicket.

For a quarter of an hour they lay motionless beneath a tangle of mangrove roots, listening to the noises of the hunt. There was a burst of excited shouting—presumably when the unconscious sentry was discovered—and then the search advanced and receded without ever approaching dangerously close. Finally it seemed to concentrate on the far side of the spit, nearer the bamboo bridge. "Let's go," Dean whispered, "and thank Christ they didn't have dogs!"

They made the dinghy without incident, and paddled silently away in the shadows of the dike. It was less than a hundred yards to the river. Once they were clear of the mangroves, they lay flat behind the craft's inflated rubber sides and let the current carry them downstream. When they passed the tip of the island, where the canal joined the river, the hunters were still out of sight behind the trees.

The return trip to the point where they had moored the launch took less than half the time it had cost them paddling upstream. The mooring rope was still hitched around the wooden pier—but the end nearest the post had been sliced through, and the Arcoa 900 had gone.

12 Alfred Daler

One of the more surprising things about the mercenary known as Alfred Daler was that although he spoke all European languages with a villainous cockney accent, his Thai was both fluent and practically accentless. "Picked it up here in the forties and fifties, sport," he told Hammer when the little Ulsterman asked him how come. "Messing around with the French, an' that. You know."

Hammer didn't know. He hadn't known that Daler had even been to Indochina before. But there was no point pursuing the matter—if Daler had been prepared to come across with any more details, he would have done so before now. The important thing was that this facility made him a natural for the liaison between Dean and Ngon Thek's security forces.

Soon after Schneider and the combat leader had returned to the city—it was not until dawn that they made the outskirts, paddling with the current—Dean called a conference at the palace.

"We have most of the dope now," he said. "More than we had any reason to expect. We know that there *is* an assassination set up; we know it's planned for the end of the parade, when the armor is rolling past the saluting base; we know five guys have been briefed to make the hit, from five different places; and we know three of the places." Dean paused and then added, "Kurt and I know three of the hit men, too—though they won't necessarily be posted in the three places we know about. Number-one priority, then, is to identify the other two gunmen. And then call in Ngon Thek's boys, the whole goddamn police force if necessary, and stick to those guys like leeches until we know where each of them will be holed up on the day of the parade."

"How the fuck d'you aim to do that, boss?" Novotny asked. "Identify the other two birds, I mean."

"Ramon said they land from the *Arethusa* tomorrow. I checked that out: the *Arethusa* is a Panamanian-registered freighter—what else!—due to dock here around noon with a mixed cargo from Jakarta and Hanoi."

"And how do we tell which of the nine thousand crew members are the two guys we want?" Wassermann demanded. "They are not going to be wearing *I Kill Kings* lapel buttons, are they?"

"This we have to play by ear," said Dean. "We arrange for the immigration people to make an extra-high-power screening of any and every person who comes ashore—and we keep our fingers crossed and hope to hell this turns up something."

"Okay, so we locate all five of the son-of-a-bitch hoods"—Novotny again—"but that ain't gonna be all that easy, right? I mean, you and Kurt, boss, you know the first three by sight. But suppose you ain't around when they hit town today? There's a hell of a lotta different roads into the city. Fuckin' canals, too, if it comes to that."

"Chan's mug will be on file," Dean replied. "They can get it wired from Interpol if it's not in the morgue here already. The other two are difficult, I admit. I don't know if I'd recognize them for sure myself without the uniforms—and they sure as hell won't be wearing those on their way into Am-Phallang. But we only have to locate *one* for a start, maybe Chan, maybe the guys off the boat; because they'll have to meet, see. They've got to. First to pick up their weapons. Ramon said that would be 'from the godown.' I'm backing a hunch that this may be Mr. Theng's place. Then they have to meet, too, for the boat men to get themselves briefed, to show them who goes where, for all the guys to familiarize themselves with the terrain, their angle of fire, and like that."

"You mean we pick up this one guy, whichever, an' we lay a heavy tail on him until he makes the meeting," Daler said, "an' when he leaves, we keep with him—but we have enough men ready to tail the other four as well? Is that it?"

"That's exactly it," Dean said.

"Yeah, but . . . I mean, like you say we pick up this

111

one guy," Novotny objected. "That's still a hell of a supposition, ain't it? How do you *know* we can? Likewise the twenty-four-hour tag if you do pick him up: shit, that's a performance, ain't it the truth?"

"Look," Dean said, "we hang a six-box on him, day and night—with cars, bicycles, UHF contact, everything. That's for the tag. So far as picking him up goes, whichever he is, we stake out Theng's godown and every other godown in town; we keep all three of the places we know of covered, again day and night; we have men posted near every single building that overlooks the parade ground, and watching all roads in the palace quarter. They have to go there sometime, after all, to check out their MO. Plus we have the chance of flushing someone off the boat."

"Christ!" Sean Hammer said. "This is a big-deal operation you're into, all right. Do we have that kind of manpower on tap?"

"That's for Daler to fix with Ngon Thek and his security chiefs," Dean said.

There was in fact only one security chief for Daler to deal with. The minister had placed Colonel Luen-Phok Chakrawongse, the head of a commando unit that had enjoyed spectacular success against the rebels in the north, in sole charge of the city's antiterrorist forces until after the parade. The colonel—a lean, solemn man with a wide mouth and a completely hairless head—could draw upon the uniformed police, the secret police, immigration officers, gendarmerie, and any militiamen stationed within the city limits. Everyone, that is, except customs inspectors on antinarcotics detail.

He was helpful and cooperative in his serious way, clearly anxious to impress Daler with the efficacy of his organization (which was an advantage: he could have been angry at the thought of a foreigner, with no specific rank, being placed in authority over him.) "But tell me, Mr. Daler," he said during their first meeting, "there is just one thing I do not comprehend: what is a six-box?"

"You can have a four-box," Daler said, "but six is better, and the tag's much less likely to be flushed. It's a system for keeping people under observation, a surveillance technique. The six tails work in pairs, one couple behind the mark and another in front, varying their distance, sometimes switching positions, with the fifth and sixth men on call—usually in a car a block or so away. They can be called in by radio if the mark tumbles, or is suspected of tumbling, to either of the other pairs. If it's done well, with a constant change of position and even the individual members of each couple altering, only the smartest of professionals gets wise to the fact that he's being followed at all."

Chakrawongse inclined his head. "I am familiar with the system," he said. "We have a different term for it, that is all."

"That's great, sport. Then you can brief the fellows on what's expected, if they don't know already. I'd like five six-man teams organized right away, in radio contact with each other and with you at some central switchboard. Detail two teams to cover the docks tomorrow; the others can stay on call until Colonel Dean's squad raises one or more of the other trio. Okay?"

"No problem," the colonel said.

The first day drew a blank. If Chan and the two rebel officers had indeed come to the city, they had passed through the cordons unsuspected. With the docks, unexpectedly, Daler was more lucky. Perhaps demoralized at the sight of three grim-faced immigration officers and a phalanx of plainclothes security agents waiting at the head of the gangway to interview crew members on shore leave, two men attempted to disembark secretly an hour after the ship docked the following day.

They were spotted by an alert member of Colonel Chakrawongse's squad who was disguised as a stevedore—two slight figures swinging hand over hand down a hawser that looped to the quayside in the shadow of the rusty-hulled tramp's stern.

As they darted away between cotton bales and sacks of rice, the security man radioed his commander, who was installed, together with Daler, high up in the glassed-in office of the harbormaster. The colonel immediately alerted the two surveillance teams and other watchers in the dock area. Daler called up the palace and asked for Kurt Schneider to be ready for instant liaison with the teams, as he was the only man apart from Dean who could identify the three known killers if they were contacted by the couple from the boat. By the time the supposed stow-

113

aways showed their forged passes at the dock gates, they were boxed in by a dozen highly trained security agents in cars and tri-shaws, concealed in panel trucks, riding bicycles, and on foot. Meanwhile the rigorous screening of the crew members continued, in case the two men were decoys.

Daler was staring out over the forest of masts and rigging and derricks and smokestacks between the office and the mole at the harbor entrance when the transceiver in his breast pocket bleeped. Dean was calling him back from the palace.

"Looks like you struck paydirt, Alf," the combat leader's voice enthused from the tiny transistorized speaker. *"Kurt's on his way: he'll wait in the central square until someone calls him in. You got both teams in action in case these two guys split up?"*

"Natch," Daler replied. The pyloned light at the end of the mole had changed from red to green: a container ship bringing machine tools from Bremen was about to berth. "Those characters are boxed in tighter than a uranium-235 core in a lead shield."

"Swell. I've been thinking: now that we know the killers' choice of time and place, we don't need to mount the twenty-four-hour watch on our royal boss. Until the day of the parade, he should be safe. In which case, I figure on attaching one of us to each of Colonel Whatsit's teams, as of now."

"There are five teams and seven of us," Daler pointed out, "if you count Mazzari."

"I want to keep Ed on a roving brief, apart from the rest of us. It's always useful to have at least one man undercover. I want to keep you as a command post, since you speak the lingo better than any of us. I shall detail Kurt to stay with one of the squads most likely to spot the guys we know, and I'll take the other. In the meantime, you coordinate with the gallant colonel. Can do?"

"Sure," Daler said. The German freighter was already surrounded by a flotsam of penny-divers, Benares brass merchants, and the sellers of sweetmeats and fruit in sampans clustered thickly along her sides. "He's got the city quartered like a railroad diagram in a signalman's cabin, flags on pins, colored lights an' all. Up in his own pad at the ministry. Soon as the crew screenin' is through, we're goin' up there. I'll be in touch."

"*Check*," said Dean. He cut the transmission.

Colonel Chakrawongse's office was a showplace of electronic software. But it was the city map that took up one whole wall above the computer consoles and video screens and memory banks that compelled Daler's attention. Five operatives wearing headsets with cans sat by the UHF receivers on the far side of the room, listening continually for the reports that came in every few minutes from the surveillance teams. A sixth man stayed tuned to Dean's frequency.

From special keyboards in front of them, the five radio monitors illuminated on the map the sectors of the city traversed by the teams and their quarry. At the same time, detectives carrying long magnetic pointers moved numbered markers representing each individual tail and each of the two stowaways. When the hunt moved into any one of a dozen key areas, video scanners hidden on lamp standards, behind shop windows, and in parked trucks flashed a picture onto the screens below the map.

There were cameras outside government buildings, in the central square, around the palace, and in most of the main streets. Once, there was an excited cry from one of the monitors: the quarry was near one of the static cameras, was about to pass into shot.

Daler saw two small men of indeterminate age—they looked as though they could have been Vietnamese—gain the sidewalk of a busy street. They were dressed like thousands of other workers, in peaked caps and dungarees. Beyond the traffic, on the far side of the street, the video screen showed the facade of a Western insurance building, a department store, palms, and the spires of a pagoda behind a high wall. He didn't recognize the street, although it was lit up on the wall map. The two men walked quickly out of shot—and Daler couldn't spot any of the tags either.

In fact, the colonel told him, pointing at the markers, there was a cyclist, a woman in a tri-shaw, three pedestrians, and a couple in a convertible on their tracks. The remaining five were circling whatever block the men traversed in a radio truck and another car.

Near the city's largest discount store, the two men split

115

up. It was impossible to say whether this was simply a routine precaution or because they suspected a tail.

One of them took a side street leading toward the redlight district by the riverside, and then ducked quickly into an alleyway running parallel with the canal. Two of the tails walked past the entry and radioed the cyclist, who made a rapid tour of the block and entered the lane from the far end, crossing the man who was being followed halfway along. By the time the cyclist emerged, the woman in the tri-shaw had descended and was walking up the alley. She paused outside a door, pretending to ring, for long enough to see which house the man entered, and then continued on her way as though she had found nobody at home.

The second man went into the store, followed by the third pedestrian. The tag went straight to a rack of jackets, took one, and disappeared into a fitting booth. Here he called up one of the men from the radio truck, who hurried into the store and took over while the first operative remained in the booth. When the mark at last came out of the store—he had bought nothing—he turned left for the main street. The tail turned right and the chase was taken over by the couple in the convertible, who had meanwhile changed cars.

At the first intersection, the mark turned left again. The couple in the car carried straight on, but the radio truck was already in the side street, and when it parked, the tag was renewed by the tri-shaw woman, who was now riding the bicycle.

It was when the man eventually returned by a circuitous route and entered the same house as his companion that Daler and the colonel knew they were on the right track.

The house was less than a quarter of a mile from Mr. Theng's warehouse. Mr. Theng himself appeared to be absent, for the tall wooden gates to the yard were closed, the godown was shuttered and locked, and a youth whom Dean found sweeping up around the mountain of scrap informed him that the *patron* had gone to Vientiane on urgent business. Colonel Chakrawongse was nevertheless asked to place a cordon around the property: there was a very good chance that this was the godown mentioned by Ramon, where the killers' weapons were to be collected

. . . and it was always possible in the rabbit warren of old buildings near the river that there might be an underground passage between the warehouse and the safe house where the newcomers were holed up. All five of the surveillance teams were placed on standby, together with Dean himself, Hammer, Wassermann, Novotny, and Schneider, within two minutes' call of the alleyway.

For the first twenty-four hours they might as well have gone to the movies. Nobody went into or left the house. It was not until the afternoon of the following day that there was any action—and even then a single tail, rather than the thirty-five available, would have sufficed.

To Dean's astonishment, Chan, unmistakably Chan, emerged into the lane. With him were two men who could have been the officers he had seen at the pottery, and the two newcomers. But gone were the workers' dungarees: all five of them were wearing sober business suits. And gone for the moment was the necessity for sophisticated shadowing. Chan called a cab and they all went to the Hilton for afternoon tea.

They stayed an hour. Afterward they behaved like tourists—strolling around the temple gardens, staring at the palace, the big stores, the waterfront bars, visiting the Muong-Thang Museum of Southeast Asian Art. They returned to the house in the alleyway at eight o'clock and remained there, so far as the watchers could tell, until the following morning, when the routine they followed was much the same.

For five days Chan and his companions continued to play the tourist role. The itinerary varied in detail from day to day, but there were three things common to all of them: the quintet always remained as a tightly knit group; the routes they took invariably crossed and recrossed the palace quarter several times a day; and they visited the rooftop restaurant at the Hilton every afternoon for tea. "Smart enough," Dean commented to Daler. "According to the colonel, they tip well, they talk with the waitresses, they're making themselves instant regular customers. That way, nobody will pay them any mind if one or more hang around on the day of the parade."

It was during the afternoon sessions at the Hilton that Jason Mettner proved of use to Dean, for the mercenary chief was unwilling to deploy any of the members of his own team—who might after all be known by sight to the killers—at such close quarters. Neither Chan nor his henchmen, however, made any attempt to reach the roof or leave the elevators and passageways that led to the restaurant. "Maybe they're leaving all that to the double agents Ramon claimed to have infiltrated into the police," Dean said sourly when the newspaperman reported.

On the sixth day there was a drastic alteration in the routine. The five gunmen emerged separately, at ten-minute intervals, and hurried away in different directions. As a ploy, having lulled any possible watchers into a state of somnolence by five days of inaction, it might well have been successful . . . had it not been for the fact that there were thirty-five highly skilled operatives waiting for just such a break.

After fifty minutes of frenzied radio activity, Daler and Colonel Chakrawongse sat back in their operations room and waited for the reports to come in as the five teams shifted at last into top gear.

With growing excitement Daler saw that the pattern made by the surveillance groups spinning a moving web around their five quarries was beginning to arrange itself in a semicircle around the parade ground where the march-past was scheduled. The killers were twisting and turning, sometimes doubling in their tracks, but within an hour it was clear that each man at last was investigating the firing point that had been assigned to him—and presumably pointed out, but only at a distance, during the peregrinations of the past five days.

Chan was the first to come in off the street. Not unexpectedly, he went back to the Hilton—but security men posted among the hotel personnel reported that he had appeared neither in the restaurant nor in the American bar. Did he have accomplices there? Dean hurried to the Samoa Hotel to alert Mettner, with a request that the newspaperman race to the Hilton with Mazzari, and stay there until Chan had been located.

One of the rebel officers ended up at the Buddhist temple next door to the Hilton. A Buddhist security man followed him inside and radioed later that—apparently with the connivance of one of the monks—he had mounted to the bell tower and was surveying the terrain from an open arch above the concentric rows of idols that surrounded the pyramid spire. His colleague was tracked to the godown. It was a rice-and-grain warehouse, the only one overlooking the palace grounds, and it was closed, locked, and barred until the rice harvest after the monsoon season. The officer used a passkey to unlock a door set in the huge wooden gates, and vanished inside. Since it was impossible to follow him there, the team shadowing him surrounded the building and kept watch in the hope that a suddenly unshuttered window high up in the facade would pinpoint the eyrie from which his shots would be fired.

The two men from the *Arethusa* took the longest time to home on their sniper's posts, although these—the two of which Dean and his men knew nothing whatever—turned out to be the simplest and perhaps the most obvious. Chan and the officers would be firing from high up, an angled deflection shot aimed at a foreshortened target; the boat men, on the other hand, had been assigned low-trajectory firing points, from which their shots would barely skim the palace wall. One was in the branches of a cedar tree in the temple gardens, the other on the fire escape of a small apartment building, outside a duplex to which the killer had the key.

"Well, cock, that's it," Daler said with satisfaction, staring up at the numbered markers that located the positions of the gunmen on the wall map. "I guess we keep the bloody bloodhounds on the trail, eh?" He gestured toward the different-colored flags identifying the tags, yellow, marked A to F, for one team, blue for another, and so on.

"But yes. Of course." Colonel Chakrawongse was definite. "One does not know what else they may do, where else they may go." He indicated the illuminated sectors on the city plan. It was noon. According to the markers—which were constantly being moved as the radio reports came in—the killers were already returning home. "Now that we do know where they are supposed to be on the day, we must keep closer to them than ever . . . first in case they should change their minds and decide upon alternative places, second because it is essential that we track them until the very moment they prepare to shoot. Only that way can we be sure there is no slipup."

"Yeah," Daler said. "What *we* have to do now, to

make sure nobody fucks up on our side, is to locate five places that give us a good enough view to knock the bastards off before they can shoot."

This was less difficult than he had feared. At Ngon Thek's suggestion, they tried three different tiers of the military pagoda that stood behind the saluting base. From this trio of vantage points, the bell tower, the fire escape, and the warehouse could be minutely covered (a late report from the team shadowing the man at the godown stated that one of the tags had observed the opening and closing of a shutter, high up beneath the eaves on the side facing the palace, while the man was inside). The cedar tree could only be sighted from a balcony immediately above the base—which was hardly suitable—or from the top of an army truck parked on the inner side of the wall. The duty officer promised to organize this. Wassermann was detailed to take care of Chan, since he was the best marksman and the only feasible place was the roof of the palace: a 600-yard shot, with the exact situation that Chan had chosen on the Hilton roof still uncertain.

"All the same," Dean said when these arrangements had been made, "I'm not entirely happy with the setup. I don't know, but . . ." He left the sentence unfinished.

"What's eating you, squire?" Mazzari asked. They were drinking at the inner bar of the Fragrant Blossoms tea-house, and the big African, together with Mettner, was pretending to interview the leader of the new palace guard.

"I don't know," Dean said again. "Something. Ramon, for a start."

"How d'you mean . . . Ramon?"

"Well, I mean it's understandable that Furneux, for example, isn't in town with these hit men. If, as we suppose, he ferried them into the country via the pottery, maybe that's where his job ended: maybe he isn't needed anymore. But Ramon was *organizing* the whole damned thing, for Christ's sake; he fixed the timetable, selected the places, and chose the men. We heard him say so ourselves. I find it mighty strange that he isn't here supervising the run-in."

"Maybe he aims to show at the last minute," Mettner said. "Like a broad laying a foundation stone or a politician planting a memorial tree. You know, somebody else

120

already hefted that stone; the tree's been prepared and all he has to do is tip the son of a bitch into a hole some guys already dug for him."

Dean shook his head. "It's the preliminary work that needs the official touch here," he said. "Checking that everything's working out according to plan. About the shooting he can do nothing."

"Maybe he *is* here," said Mazzari. "Keeping a low profile."

"Sure," said Dean, unconvinced. "I certainly hope so."

Whether or not Ramon was in town, he made no appearance so far as Dean and his men were aware during the next forty-eight hours. There was of course the possibility—since the local security forces did not know him and Interpol could provide no photo—that he was there and they had simply missed him. But since Chan and his fellow conspirators remained under full six-box surveillance, and none of the shadows reported any of them meeting anyone, it seemed unlikely. The killers in fact emerged seldom, and then only to repeat their tourist roles: during the time that the mercs, in their turn, were familiarizing themselves with trajectories and angles of fire from their chosen posts, they did not once revisit any of the hideouts located by Colonel Chakrawongse's operatives.

Dean was once more obscurely worried by this. It was entirely possible, of course, that they were so confident, so efficient, that they had no need to make any visual recap. This was certainly true of Chan himself . . . but he was the one man out of the five, and by far the most dangerous, whose precise choice of position remained unknown. At nine o'clock on the morning of the parade, they still had no idea what part of the Hilton roof he would be firing from, or how he planned to insinuate himself through the police cordon surrounding the place. "He's *got* to be located and put down along with the others," Dean said forcefully. "We could poleax the others in a single second, and one round from that guy could mean we might just as well never have quit the U.S. of A."

"If we load the goddamn roof with enough cops," Novotny said, "he won't have a chance to fire that round anyway."

"That's just what I don't want," Dean replied. "Like I

said before, we have to leave him the opportunity to try—and best him at the moment he sights the gun. Make it impossible for him to attempt the shot, and he could fall back on some alternative place or plan that we don't know of."

Wassermann said, "So what should we do?"

"Play it by ear—and keep our eyes peeled like they never were before," Dean said. He detailed Sean Hammer, Schneider, and Daler to position themselves in the pagoda and cover the fire escape, the bell tower, and the godown window respectively. Novotny was to be concealed beneath the observation blister of a command truck parked inside the palace wall. His target was the sniper in the cedar tree. Dean himself was to accompany Wassermann on the palace roof, and Mazzari too was brought into the royal enclosure so that there would be three of them anxiously, desperately scanning the facade of the Hilton for the elusive Chan.

The parade was scheduled for eleven o'clock. An hour before then, after a final tryout on the range with their high-precision rifles, the mercs moved into position.

The only hitch in the plans for the day was on the side of the opposition. At a quarter to eleven there was still no sign of Chan . . . and Colonel Chakrawongse radioed from his operations room that, according to his surveillance teams, not a single member of the assassination squad had left the house in the alleyway near the canal.

13 Marc Dean

The weather had been disagreeably hot for two weeks before the military parade at which the Emperor Kao Dinh was to take the salute. On the day of the march-past itself, it was insupportable.

The sun blazed down so furiously out of the brassy sky that it seemed to bleach all the color from the banners and paper lanterns strung across the streets, and the flags hung limp as burned leaves above the government buildings. Prone behind a carved Oriental balustrade on the palace roof, Abe Wassermann squinted for the hundredth time through the telescopic sight of his EM-2 at the distant facade of the Hilton Hotel. His face was shadowed by a large straw coolie hat, but sweat from beneath his hair ran down continually into his eyes, the bush shirt clinging to his shoulders was dark with moisture, and he wiped his right hand constantly against the seam of his pants lest the perspiration bathing his finger should make it slip on the scorching metal of the trigger.

There was still so much humidity in the air that the ferroconcrete parapet of the hotel trembled in the circular eyepiece. When Wassermann laid down the rifle and focused a pair of powerful Zeiss field glasses, the figures behind the parapet shimmered and swam in the heat waves rising from the stone like fish in a tank of cloudy water. "Shit," Wassermann said feelingly, "a day like this, you need three pairs of cross hairs you should be able to draw a bead on a single guy!"

Kneeling beside him in the full glare of the sun, Marc Dean smiled absently. There were perhaps a dozen people on the Hilton roof, most of them police. At his insistence, Ngon Thek had ordered the top three floors of the hotel to be evacuated and the windows shuttered. It would be normal procedure on such a day, as would the posting of cops on the roof; Chan would expect it, would have made his plans taking it into account, and would have organized his approach to his firing point so that he avoided surveillance on the way.

If he was on the way.

There was certainly no sign of him so far. Dean scrutinized the roof once more through his own binoculars and then glanced at Edmond Mazzari, who was stationed at a curve in the balustrade twenty yards to his right. Mazzari had laid down his EM-2 and was surveying the hotel through a telescope on a low tripod, swinging the lens this way and that as he searched for the gunman. He shook his head. "Absolutely not, squire. Not a bloody sign."

"What the hell can the man be doing?" Dean muttered angrily. He stared over the coping. The parade was due to start in five minutes. Already an expectant hush had fallen over the chattering crowd swarming on distant rooftops, windows, walls, and lamp standards and clustered fifty deep outside the wrought-iron palace gates. Below, beneath the striped awning of the saluting base, Kao Dinh—resplendent in a blinding white uniform crossed by the jade-green sash of the Imperial Order of Muong-Thang—stood at the top of red-carpeted steps in front of his two hundred guests. Away on the far side of the parade ground Dean could see the first companies of infantry forming beyond the gateway to the royal stables.

He raised his transceiver abruptly to his ear and pressed the Send button. "Colonel? . . . Dean. . . . What news? No sign here. . . . No, nothing at all."

Wassermann couldn't distinguish the words of Chakrawongse's reply, only Dean's startled response: "What? *Still* no sign of anyone leaving that house? But this is crazy! . . . I know: on a day like this, with half the streets closed and the rest crowded to hell, half an hour at least. . . . I can't understand what the hell goes on."

He snapped off the little radio and turned to Wassermann. Before he could speak, the transceiver bleeped urgently. He held it to his ear again and then called excitedly to Mazzari, "Ed! Hammer just called from the pagoda: the godown window has opened and there's a guy with a gun behind it. See if you can spot it. Top floor."

Mazzari nodded and swung the telescope toward the

tall warehouse that rose above the scalloped roofs a block away. "Got him!" he called. "Fifth window from the right. He's in deep shadow, but you can see the shutter's been pushed open just enough to make room for an arm and a gun."

Dean focused the field glasses and nodded. The radio was bleeping again. "They located guys on the fire escape and in the bell tower," he reported when he had listened to the message. He swept the glasses downward and trained them on the plexiglass blister of the command car parked on a ramp inside the palace wall. It was less than two hundred yards from the trees in the temple gardens on the far side of the street. Inside the curved, transparent dome, he could just make out the figure of Novotny. As he watched, the Pole gestured toward the trees and then turned toward the palace and held up a thumb.

"All except Chan!" Dean groaned. "We *must* locate that bastard!"

"How come those guys made their hidey-holes when the colonel says they never left home?" Wassermann inquired.

Dean mopped his forehead with a Kleenex. "Search me, Abe. They must have passageways through other houses—or a pretty long tunnel if they surfaced outside the whole damned cordon around that house. Where *is* that fucking Chan? For Christ's sake, keep looking."

Wassermann nodded and picked up his binoculars again. Mazzari and Dean, too, scanned the distant facade afresh.

Moving the focus wheel with his middle finger, Wassermann felt the sweat from that slight movement run over his palm and down his wrist. It was coursing in rivulets between his shoulder blades and over his sides. The heat of the sun was hammering inside his skull, building up pressure behind the eyes. Through the misted eyepieces, the now familiar outlines of the hotel and its watchers wavered and slid. His gaze swept past the police, the hotel servants, the favored and screened guests, along the parapet beneath the stacks and the air-conditioning vents; back lower down past the first row of shuttered windows; along again . . .

Wassermann stiffened. What was that? Something unexpected, something that shouldn't be there.

125

A sudden flash of sunlight where nothing should be moving.

He swung the glasses back, cursed, wiped the lenses with Dean's Kleenex, made a fine adjustment to the focus, and . . . Yes, by God! "Colonel!" he yelled. "I got him! Not on the roof at all!"

"Jesus!" Dean shouted. "Where? Where?"

"Window. Second story down from the parapet. It's . . . let's see: one, two, three, four, five, six . . . yes, the seventh from the left. Bastard!"

"I don't see anything," Dean said, adjusting his own glasses.

"They got those fuckers with slats . . . venetian blinds? . . . yeah, venetian. He pulled up the bottom ones, so there's a gap about six inches between the blind and the windowsill. They're polished white and the sun caught the son of a bitch when he moved it."

"You're right, Abe," Dean said slowly. "By Christ, you're right. He must have accomplices inside the hotel, then."

"Or inside the police."

"Right. Or inside the police. Well, we know where he is, but he's too smart to show himself: he's gonna poke that gun through the gap and sight it unseen and . . . bingo! So we've all three of us got to aim for the center of that gap and hope we blow him to hell!"

Wassermann sighed, shifting his body in an attempt to separate his sodden shirt from his back. "Just so long as I haven't melted clean away before he shoots," he said.

There was a blare of brass-band music from the far end of the huge parade ground. Someone, somewhere, was setting off firecrackers. The first detachments of infantry goose-stepped through the gateway from the stable yard, their burnished equipment glittering in the relentless sunlight. Kao Dinh walked forward and stood at the top of the red-carpeted steps leading to the royal box.

Dean was speaking tersely into the transceiver. "Calling all posts: ready for action as of now. Estimated time lapse before the armor begins to pass the saluting base, twelve minutes. Hold your fire until you see their guns aimed. It's over to you guys now. . . . Colonel Chakrawongse? . . . Dean here. We now have all five clients covered.

126

God knows how they got through your cordons, but they did. . . . Okay, we'll keep in touch."

He eased himself facedown on the hot stone of the roof, shuffled back a little so that the barrel of the EM-2 did not project too far through the balustrade, and cradled the butt against his right shoulder. The cross hairs of the telescopic sight centered on the gap below the venetian blind more than four-hundred yards away. In the darkness behind the gap he was aware of a slightly paler blur, but there was nothing he could positively identify as a man, as Chan. Farther along the rooftop, partially sheltered by the drooping folds of a flag, Mazzari leaned his elbows on the coping and prepared to aim and fire from a kneeling position.

Several companies of infantry had now passed below them and were circling the far side of the parade ground. The king stood rigidly at the salute—wide, chunky, a pale and perfect target against a dark background. The band passed, instruments flashing in the glare. It was followed by guerrilla formations with netted helmets and camouflaged combat gear, a regiment of machine-gunners, another of mortar crews, and a third operating bazookas, all mounted in jeeps, and after that the armor.

The whir of powerful motors and the threshing of Caterpillar tracks increased to a roar as the first vehicles emerged from the haze of dust that was now hanging over the gateway at the entrance to the parade ground.

M-113 armored personnel carriers headed the procession, perhaps a hundred of them, followed by two squadrons of AMX-13 light tanks inherited from the French. After these came Saracen armored cars, originally shipped to Malaya for antiguerrilla reconnaissance work and then sold off at a discount when the country achieved independence. And finally the up-to-date hardware from the United States for which the entire ceremony had been staged as a shop window.

Self-propelled howitzers led this last section of the parade—the M-109 model armed with 155mm guns and driven by 400 hp turbo-assisted diesel motors. The ungainly vehicles rumbled past the base, commanders erect in the open turrets, eyes-right toward the figure of the king as the flashguards on the ends of the long barrels dipped and swayed as though they too were saluting.

Behind the howitzers came 88mm artillery trailers, and then a regiment of XM-723 mechanized infantry combat vehicles. These machines, in service only since 1980, had been designed for the U.S. Army not simply as a means of transporting troops from one sector of a battleground to another, but as mobile strong points from within which soldiers could continue the fight. There was space for eight fully equipped men behind the armored hatches and firing slits, and above the cabin housing the three crew members there was a turret-mounted 73mm automatic-loading gun. A 7.62mm machine gun was fitted coaxially with this. Each MICV carried six smoke dischargers and a rail for SAGGER wire-guided antitank missiles.

Kao Dinh's military advisers were confident that the new MICV's would be invaluable in upcountry operations against the rebels and their foreign "volunteers," but the weapons they hoped might be decisive in the civil war were those at the rear of the procession. The pride and joy of Muong-Thang's army was a battalion of MGM-52C Lance surface-to-surface missiles. There were three batteries of these, each comprising three firing platoons. The passage of the slender, finned, two-stage, liquid-fuel projectiles with their sinister high-explosive warheads was timed to coincide with a fly-past by Chinook helicopter gunships and a swoop of Phantom jets. It was at this moment, when the noise volume and the excitement were both at their height, that the assassination attempt was expected.

In the command truck on the ramp, Emil Novotny slid aside the transparent panel on the blister and eased off the safety on his EM-2. Even the hot, damp air of the parade ground was a relief after the furnace heat inside the steel hull of the truck. He could see the killer in the cedar tree quite clearly; he was wedged into a fork, with his left forearm braced against a branch. Novotny had not taken his eyes off the man since he climbed up there fifteen minutes ago.

He was aware of distant cheering, the swell of mechanical noise, a pulsating drone as the missile tractors entered the parade ground and the helicopters approached overhead. The man in the tree raised his rifle to his shoulder.

It was too simple, really, almost perfunctory, a cause-and-effect situation as automatic as lighting a cigarette or twisting the ignition key of an automobile. Novotny centered the cross hairs of his telescopic sight on the sniper's chest. He squeezed the trigger. The butt recoiled as the report reverberated around the blister. The sniper's gun dropped. The man fell out of the tree.

For a moment he lay draped across one of the lower branches; then hands reached up and dragged him down out of sight behind the wall. Novotny turned around to watch the end of the parade.

On the upper tiers of the pagoda, obliquely across the vast open space, Hammer, Kurt Schneider, and Daler crouched in their respective openings, each alert for the slightest move from his quarry. Dean had ordered that the rifles were not to be brought up into the aiming position until the last minute: too long a concentration could unsteady the hand, cause the barrel to waver, and ruin the accuracy of the shot.

Schneider was the first to shoot. The dimly seen figure in the arched opening of the bell tower half-rose and its gun came up. The first row of missiles was slanting past the base. Schneider sighted the EM-2, held his breath, fired. The figure disappeared. A single note boomed out sonorously as the high-velocity slug terminated its flight against the great brass bell cradled behind the arch.

The noise was drowned by the clatter of helicopter rotors. The first of the Chinooks was directly overhead when Sean Hammer pressed the trigger of his EM-2. Even that would hardly have eclipsed the rifle shot, but the report coincided with the scream of the first flight of jets arrowing overhead, and Hammer felt for a moment as though he had fired into a wall of silence, watching his target crumple and fall. By the time the ringing in his ears had subsided and he could hear again, Daler too had gunned down the killer whose weapon had just appeared in the space between the suddenly opened shutter and the wall of the warehouse. The man had slumped forward over the windowsill, his arms trailing emptily.

On the palace roof, Wassermann cursed for the fifth time in the past sixty seconds the sweat that was misting his eyes. He knew better than to make them sting by knuckling them with hot hands, but the moisture was blurring the image in his sights. He opened the lids wide, flexing the muscles, and then willed the tears not to form while he concentrated on the section of window visible beyond the circular rubber eyepiece.

In the six-inch gap separating the stone ledge from the lowest slat of the blind, the blued steel muzzle of a rifle appeared. Wassermann held his breath. He imagined the marksman settling the point where the hairs crossed on the king's bemedaled chest, shifting his grip fractionally, pulling the butt into the hollow of his shoulder, caressing the trigger gently, lovingly, as he took up first pressure . . . Wassermann pulled steadily on the trigger of his own gun.

The foresight jerked as the automatic rifle roared. Beside him Dean's EM-2 spat flame, and an instant later they heard Mazzari's gun crashing out its stream of lead.

The venetian blind shivered and flew up. Shattered glass showered in the sunlight like a fountain falling to the street. For a timeless moment Wassermann saw the figure framed in the embrasure—was it really, horribly, abruptly blotched with red, or was his imagination working over-time?—and then it vanished into the darkness of the room.

Dean was on his feet, shouting. "We made it! By Christ, we zapped the bastard; we made it!" Down below, there was some kind of commotion. Doubtless Ramon's agents were going ahead with their "diversion" even though the shooting had been blocked. Wassermann rolled over into the narrow band of shadow cast by the balustrade and wiped a damp sleeve across his eyes. "Jesus!" he said. "That sun!"

Colonel Chakrawongse would already be at the Hilton, his men investing the other hideouts. Ngon Thek had been insistent that the dead killers should be found—and seen to be found—in place for propaganda purposes. The police must be there before the public—or rebel agents—had a chance to spirit the bodies away. Five minutes later the security chief's bewildered voice was crackling in Dean's receiver.

"Colonel, I do not understand. Here at the hotel the man is shot to pieces, but he is not—was not—Chan. His gun is no precision weapon but a Short Lee-Enfield Mark IV: an ancient bolt-operated rifle the British discarded before World War II."

130

"You're kidding!" Dean exclaimed. "What about the others?"

"The man in the tree was pulled down by an angry crowd. Trampled to a pulp before we could get there. But the one on the fire escape was just alive: we spoke to him before he died. He was an illiterate peasant from the north. So, apparently, were the rest of them: none were the men we have been following. We checked out the remaining three. All of them had obsolete guns like the fellow at the Hilton."

"I don't get it!" Dean muttered furiously. "I just do not get it. With guns like that, at that distance, they couldn't possibly have hoped to make a hit. Not even Chan could have done it. And why the hell——?"

He broke off as Jason Mettner stumbled up the stairway leading to the roof. The newspaperman was flushed and out of breath. "Brother," he panted, "somebody's been stringing you along, but good."

Dean seized him by the arm. "What do you mean?" he demanded fiercely.

"One of those MICV's ran out of line," Mettner said. "Six guys with guns piled out when it approached the base. They jumped his royal person and bundled him into the back, and then roared off before anyone realized what was happening." He paused, breathing hard. "While you guys have been doing cartwheels to block a shooting, the opposition have waltzed in and kidnapped your fucking client!"

II

The Sick-Rose Syndrome

O Rose, thou art sick!
The invisible worm,
That flies in the night,
In the howling storm,

Has found out thy bed
Of crimson joy;
And his dark secret love
Does thy life destroy.
—William Blake

14 Marc Dean

"A setup!" Dean exclaimed bitterly. "The whole damned thing has been a setup from beginning to end. And I was dumb enough to fall for it. All the fucking way!"

"Ah, c'mon, Marc," Sean Hammer said. "There's no sense blamin' yourself, sure. You couldn't be expected to see—"

"I saw plenty," Dean interrupted. He was very angry. "But I was too much of a smart-ass to pay what I saw any mind, and that's the truth."

"You are all the time saying something smells, that you are unhappy because things do not stack up so good," Schneider agreed.

"Too right I was. But I didn't read the signs right, did I? I should have tumbled that it was all too goddamn easy."

"Too *easy*?" Novotny echoed.

"Yeah, too easy. That creep Furneux just *happening* to be in the Fragrant Blossoms when Sean was there . . . just *happening* to be smashed out of his mind, or pretending to be . . . just *happening* not to know why Sean was in town, and letting slip the monastery clue." He shook his head. "It makes me sick to my stomach to think how easily we fell for it. Ramon must be laughing his bloody head off!"

"Me, I don't exactly see why," Wassermann objected.

"Look, they bait the hook with that Canadian bastard's careful 'indiscretions'; they allow me to think there's something phony about this monastery by having Mr. Theng get all evasive about the place; when I go there— and it's all nice and laid on, slow and easy—when I go there, the old French guy makes me more suspicious still. So I decide to go back again, at night, to see what cooks."

"Okay," said Novotny, "but—?"

"Listen. While I'm away, they wheel in Furneux again to say his second piece. Ed and Mettner here catch it this time. And this time he lets slip there *is* to be an assassination attempt . . . and there's to be several hit men on the contract. So when Kurt and me make it to the monastery that night, we're all primed to hear the scenario that's been prepared for us."

"*Scenario*?" Schneider exclaimed. "Are you saying . . . ?"

"We were expected there, for Christ's sake! That's why it was so goddamned easy to best those guards; that's why none of their shots winged us: they weren't meant to. That's why the search party never tumbled to the rubber dinghy: they took good care to keep away. One guy got knocked out, but that was a small price to pay for the dividends. By allowing us, as we thought, to eavesdrop, they put over the idea they wanted to put over: that there were five killers coming into town, with five different hideouts organized that they could shoot from. And I swallowed the whole story."

"Jesus!" Novotny said. "They sure put some fucking brainwork into the son of a bitch, I'm tellin' you!"

Dean said, "Ramon was a *professor,* teaching terrorists how to dope out this kind of deal. There were some nice touches: I'll give him that. The camouflaged combat fatigues that were not *quite* hidden in the monastery dormitory; the guys I glimpsed stealing through that bamboo thicket; the two men off the boat; only letting on about three of the five hideouts and leaving us to nose out the other two."

Daler said, "They knew the security boys would have sussed out there was some kind of hit in the wind, so they figured it'd be best to give them something to work on, to keep them occupied? Is that it?"

"Right. Once they knew we'd been hired, it was obvious that special arrangements were being made. The scenario they organized took care of the maximum number of operatives for the maximum amount of time—all that shadowing, locating the firing points, and so on: it kept the whole security force busy while they went ahead and planned what they really wanted to do. They even covered themselves for the confusion the snatch would cause, talking about a diversion they'd fixed during the marchpast."

"But these guys . . . the poor bastards we shot," Novotny began, "where the hell do they fit in, for God's sake?"

"Cannon fodder," said Dean. "Ramon and his kind shoot off their mouths all the time about liberating the masses, but the masses are one hundred percent expendable when it comes to this kind of deal. Those characters were put in there to be zapped. They were set up for us to knock off. Whether the poor bastards thought they were going to kill an oppressor, I've no idea—but they had to be given some kind of gun, so we'd be tempted to shoot them. I guess they were given old models because the current stuff's too expensive and too hard to come by."

"So we shot them already," said Wassermann. "I still don't see . . . ?"

"I fancy," Mazzari said, "that the story line would run somewhat as follows: we spend all this time tracking these blokes down, as per leaked information; we lay on a big-deal electronic-surveillance routine; we make elaborate plans to help these johnnies shuffle off this mortal coil, once we've found out where they'll be; we're given special orders to watch them like bloody hawks and not shoot until the last minute. But if they're not there to shoot—and not visible for some time before that—we might smell a rat and start looking someplace else. Which would spoil dear Ramon's little plan. Am I right?"

"Right you are, Ed," Dean said. "They were using exactly the same reasoning we were . . . in reverse. We held off firing until the very last minute, in case it tipped them off that we were on to them and they activated an alternative plan; they in turn had to keep *us* occupied until the very last minute in case *we* started looking for an alternative."

"There are a coupla things I don't understand, but." Sean Hammer was looking puzzled. "They decoyed you out to that island, deliberate. They most likely had you shadowed from the moment you stepped ashore. So what the hell was the idea swiping your bloody launch? Where did it get them? I mean, you'd already left the place, had you not?"

Dean smiled. The Arcoa 900 had been found, neatly moored at its own berth in Am-Phallang, the following morning. "Simply to delay us," he explained. "So that Chan and his two rebel friends could get back to the city and go to ground before we returned to spread around the story they'd laid on us and Chakrawongse put his cordons out."

"Number two, the ambush you ran into. What was the point, trying to knock you off when you left the monastery the first time? After all, they *wanted* you to go back—to hear the story they'd cooked up—didn't they?"

"I think the ambush was a coincidence," Dean said. "After all, as you say, there's a civil war on. It could have been a stray rebel patrol, guys who weren't into the plot concerning us. Or, as I thought at the time, just bandits profiting from the conditions."

Schneider said, "What about this threat of Furneux's—a special squad, he said, to take care of us before the parade."

"Window dressing, like the attack on Sean at the fountain."

"Thank you very much," said Hammer. " 'Apart from that, Mrs. Lincoln, did you enjoy the show?' "

"The bomb they chucked at the Toyota, cock—that wasn't window dressing, was it?" Daler asked.

Dean shook his head. "No. If they'd pulled that one off, they probably wouldn't have needed to organize this setup at all."

Mettner spoke. It was the first thing he'd said for some minutes. "You haven't touched on the sixty-four-thousand-dollar question," he observed.

"And that is?"

Mettner shrugged. "Just why? Why all this second-rate private-eye routine? *Why* did they snatch the king? Not to kill him: they could have done that then and there, the way it happened with Sadat. Why do folks get kidnapped? To be held against a ransom demand. Not 'Your money or your life,' the way the highwaymen used to play it, but 'Your money or *his* life.' Okay, they got him. So what do they want for his return, in good condition and untouched by human hand? What's the ransom?"

"We'll be hearing from them," said Dean. "Until then, we wait and see. In the meantime doing our damnedest to find out where he is and get him back."

But there was in fact another question, to him even

more important then any of those posed, that remained unasked.

How much responsibility did the girl Golden Dawn bear for the abduction of Kao Dinh? How far, if at all, was she involved in the plot that had made monkeys out of him and his men?

15 Jason Mettner

Dean was mad as hell, of course. He'd been hit where it hurt most: in the pocket where he kept his professional pride. Not only had he fallen down on the job, but he'd been made to look a charlie, a jerk, a clown, as well. What burned him up more than anything—he told me this himself—was the idea of a cheapskate like Furneux pulling in the big laugh, telling the story around the mercenary circuit. For this reason alone, he'd sworn to even the score and get back the king at all costs—even if it meant hiring a fresh band of mercs and paying them out of his own pocket. Yeah, the same one, okay.

I was raring to follow this story up—shit, the exclusive I had so far was a three-decker on page one!—but something else broke in my sector and the proprietor wired me to take off for Hanoi. It seemed that a group of what the French call Pirates of the Air—skyjackers to you and me—had taken over a Pan-Asiatic Airlines Boeing 747 on a scheduled flight from Tokyo to Cairo, and forced the captain to land the ship in Vietnam. Don't ask me why; the message just said "Go Hanoi soonest."

I was feeling kind of choked—these damned air hijacks were becoming so frequent we considered running a list on the sports page, along with the baseball results—when the second message came in. This one wasn't strictly for me. I mean like it was on a radio news bulletin, a private one for Dean; office of origin: New York City. According to the information, the hijacked Boeing had taken off again. Its destination? You guessed it: Am-Phallang.

I called the travel agency and canceled my one-way to Hanoi.

"I don't get it," I said when Dean told me. "I mean, why would they fly here? There's a civil war going on. It's only a whistle stop from Hanoi anyway. Plus there ain't no head of government to deal with them or grant them asylum or whatever it is they want. What do they want— just as a matter of interest, you understand?"

He grinned at me. "Off the record?"

Bastard. "All right," I groaned. "Off the damned record."

"They'll communicate their demands when they get here," he said. "Right now, all we know is what they're offering in return."

"The ship and the passengers, I guess," I said. "How many?"

"There are 246 passengers and nine crew aboard," he replied. "And a king."

I stared. "You don't mean . . . ? You're not telling me . . . ?"

Dean nodded. "Our very own monarch."

"But . . . Christ! It was only yesterday . . ."

"Just time to get from the parade ground to the nearest waterway, unload him into a fast powerboat, make the Khmer border, and then fly him to Hanoi in a Cessna or something like that. This is a big-deal operation, Mettner. Kidnapping, skyjacking, all nicely worked out and dovetailed: the only reason they landed the Boeing at Hanoi was to take Kao Dinh aboard. It increased the value of the merchandise, having a royal along."

"And that's why this whole operation . . . ? *That's* why he was snatched? Just to make extra weight as a bargaining counter?"

He nodded again.

I felt like a flyweight climbed into the ring and found he'd been matched by mistake against Muhammad Ali. I stammered, "But why . . . why . . . why the hell bring him back here? Why take him there? Why not land the 747 here in the first place? What kind of demands can they have to go that far before they even ask?"

"I guess we'll find that out when they touch down here," Dean said. "As to your other questions, the main runway here at Am-Phallang's a thousand yards too short for jumbos. A 747 would run out of road and flatten half the town if it tried to land."

"But you just said—?"

"I said the main runway *here*. At Am-Phallang. You're forgetting there's a new international field under construction at Phra Pradeng, fifteen miles out of town. The main runway's down, though the airport's not in operation yet. That's where they've told the pilot to put down."

"And we're going to go on out there?" I asked hopefully.

Once more he nodded that rugged head . . . and sighed. "They landed fifteen minutes ago," he said.

Phra Pradeng field was slightly smaller than the state of Colorado. On the other hand, it was considerably flatter, so maybe that evened things up. There was a macadam perimeter track with dispersal pans and—so far—only this one main runway stretching northeast to southwest from horizon to horizon. Just visible over the curvature of the globe were the terminal buildings, and these were flanked on either side by a mess of cranes, bulldozers, trucks, dumps of construction materials, and earth-moving machines where they were putting up repair hangars, maintenance units, storage sheds, and all that stuff.

The Boeing was parked right down at the far, southwestern end of the runway. Even at that distance—it must have been all of two miles away when we came through the gates—in all that space, it still looked enormous. Hell, they *are* enormous: didn't someone say the pilot's eyeline is around forty feet off the ground? I mean, Jesus, imagine trying to maneuver that into a gap between the automobiles double-parked in the Loop—even by a fireplug! At least the cop on the beat would have a hard time slipping the parking ticket under the windshield wiper.

There were no vehicles near the hijacked plane, but several army trucks, a command car, and a dozen civilian sedans were scattered around the parking lot inside the main entrance. There were three Phantoms in one of the dispersal pans and a couple of executive jets among the light training aircraft around the control tower. Otherwise the field was bare of planes. Inside the terminal, the situation was about what you'd expect at an uncompleted airport. That is to say, all the electronic gadgetry in the tower was in working order, and so were the cafeteria, the baggage-claim carousel, the newstand, the cigar store, and the men's room—but there were no landing lights, radio masts, check-in counters, baggage trolleys, or immigration desks. Everything for the passengers' safety and comfort, but no means of flying him in or getting him away. Maybe it didn't matter too much: the field was in the bottom-left-hand corner of the country, the nearest region to the Thai border and the farthest from the fighting. And there was a full week before it was due to be open to international traffic.

It was kind of creepy inside—all those rubber-tiled acres with no girls' voices crooning over the PA system, no guys in raincoats pretending not to read the girlie magazines at the newsstand, nobody shouting at the information desk. We walked past the empty counters to what looked as if it might one day be the transit lounge. A group of guys was standing just inside the glassless swing doors: the security minister, Ngon Thek, and a collection of top brass from the police and the army, including this Colonel Chakrawongse, the poor Asiatic's Yul Brynner. We were only a few miles from the King of Siam's domain, too.

Ngon Thek—he was the one looked like a walnut in a sharkskin suit—came up to Dean with a face as cheerful as Tutankhamen's grandpappy. "I think we had better retire to the control tower, Colonel," he said. "I am afraid this looks very grave."

They took a powder, the whole lot of them, through a door marked "Private" (that's always the first one they install), and left me in the deserted lounge. I went to look at the girlie magazines on the newsstand.

I'd salivated over three busty centerfolds and fourteen pages of pubic hair before any of them came back, and then it was only Dean and Ole Walnut Face. It was clear at once that, so far as the Minister of Home Security (or whatever he was) was concerned, Mettner, J., Jr., Our Special Correspondent in Muong-Thang, was nothing but bad news. Dean had to pitch him quite a line about the way I'd been helping out before the guy even condescended to sneer at me.

All I was allowed to learn then was that the tower was in radio contact with the skyjackers, that certain demands had been made, and that the Boeing was staying put until they'd been given some kind of reply. "Big deal," I said bitterly. "I'll wire them to hold the front page. You wouldn't like to add something really sparkling—like the police are confident of an early arrest?"

Of course the Lord High Spy had to take it for real. "I

am afraid there is no question of an arrest, Mr. Mettner," he said. "And no question of press telegrams leaving the country, at any rate for the moment."

"How's that?" I asked, startled. I heard later that the government troops had suffered a setback in a battle with rebel guerrillas somewhere in the north, so maybe he had too much on his mind. But a total censorship block? He had to be joking.

Naturally, I'd filed when the king was snatched, like Hal Schenk and every other newsman in town. The office was screaming for copy and all the agencies were hot on the trail, so what the hell did he mean, no telegrams?

"All telephone and cable services have been temporarily suspended," he said.

"You can't do that!" I shouted. "The whole damned world will be crying out for the latest news of the king; they'll want to know exactly how the hijackers and your men in the control tower—"

"Mettner!" Dean interjected. "Cool it, will you? The whole damned world doesn't know a damned thing about it."

I stared at him. "What the hell do you mean?"

"Nobody outside Muong-Thang, and very few people inside it know that the plane is here. All they know is that it was hijacked, landed at Hanoi, and took off again for an unknown destination. Nobody at all knows they have the king aboard. Not even the airport authorities at Hanoi."

"But . . . but how come?" I was stammering again. "I mean, surely the air-traffic controllers . . . ? And how did the king . . . ?"

"The king was whisked aboard with two guys who sounded like Ramon and Chan. Probably drugged. The authorities figured all three of them for guerrillas: it was part of the deal; the pirates threatened to knock off some of the hostages. So far as the air-traffic people are concerned, we're too near Hanoi for the ship to have been plotted in any other zone. For the moment, so far as the rest of the world knows, it's simply missing."

"Like the king?"

"Like the king. No news on either front. And no connection. That's why there's to be no question of cables."

"But for how long? No news on the snatch, okay: it

happens in kidnap cases. But you can't black out the plane indefinitely."

"Why not?"

"Because of the people, Dean. Those 246 guys and dames, those crew members, they got families—parents, children, sweethearts. You can't let all those folks believe they lost their dear ones in another plane disaster. Without even any news of where."

"Stop talking like one of your own sob sisters," Dean said. (He was right: I'd been mentally doping out an intro for a Sally Miles Fem-Point Panel.) "In any case, is it any worse than knowing they're in the hands of terrorists who may blow them to hell at any moment?"

"Is that what they're threatening?"

"That's all I have to say to you, Mettner," Dean lied.

In fact, once we'd gotten rid of the nut-faced panjandrum, on the way back to town he came across with the lowdown on what had really happened in that control tower. Off the record, natch.

"It's one hell of a delicate situation," he told me. "The terrorists are asking . . . well, what they're asking is crazy."

"Release of political prisoners?" I suggested tiredly. "The usual routine? Cash? A plane to take them someplace where they get asylum?"

"Yeah. All that. But *what* prisoners? This is where they get really insane. They want the release of convicted terrorists from prisons in Britain, Israel, the United States, and Ireland, plus half a hundred dissidents from Soviet labor camps!"

"Jesus!" I said. "That's quite an order."

"You can say that again! Then, as an additional sweetener, they'd like certain political prisoners, as you say, set free in Guatemala, Chile, Argentina, and Brazil. And, for afters, a plane with enough fuel to get to South America, and the small sum of ten million dollars!"

My mouth opened but no words formed. Finally I managed to gasp out, "But that's lunatic! The conditions are impossible! Nobody would ever—"

"Especially when you know who's on board," Dean cut in.

"Apart from his majesty?"

"Apart from H.M."

"Namely?"

145

"The names are not important—I don't have a passenger list anyway—but it's *what* they are and where they come from." He took a hand off the wheel and held up a finger each time he quoted: "Oil sheikhs from the OPEC Council, Communist Arabs from Libya, a gang of highly placed Cubans, senior dignitaries from the EEC, Russian athletes returning home from some Oriental games in Tokyo. Can you imagine a more disparate group of VIP's?"

"You mean they're all on different sides of the fence?"

"Sure. *And so are the people they want released.* You see what that means?"

I fished a pack of Chesterfields from my pocket and lit a cigarette. "You mean . . . like the Europeans would want to save their ministers but they'd balk at freeing left-wing terrorists; the comrades would jib at the release of fascists in Latin America; the Israelis or the oil kings might think of raising the loot, but they'd think twice if it meant helping Qaddafi's Libya?"

He nodded. "Impossible to get all those interests to agree—and if anything was done without full agreement, there'd be half a dozen brickbats for every bouquet when it was all over. You can understand why Ngon Thek doesn't want to know."

"He won't treat?"

"Says he hasn't the mandate: it's an international responsibility. Won't discuss things with the terrorists at all."

"It's a Pan-Asiatic Airlines ship," I pointed out. "Isn't that an American concern?"

"The planes have U.S. registration, but fifty-one percent of the shares are held by a consortium of bankers from Thailand, Indonesia, and Japan. Washington's terrified of touching it. They've been the world's whipping boy long enough: you can see that anything the administration did would be wrong." Dean grinned. "And just for good measure, it's an election year—and at least two of the pirates are said to be black!"

I cleared my throat. Smoking endangers my health. It says so on the pack. "I guess you could call the situation . . . sensitive," I said. "I can see that Washington would never be able to persuade all those other countries, so many words apart politically, to release their prisoners.

And who the hell could authorize the payment of such a huge sum? Just the same, if our country won't negotiate, who the fuck will?"

Dean said, "For the reasons you just cited, there's no question of negotiating, no question at all of giving in to their demands. On the other hand, they have threatened to kill the passengers one by one and then blow up the ship if those demands are not met . . . and the death of Kao Dinh or even one important foreigner could have unthinkable results."

"I get the picture," I said. "Stalemate. And so . . . ?"

"So there are only two choices: talk them out of it or mount an Entebbe-style raid."

I laughed. He had to be joking. "And who exactly is the lucky guy destined to make *that* choice?" I asked.

"It's been suggested that I do it," he said calmly.

Funny joke. I didn't say anything, just went on staring.

"On account of the assassination threat," Dean explained, "I have a hot line to the U.S. Contact by the name of Quinnel. Something to do with the CIA."

"I think I met the guy," I said. "Tall, thin character, looks like a jumbo-size kid from fourth grade who outgrew his strength?"

"That's the one. The Agency was going to be happy if we kept the king alive; it'll be happier still if we can get him—and all the other VIP's out of that plane. I won't go into details, but if the pirates can't be talked out of it and we have to mount an assault, someone like me—a professional, a mercenary if you like—can be disowned by everyone, whether the raid succeeds or fails. Nobody knows who hired me, so there's no target for the brickbats, and faces are saved all around."

I said, "It wouldn't take a genius to guess who hired you."

"Guessing isn't proving—and the principle remains. In brief, I can name my own price—short of ten million dollars, that is!—if I organize an assault group and carry out the raid in the case of talks getting nowhere."

"You're going to accept?"

"On one condition—and it's a tough one."

"Specifically?"

"That I handle the talks, the bargaining with the pirates, as well. That I have absolute and total command of

147

the whole deal from beginning to end—that it's up to me to decide when and if the talks have failed, when and if to go in with the guns, and like that. Also, if the deal's accepted, that I can't be overruled by *anyone*, no matter how rugged it gets."

"Boy," I said, "you really want to wear the hair shirt, don't you! And who says yes or no to your proposition?"

"Unofficially, I deal only with the Agency. But I guess they'd sound out all the other interested parties before they agreed. Officially, of course, they'd know nothing about it. The one good point—the only one—is that the terrorists won't have the backing of any country or bloc. With the selection of hostages they have, they alienate just about everyone except the Red Brigades, the anarchists, and first-year students of political science!"

"Why did you insist on that condition?" I asked curiously. I never did quite find out what made this guy tick. "It's a hell of an extra responsibility, for Christ's sake."

"Because I hold very strong opinions on the taking of hostages," he said. "And if I can't play it my way, I'm out of the game."

I turned in my seat to look at him. Suddenly there had been an edge, a relentless and unsparing hardness to the voice that gave me a new slant on the guy. Perhaps for the first time I really saw how forceful and tough this man was. "I believe," he said tightly, in that flinty manner he can switch on, "that ransom demands should never, ever be met; that if necessary, however regretfully, hostages should be sacrificed; and that skyjackers and kidnappers should be ruthlessly eliminated—without trial, if they're caught red-handed with their victims. To put it another way, if six men hijack a plane and put the lives of several hundred innocent people at risk, maybe even kill one or two just to show they mean business; and if those six men are caught while they're still aboard that plane, so there can be no question of mistaken identity—then I say they should be summarily executed, like looters in wartime. Shot right away."

"Hard words," I said.

"It's a hard life. And one of the toughest things we have to deal with right now is this rash of terrorist violence. It's happening all over the world, not even for political ends anymore. Not always. And like most forms of

148

corruption, it's self-perpetuating: once you give in to the motherfuckers, there'll be another bunch along with even more outrageous demands. And then another and another. Finally you get to a state where John Citizen and his wife are afraid to go walking in the street in case they're snatched by some teenage hophead who threatens to knock them off unless he gets fifty dollars for a fix. It's going that way in Italy already."

"Okay," I said, "but how do you plan to—"

"The Israelis know the answer," he cut in. "One Entebbe raid and it's months before there's another skyjack. You have to break the rules to beat them: Ramon himself told me that when he was teaching at the terrorist school I smashed in Corsica."

"There were hostages killed in the Entebbe raid," I pointed out.

"Sure there were. You can't win a battle without losses. But that's the sacrifice the civilized world has to make if it's not to be blackmailed into total anarchy by these bastards."

"I was going to say: if they do give you the go-ahead, how do you plan to deal with this particular situation?"

"There are two different kinds of kidnap syndrome," Dean said. "The old-fashioned routine, where someone is snatched, kept hidden, a prisoner, and nobody knows where they are until the ransom is paid and they are released. You hope. The second kind, where a group of people are held hostage in a bank, an office building, or, like here, a plane—this kind brings a new dimension to the problem. Because here *everybody* knows where the victims are. Demands are made and messages exchanged between the villains and the authorities in each case . . . but in the second, the whole deal takes place in a blaze of publicity. Instead of being shadowy figures leaving furtive notes in telephone booths, the kidnappers are on television, in the newspapers, on film. Even if they aren't seen personally, they are stars."

"True enough," I said. "But—"

But he had the bit between his teeth now. Except that he was the one *riding* the hobbyhorse! "I believe," he said, "that the best way to deal with hijackers is, so far as possible, to ignore them. To deny them the center of the stage, the worldwide publicity they crave. If nobody wants to talk to them, if nobody seems to give a shit whether they knock off their hostages or not, if the TV crews are someplace else . . . well, finally they begin to feel insecure. And it's the negotiator's job to play on that insecurity until they're only too glad to give up. Or until they reach a stage where a lightning raid has a good chance of success—and if anyone gets killed, too bad."

"How are you supposed to know when that stage has been reached?"

"You can occasionally tell from altered speech patterns, more often from stress readings in the voice itself; psychologists specializing in this kind of work have perfected machines that can record these. That's one of the advantages of the hostage situation over a simple snatch: you are in actual verbal communication all the time, and that can tell you a lot."

"You got strong feelings about this," I said.

"Yeah, damn right I have. It may seem kind of screwy to you, Mettner: after all, I'm a soldier; I'm paid to do violent things; that's the main reason my wife left me—because, in a sense, killing is my business. But the violence is directed against other guys in the same business. What burns me up is when ordinary folks are involved, especially when their fear and their suffering, and the threat of both increasing, are cynically used as bargaining counters."

Dean shifted down and turned in the palace gates. The green-uniformed sentries saluted as we swept past toward the pagoda. "We got one or two things working in our favor here," he said quietly. I realized that he'd been progressively raising his voice while he was delivering his lecture on "The Snatch and How to Foil it." "If they agree to my terms, the plane will simply be reported missing somewhere over the China Seas, and too bad about the distress to passengers' relatives. It will be completely isolated out at Phra Pradeng. As you saw, the airport's incomplete: there's no traffic and it's in the middle of a million miles of paddy. Ngon Thek's police can easily keep any rubbernecks away from the jumbo at the end of the new runway."

"You're keeping a total press blackout on this?"

"Total. You're favored, and I'm counting on you not to abuse that position."

"Okay, okay, okay," I said. "Until you lift the embargo, I'm as *shtoom* as the three brass monkeys. An honorary merc, yet!"

"We'll talk to them from the tower on CB radio," he said. "All they'll hear on regular news bulletins will be the report that the plane is missing. After that, zero. Later on, I may even jam every wavelength except the one we're speaking on. That should give them a taste of real isolation."

"Suppose they start murdering hostages? It's happened."

"Then it becomes a game of poker . . . bluff and counterbluff to see who can hang in the longest."

I suppose the guy was right, but I'd have been happier if I'd known who was dealing the cards.

16 Marc Dean

Quinnel flew in the following day. A military jet, Colonel Chakrawongse's man at the old Am-Phallang airfield told Dean. Very rapid. Very short takeoff. He wasn't familiar with the make or type.

The CIA man checked in at the Hotel Samoa, where he was given the room next to Mettner's. Dean visited him at the beginning of the afternoon; it had been agreed that Quinnel should remain strictly incognito: for a number of reasons, most of which Dean had quoted to Mettner, it was most important that nobody connected with the Agency should be seen to be involved in any way with the hijack situation. There was no question, therefore, of Quinnel going anywhere near the new airfield at Phra Pradeng; his principals, however, had made it a condition, in accepting Dean's terms, that there should be a man on the spot rather than in front of a radio transmitter eight thousand miles away.

The heat had now become insufferable. No ghost of wind stirred the drooping fronds of tamarisk and palm in the hotel garden, the flags in front of the government buildings hung limp beneath the leaden sky, and the rank odors of stagnant water and rotting vegetation lay heavily over the smaller canals. There was no air conditioning in the Samoa: the six-foot blades of the slow-moving ceiling fan in Quinnel's room seemed barely to disturb the humid air. Quinnel himself was still wearing his thick gray flannel pants; in shirt sleeves he sprawled in a rattan chair, the skin already flushed over the bony bridge of his nose. "Score out at the field?" he asked. "New since we liaised on the radio last night?"

Dean shook his head, repressing a smile. Under stress, Quinnel's delivery became more laconic than ever, dispensing with auxiliary verbs right and left. "For the moment," the combat leader said, "I'm letting them stew. It must be like a furnace out there in the open, in this heat. There's more than 250 people in that ship, and the batteries won't last forever. Not the best conditions for heroics—even by fanatics."

"Spoken to them at all today—hijackers, I mean?"

"Yeah. Early this morning. No change in their demands. They want food sent out, but I'm making them wait for it until sundown. Tough on the hostages, but bad conditions work in our favor. They called the control tower back, twice they tell me, but we gave them no reply. Part of the Marc Dean isolation service!"

"Anything else?" Quinnel fanned himself with a copy of the previous day's *Washington Post*. Outside the shuttered window the city was quiet. Even with their king abducted, the heat was such that the usual chattering crowds had stayed home until it was cooler. An occasional car swished past, its tires sucking at the melting asphalt.

"Sure," Dean replied. "One thing. I sent Hammer and Mazzari—two of my guys—away to drum up some trade."

"Trade?"

"I only have six men here. It was a bodyguard job, remember. And I fucked up. I don't intend to do the same again. I'll need a commando of at least twenty to storm that plane—and I want them here, trained, briefed, and ready."

"You figure it'll come to that?"

Dean shrugged. "You tell me. But we have to be ready."

Before he left, he arranged for Quinnel to be in the Fragrant Blossoms bar later that evening. It was important that there be no visual connection between himself and the CIA man, but Daler would be there. As two Anglo-Saxons in a foreign country, they could believably get into conversation—and Daler would then pass on Dean's report on the Phra Pradeng developments during the afternoon. If there was anything to report.

Of considerably more interest in fact (though, not unnaturally, it was reported to no one) was the situation awaiting Dean when he left the Samoa. In the front passenger seat of the official palace Toyota he was using, gorgeous tropical birds circled oversize hibiscus blooms above the cloth upholstery. The birds and the flowers were printed on silk. The silk, elegantly cut, sheathed the nubile body of Golden Dawn.

"You have not been to see me," she said reproachfully.

Dean climbed in beside her. Beneath the soft top, the atmosphere was like the steam room of a sauna, but the girl looked as cool and crisp as a model in a Paris fashion parade. "I imagined you might understand why," he said expressionlessly.

She gave him a swift sideways glance, a look of apparent bewilderment.

"There have been a certain number of things happening," he said. "Quite apart from the abduction of a king. Just how does Jean-Paul Albi happen to be your uncle?"

"I do not understand."

"I mean how exactly is he related to you."

"He is my uncle. You just told it. I am his . . . how do you say? . . . his niece."

"Sure, sure. Okay. But which side of the family?"

"Oh. If it is important. His youngest brother was my father; my mother was from Cambodia."

"It might be important. I don't know how much you've been told—how much they let you know before they briefed you. About my job, I mean. But if the French connection is on the male side and extends back to colonial days, there might be a discoverable reason for an involvement with the invaders. A grudge, perhaps; a feeling that talents had been overlooked. Some kind of jealous—"

"I do not think I like what you are saying," Golden Dawn interrupted.

"I'm not at all sure that I like what you are doing . . . or at any rate were doing."

She twisted around in the seat until she was staring him full in the face. For a moment he thought that her eyes looked misty, but it could have been the damp heat in the vehicle. "What are you trying to suggest?" she demanded. Her voice sounded angry.

"Come off it, baby," Dean said roughly. "There's no percentage trying to act dumb with me. Everything was just a little too neat and pat."

"I do not know what you mean. Why do you speak harshly to me, *chéri?*"

"Somebody's tipped off to put me in touch with Mr. Theng when I investigate the smoking den above the

Fragrant Blossoms. Mr. Theng is in the import-export business—mainly of drugs. Mr. Theng is angry because the king has leaned on the drug business since his accession and wants to stop it. The absence of the king would therefore be of great advantage to Mr. Theng."

"What has this to do with me?"

"You tell me. But wait. Another set of facts. A crooked Canadian tells one of my men that something to do with mercenary work and the expected assassination attempt goes on at the old monastery—your uncle's place. Mr. Theng confirms by implication that this may be true, and I decide to go there and find out for myself. What happens then? Surprise, surprise! A kind and—shall we say accommodating?—lady shows up unannounced and offers just like that to take me there. She has doubtless been furnished as part of the setup by Mr. Theng . . . because as a result of the visit I fall for this whole complicated routine and plan for a murder attempt when of course the real aim is simply to kidnap the king. To the delight, surely, of Mr. Theng—who curiously enough disappears at the same time as Kao Dinh."

She had turned away from him and was staring out the window at the heat haze shimmering above the sidewalk on the far side of the empty street. "Who is this Mr. Theng?" she asked distantly.

Dean ignored the question. "You don't think," he asked instead, "that your own role at the center—as the pin, in fact, that holds the whole thing together—could do with a little explanation? And I'm not even mentioning the way you managed an immediate traverse of that river unscathed while I was being shot at in the water."

Golden Dawn kept her back turned and said nothing.

"Nor," Dean pursued, "am I making a point at this moment of the way, admittedly agreeable, in which my return to the city was delayed—"

"I suppose you think I organized the rainstorm?"

"—or the real business carried on by your uncle at the old monastery."

She did look at him then: an astonished interrogatory glance over her shoulder.

Dean said, "I didn't use the phrase 'French connection' just now at random. I'm not so dumb that I'll swallow a story asking me to believe that crystals of salt will remain unchanged after a spell in a pottery firing kiln. The white powder that came out of the pot that kid broke was refined heroin, wasn't it? The band of dark blue glaze at the bottom of the pots conceals a false bottom, fitted after the original firing, and the space in between is filled with the drug? Albi told me himself: the jars are exported to Rangoon, Bombay, Pakistan, and the Middle East one way, to Indonesia the other. The classic narcotics routes to Europe and the U.S."

"You should be a writer of detective stories," she said.

"Trouble is, like most illegals, the guys are getting greedy. Or that's the way I read it. There were those lights on the top floors of the monastery; I figure I *wasn't* supposed to see those. Albi runs a drug factory on those stories that are supposed to be blanked off, doesn't he? He's installed a lab for changing morphine base into pure heroin. That's why he blew his top when I did see the stuff among the fragments of the broken pot. And the pots are no longer efficient enough to shift the amount they want to move. They want to do it in bulk—and *that's* the real reason, I guess, for the abduction of the king."

Dean said nothing about the hijacked Boeing and the fact that the king was on it; he had hoped to find out whether or not she knew it had come to Phra Pradeng, gambling on a slip of the tongue or some telltale phrase indicating she was wise to the move. But all she said was, "In brief, you think I was . . . nice . . . to you because I was part of some plan to distract your attention? That I am part of a conspiracy leading you—shall we say?—up one garden path while the king is kidnapped along another?"

"I couldn't have put it better myself," said Dean, ignoring the mockery in her voice as she mimicked his own delivery a short while before.

She swung back toward him so forcefully that she bounced on the seat. "Well, you are wrong, *Mr*. Dean! You are completely wrong!"

Dean shrugged. It was possible. Anything was possible in this country.

"I can prove it!" Golden Dawn cried fiercely. "I can, I can!"

"Prove a negative?" He was skeptical. "I'd like to see you try!"

"You shall. I have proof; I will show you. You shall see."

"Frankly, I *don't* see how you could possibly—"

"Come to my apartment. Now. I will show you," she repeated.

Dean glanced at his watch. "How long will it take?"

"As much time, or as little, as you can spare."

What the hell, he thought. They could wait a few more minutes for him at the airfield. Wassermann, Daler, Novotny, and Schneider were all at the control tower. He wasn't expected at any particular time. Maybe whatever the girl had to show him would throw some light on one part or another of the mystery he was involved in. "You'll have to show me the way," he said.

The apartment was in a modern building on a quiet street between the port and the government quarter. It was completely neutral: Indian rugs on a terrazzo tiled floor, Scandinavian-style contemporary furniture, reproductions of Japanese classical paintings on the white walls, most movable objects behind sliding glass panels. It could have been a flat hired for the day, or a suite kept by one of the multinationals for the use of visiting firemen. It could equally well have been home for a girl whose interests all lay entirely within the sphere of her work.

Listening to the subdued roar of the air conditioning while she went out to fix him a drink, Dean stared through white net drapes at the top of a palm tree and realized that he had no idea what kind of work Golden Dawn did do. If she worked at all. There wasn't a book or a magazine in sight. He would ask her when she came back.

Three minutes later she returned to the room carrying a bamboo tray on which there were two tall glasses. The rims, ice cold to the touch, were beaded with moisture; thin slices of orange floated on the surface of the greenish liquid within. "Gin with fresh grapefruit juice," she told him. "I hope you find it . . . refreshing." She handed him one of the glasses.

"Tell me," Dean said abruptly, "what do you do?"

"I make you the proof that I am not a conspirator. I tell you."

"No, no: I don't mean what are you doing now; I mean what do you do for a living?"

"A living?" The ivory brow wrinkled; it was not a term she knew.

"Where do you work? What is your profession?"

"Ah!" She smiled, understanding. "I am becoming a lawyer. I study at the faculty here in Am-Phallang. Now is a holiday because the monsoon is coming, but after there will be much work." She put down her glass, untasted. "I will be back in a minute." She disappeared through a door on the far side of the featureless room.

Dean heard water running. Feeling rather foolish, he strode silently across and switched glasses. It seemed melodramatic, but shit (he thought), stranger things than a doped drink have happened before; better safe than sorry, as they say. The drink was good.

Golden Dawn was back in the room. "Great," he said, holding up his glass. "Now, where is this 'proof' you have to show me?"

"Here," she said. A swift movement of the arms, and the birds flew up and around and then settled on the floor. The red flowers dropped; she stood naked before him.

Dean was astounded. It was the last thing he had expected. Did she really think . . . ? Did he himself give the impression of being such a pushover? He gaped, trying to find a logical reason for her behavior. Finally, "Very pretty," he said evenly. "Should I applaud?"

"Am I not desirable?" She stepped out of the pool of birds and flowers and came very close to him.

"Very."

A faint exotic fragrance, elusive yet reminiscent of something he could not quite place, rose from the dark cap of hair. "You do not touch me?" Golden Dawn said. She cupped her small firm breasts in her own hands, pushing them upward. Her warm breath, scented with almonds, played on his chin. "Yet I have not changed."

Dean stared for a moment into the flowerlike, uptilted face. Then he swung on his heel and strode away from her. "Look, baby," he said. "Quit horsing around with this vamp routine, would you? I'm not in the market, not anymore." Yet even as he spoke, he knew that he was ly-

158

ing, to himself as well as to her. Like it or not, he was very much in the market. Despite his doubts, despite the near-certainty that she was up to her neck in the web of deceit and treachery surrounding him, he felt desire stir as he looked at the purplish points of those breasts, the subtle curve of belly above that dark triangle of pubic hair. Despite his determination not to fall for any kind of sex maneuver, he was powerless to control the impulse that tightened the fabric of his pants across his loins. "I came here to see some proof that you weren't mixed up in this racket," he growled. "You said you could show me."

"Am I not showing you?"

"You're showing me yourself. I don't see any connection between that and a proof—"

"You do not understand *anything,* do you?" she interrupted impatiently.

"Apparently not."

She sighed in exasperation. "Look!" She lowered her hands to make a gesture that would have been inexpressibly obscene in anyone less delicately made. "This *is* the proof. Can't you see?"

It was evident from Dean's expression that he could not.

"They tell us in school that you are not a subtle people," Golden Dawn said. "They are right. No Oriental would mistake the logic of my reasoning; no Asian would require it to be explained."

"All right," Dean said woodenly. "Explain it for the benefit of this dumb American."

"It is so simple. You suspect that I loved you with an ulterior motive, to aid those plotting to kidnap the king. Well, now the king is kidnapped; the plot is over; it was successful. Yet I am offering still to love you. Since this cannot be to assist with a plot that no longer exists, it must be for the pleasure it gives me, or simply because I like you. It follows, therefore, that if I love you now for the sake only of love, then it must have been the same also the first time. You see?"

Faced with such a devastating naïveté of reasoning, Dean found himself momentarily at a loss for words. More to allow himself time to think than because he expected a positive answer, he asked suddenly, "What would Ramon say if he heard you speak that way? Or Chan?"

"Ramon?" She was smiling to herself, pleased with her exposition, certain that Dean would be convinced. "Chan? I am afraid I do not . . . ?"

The hell with it, Dean thought. *In at the deep end, off the high board. What have I got to lose?* He said, "Yes. Ramon and Chan. With their hostages. On the plane at Phra Pradeng"—watching her face closely for the flickers of reaction, of recognition.

She said, "Hostages? I do not understand what you say. In any case, there cannot be a plane at Phra Pradeng. The airfield is not yet completed."

Either she genuinely knew nothing of the Boeing and its hijackers, Dean was forced to conclude, or she was the best actress the Am-Phallang law school ever produced. Before he could find anything more to say, she crossed the room, reached up, and twined her arms around his neck. She draped her naked body against him, thrusting a little with her pelvis. "See!" she murmured. "You do desire me. I can feel."

Dean, knowing something of the battle of wills that lay before him and the terrorists at the airfield, was in his usual preaction state of tension—nerves stretched tight as an E-string, vibrating with energy, full of an explosive power that clamored for release. With a smothered curse, he picked her up and carried her over to a divan that filled an alcove near the door.

17 Chloe Constantine

The sun had disappeared behind a violet haze that veiled the western horizon before the food trolleys were wheeled out to the stalled 747 at Phra Pradeng. The trolleys were made of polished aluminum with nests of drawers and heavy covers to retain the heat in the hot-food wells. They were pushed by members of Ngon Thek's security corps, wearing the white mess jackets of the airport restaurant personnel. Two of the hijackers lowered a ladder through the hatch beneath the Boeing's tail so that the contents could be brought aboard.

There were seven of them altogether. One was posted permanently on the flight deck to cover the crew; another guarded the first-class compartment up front; Ramon and Chan—the massive Chinese with the cold, hooded eyes—stayed mainly by the radio. Chloe Constantine, the senior of the plane's three stewardesses, thought that the black girl was probably the most ruthless and the most dangerous of the pirates. She had been brought aboard in a wheelchair—a big-hipped Caribbean with a strong chin and large teeth, faking a paralysis that no longer permitted her to walk. She was walking all right now, pacing the cabin like a caged panther looking for a goat to eat.

The guy who had acted the part of her male nurse was a thin, gangling Puerto Rican who still wore his hair in an Afro. His moose-skin vest was festooned with necklaces and beads and medallions. Once the Boeing was in the air, they had managed secretly to dismantle parts of the tubular steel chair and reassemble them as the burp guns that armed the three Arab members of the commando. They themselves had produced Browning automatics chambered to take 9mm ammunition, and it was with these that they had menaced the crew and taken over the ship while the Arabs held the passengers at bay. Ramon and Chan had toted their own weapons when they came aboard with the third man at Hanoi: a Uzi submachine gun and a Walther automatic for the leader, a Russian Stechkin pistol for Chan.

Chloe came from Phoenix, Arizona, and she had spent twenty of her twenty-five years in the rarefied atmosphere of that city. For her, more perhaps than anybody else on the plane, the suffocating heat and humidity were rapidly becoming intolerable. She had always hated the Tokyo-Cairo run; the great circle routes to northern Europe were much better. But it was part of the job not to panic, whatever the conditions—and apart from the heat, conditions in the Boeing worsened every minute. The odors inseperable from the confinement of a large number of people in a relatively small space, with failing ventilation, already had passed from the disagreeable stage to that of the barely supportable. A teenage girl had thrown up in one of the aisles, the chemical toilets were exhausted, and the fetid stench of sweat, stale cigarette smoke, and fear penetrated every corner of the cabin.

Chloe was sitting with a child who was traveling alone—a young American boy only seven or eight years old. He appeared to be unworried by a situation that terrified other children on the plane and traumatized their elders, concentrating his attention on an expensive radio-cassette player which had been (so he told her) a birthday gift from his father. Of the half-dozen babies in arms in the tourist-class cabin, at least four seemed to be crying at any given time, and several other children of varying ages were complaining loudly of boredom or screaming in tantrums. The stewardess—she was a slender, pretty girl with a fresh complexion—got up from her seat and went to the galley behind the toilets in back of the cabin.

The young black woman was standing there with one of the Arabs. Their weapons were very much in evidence, "Could I maybe start in preparing the food trays?" Chloe asked.

The black girl scowled at her. "No way."

"But it's hours and hours since anyone ate. The passengers will be—"

"Fuck the passengers."

"You don't have to treat them like animals, just because you have some political—"

"Damn right I don't. I don't *have* to do anything."

"I could always make a beginning, getting out the plastic-wrapped knives and forks and spoons. I could set up the—"

"You can piss off back to that cabin," the black girl snapped, "unless you want that pretty face marked up with a pistol whippin'."

Chloe compressed her lips and returned to her place. One of the other stewardesses hurried down the starboard gangway and approached her. "There's a woman sick up front," she whispered. "She looks pretty bad, Clo-clo. Is there anything we can do?"

"Does she have a fever?" Chloe asked.

"She sure does. Temperature's up over the hundred mark, and she has pains in her guts. Think we could persuade them . . . ?"

Chloe shrugged helplessly. "I'll try," she said.

The American boy was playing a tape. A man's voice, reading out some story about a bear, an owl, and a donkey. "My dad recorded them for me," the boy said proudly. "These tapes are only kid stuff—Winnie-the-Pooh and Alice and like that. He did some far-out space-age ones too, but Mom said it'd be better if I left them home. Will these hijackers kill us, do you think?"

Chloe contrived a laugh. "We must hope not," she said.

Although the crew were confined to the flight deck, the pirates allowed cabin staff a certain freedom of movement: it was the only way to keep passenger discontent within manageable proportions. She walked down past the five-seat-wide center block and climbed to the deck. Ramon was sitting at the radio unit—a tall, seamed man with a heavy mustache. He had lost the lobe of one ear during a shoot-out with military police in Guatemala. "There's a woman in Tourist sick," Chloe said. "Temperature more than a hundred, with abdominal pains. Could be an appendix or a burst ulcer. Or just renal colic. But I think she should be looked at."

"Is there a doctor on the plane?"

"Apparently not. The other two girls asked—"

"Too bad." The Central American's voice was cold.

"But. . . it could develop into peritonitis. She might die, And there's the effect on the other passengers. I believe it's usual in . . . in hostage situations . . . to release seriously ill persons."

"Not in this situation. Get back to the cabin."

"Oh, but please! . . . She's in terrible pain, and—"

"Shut up. Get back in there or I'll have you locked in one of the toilets." Ramon turned to the radio and reached for a tuning knob. The long-barreled Walther lay close to his hand.

Chloe walked through the first-class compartment with her head bent. The Cubans and the oil sheikhs and the other VIP's sat staring in front of them, still wearing expressions of outraged disbelief. In a corner seat by one of the ports, the wide, chunky Indochinese who had come aboard with Ramon and Chan at Hanoi slumped against the bulkhead, seemingly asleep. Or drugged? She had thought at first that he was another hijacker, but he had been pushed roughly into this seat and had scarcely moved since the plane took off.

In the tourist cabin, the sick woman moaned and writhed. The two other stewardesses—watched closely by the man with the Afro and one of the Arabs—swabbed the perspiration from her forehead with napkins soaked in tepid water and murmured soothing words. Somewhere farther back, a high, hysterical sobbing was audible over the shocked buzz of conversation. Chloe shook her head helplessly as the girls looked up with inquiring expressions. She went back to her seat by the American child.

He had stopped playing tape cassettes and was fiddling with the radio. "It can send as well as receive," he told her, sliding the tuner along the scale. "My dad fixed a mod to the tape input. I mean, for the mike, where you record—"

He stopped in mid-sentence, staring up at Chloe, who had suddenly gripped his arm and laid a finger to her lips. "Leave it there," she whispered. "Don't move it . . . but keep the volume down. You must have hit the frequency they're using to contact the tower."

She was right. It was unmistakably the emotionless voice of Ramon coming from the small speaker.

" . . . repeat, that if our terms are not met—or at least if we have not heard that negotiations with the various countries named in our ultimatum have started—then hostages will begin to die. We have more than 250 available, so don't kid yourselves there are no cards in our hand."

Then another voice, speaking English with a faint cockney accent. *"I have no authority to open negotiations with anyone. Your terms will not be met. You cannot get away: the field is surrounded by military vehicles, some of them carrying missiles. Why not chuck it in and give yourselves up before it's too late?"*

Ramon: *"Don't waste time trying to bluff. You know who we have aboard. We will not hesitate to shoot. You have one hour more."*

The voice: *"We're not even prepared to talk. You cannot win. Nobody knows you are there; the plane has been reported missing over the South China Sea, as you must know if you listen to the radio—and no more mention will be made of it. To the world you are already lost."*

Ramon: *"I warn you. I am not joking. People will die."*

The voice: *"Let them. It is you who will suffer. I may remind you that the death penalty still exists in Muong-Thang. The method of execution is not pretty."*

Ramon: *"Let me talk to the man in charge, whoever he is."*

The voice: *"He is not available. And will not be until sometime tomorrow."*

Ramon: *"Get lost, then."* There was a click and the transmission ceased.

"Remember the reading," Chloe murmured to the boy. "I don't quite know how, but it may be useful—hearing what they say."

The black girl came out from the galley. "What the hell's that?" she demanded. "We told you people no radios."

"It's not a radio," Chloe said quickly. "Cassettes. Kids' stories on tape, recorded by his father. It keeps him quiet."

The girl shrugged and passed on.

Chan came through from first class and the two of them stood talking at the far end of the cabin. Outside the ports, night had fallen; the misty outlines of the airfield and the military vehicles now surrounding the Boeing had merged into the blackness, and only the thin strip of light marking the window of the distant control tower penetrated the dark. Inside the plane the odorous heat was stifling.

Suddenly there was an outcry from halfway along the aisle. The teenager who had thrown up seemed to be having an altercation with her mother—a fat woman in a flowered dress with crescents of sweat darkening the material beneath the arms. The girl pulled free and ran screaming up the aisle. The eyes in her tense, pale, neurotic face were staring. She hurled herself at the black pirate, hammering with her fists at the woman's chest. "Let me out, let me out, let me out!" she shrieked. "I want to get out of here! You can't keep me here, you can't—"

The black girl slapped her face and swung her away, slamming her against the bulkhead. Chan raised his Stechkin pistol and shot her calmly, coldly, through the head.

The sound of the shot was deafening. The girl dropped to the floor, leaving a huge smear of blood, glistening with gluey fragments of brain, to slide down the gray bulkhead.

For an instant, as the report rang in their ears, the passengers remained in stunned silence. Then there was pandemonium. The mother erupted in screeching hysterics. Amid the outraged uproar, screams, tears, cries of horror, and shouts of fury combined to form an indescribable storm of noise.

Chan hit the mother scientifically on the jaw and knocked her out. Ramon burst into the cabin. "*Shuddup!*" he roared. "Stop this row this instant! For every minute it goes on, another person will die! Do you hear me? Another of you will *die!*"

A shocked and sullen hush. Passengers who had been on their feet subsided into their seats. The black girl pushed up the bars and swung open the main door forward of the wing root. Chan picked up the dead girl and dropped her body into the night.

"Well, they killed *her*, didn't they?" the boy said to Chloe Constantine.

18 Phra Pradeng

The body of the murdered girl was not discovered by the people in the airfield control tower until dawn. Ramon had demanded a fresh consignment of food. There were still scarves of white mist wreathing the field, and it was only when the disguised security men pushing the trolleys neared the plane that Wassermann saw the shape slumped beneath the pod carrying the inner port reactor.

"The bastards!" he gritted, adjusting the focus wheel of his field glasses. "The murdering, motherfucking, bastard sons of bitches! And only a kid, by the look of it, at that."

"Whatever you do"—Dean, summoned from the pint-size office where he was sleeping, impressed on the four mercs—"whatever else you do, you hide at all costs the revulsion and horror you feel. Is that clear? Whichever one of you is spelling me at the radio, you play it ice cold and you wrap up your disgust so it won't show when you talk. Okay?"

"But, Cap," Novotny protested, "Christ, I mean, this is cold-blooded fucking murder!"

"A man should button his lip he sees a sin against humanity? This is the way Hitler started!"—Wassermann.

"We must be telling such people, surely, that the world has no place for this kind of atrocity?"—Schneider.

Daler said, "We can't, you know, just pass the bloody thing up. This kind of conscienceless shithead . . . I mean, the buggers must be told they won't get away with it, that they'll be made to pay."

"They'll be told nothing of the kind," Dean rasped. "Because, that's exactly what they *want* to be told. They *want* to shock and outrage and disgust what we call decent people. It's their strongest weapon; it gives them confidence when they're called names; they feel that all they

167

have to do is commit a few more atrocities and we'll cave in. *That's* the way Hitler started, Abe. Telling this kind of terrorist what you think of him only plays into his hands."

"*I warned you*," Ramon told Dean later over the two-way radio. "*I warned you last night, and you chose to ignore my warning.*"

"It will bring you nothing," Dean said. "You cannot win."

"*My ultimatum stands. If I have not heard by ten o'clock that negotiations have begun, another hostage will die.*"

"You can murder the whole planeload, you can be knee-deep in bodies," Dean said indifferently; "we'll still move in and get you in the end."

"*I demand to be put in contact with the competent authorities. I demand that my terms be considered in the proper quarters.*"

"You are not in a position to demand anything. I am the only competent authority here and I refuse to negotiate. Either you stay where you are, or you give yourselves up."

"*There are important people on this flight. When their governments realize—*"

"They will realize nothing," Dean cut in. "Nobody knows you are here. The VIP's are already regarded as lost. The plane was reported missing over the sea, remember? That was your big mistake, coming here, where you can be completely isolated."

He switched off before the terrorist leader could reply.

The mercs were looking at him dubiously. It was clear that they remained unconvinced of the rightness of his thinking. "This is exactly the strength of guys like Ramon," he told them. "Hoods who make up their own rules. You're already thinking, maybe we ought to treat, aren't you? As soon as you think *maybe*, you've lost out. You have to resist the moral blackmail and think no— and as soon as you decide that, *he's* lost. It may take time, but he's lost."

"Yeah, but there's guys and dames getting rubbed out; all those people out there—" Novotny began.

"Sure, it's rugged for them," Dean agreed. "But the tougher we are, and the harder we stick to our line, the less they'll have to suffer."

He tuned the radio to a commercial station broadcasting out of Bangkok. They caught the last few minutes of a news bulletin. West Germany had won a contract to build a nuclear-power station in Assam. An abbey had been attacked and thirty monks slaughtered in Nicaragua. Members of the OPEC states had decided to raise the price of crude by $1.95 a barrel. India's cotton crop would give eight to nine percent less than the yield anticipated, but rice in the whole Southeast Asian region would be up to expectations. Typhoon Terry, the first of the premonsoon storms, had ravaged an island in the Indian Ocean. In the same area, the search for the missing Boeing 747 had been called off. "There you are," said Dean. "One up for us."

On a sudden impulse, he left the control board, with its switches and diagrams and pilot lights and riser mikes. At the back of the room, by ground-glass video screens and a talk-down console, there was a PBX switchboard that was connected to the Am-Phallang telephone exchange. "Get me Colonel Chakrawongse at security headquarters," he told the operator.

He waited impatiently, staring out the window at the distant jetliner centered in its ring of army vehicles. Despite the green tint to the glass surrounding the tower, the glare of the sun was still painful to the eye. "Hello?" he called at last. "Colonel? . . . Good morning. Dean here. Look, do your telecommunications people have the equipment to jam the whole spectrum of radio reception and transmission from CB to ultralong wave? . . . They do? . . . Swell. I guess this can be done on a purely local basis? . . . Okay, yes, I'll hold."

He grinned at Wassermann and the others, cradling the handset between chin and shoulder as he reached for a cigarette. "It occurred to me that he might try to use the plane radio to contact someone else," he said. "You know—if we deny him the publicity he expects, he could try to make it in some kind of sensational way, calling up Rangoon or Hanoi or Jakarta. And once the news got out, half the chips on our side of the table would be gone."

He turned his attention back to the phone. "Colonel? . . . Yes, still here. They can? That's great. Now, listen, here's what I want them to do. I don't care how localized it is, but so far as that plane is concerned, I want every frequency across the board jammed, in and out—all except the band we're using to link the ship and the tower. Okay?" He listened for a moment, chuckled, and then added, "It won't hurt at all for Master Ramon to find there's a total blackout on incoming transmissions as well!"

He replaced the phone and turned back to his companions. "From now on," he said grimly, "that murderous bastard is cut off from the whole goddamn world. The only way he can get any news at all is through us."

Aboard the Boeing, tension among the hostages was approaching fever pitch. Twice, food had been delivered to the stalled plane—they had seen the trolleys through the ports—but none had been served. The stewards and stewardesses were powerless to help. The hijackers refused to talk, to explain; they remained deaf to all entreaties, although hunger now was making their prisoners desperate. Children were screaming. The sick woman rolled from side to side in her seat, clutching her belly. The mother of the murdered teenager moaned into the hands clasped over her face, shaking off horrified neighbors who tried to soothe or console her.

The boy Chloe Constantine was looking after seemed almost the only passenger oblivious of the privations imposed upon them. He was absorbed in his radio-cassette player, switching from wavelength to wavelength, listening to Thai *samisen* bands, trying to guess which language the newscasters were speaking, smiling happily when he heard a song he knew. From time to time he tuned in again to the band on which they had heard Ramon speaking. "Hey, did you know we'd been reported missing over the ocean?" he asked the stewardess excitedly. "Nobody will ever come to rescue us now. How long does it take to die of starvation, do you know?"

Toward the end of the morning (she had just come back to the seat after a fruitless attempt to have a doctor called to the sick woman) he looked up at her with a comically woebegone expression. "It's broken," he said desolately. "I didn't do anything. I didn't. But I can't get *any* station at all now. Listen."

"That sounds more like deliberate jamming to me," Chloe said when the same high-pitched burble, laced with

170

a crackle of static, resulted from a dozen different settings of the tuner. "Unless, of course, the batteries are all through."

"They sure aren't," he said indignantly. "Mom bought me new ones the day before we left, and they last for *weeks*."

"Well, turn the volume all the way down when you try. It's supposed to be just a cassette player: that's our secret, remember?"

He nodded. "I guess I'd better just *play* the old cassettes. Gee, Mom will be real mad at me if it did somehow get broken."

The girl nodded absently. She was watching a group of men at the far end of the left-hand aisle. Two of the Arabs had pulled a passenger from his seat. Chan and the man with the Afro beckoned from the gangway separating the tourist from the first-class cabin. Ramon's bleak face was visible beyond.

The passenger, a fleshy Japanese with shell-rim glasses, was protesting. When he had been dragged level with the main exit door between the two cabins, he started to struggle and shout. Ramon swung back the bars and shoved the door open. The Japanese fell to his knees; his pleading cries rose up the scale.

The Arabs stepped back. Chan raised his arm. The gunshot seemed less loud than the first because of the open door. The man with shell-rim glasses fell from sight.

The hijackers pulled the door shut and swung around to cover the passengers, most of whom were on their feet yelling abuse, shaking their fists, or just screaming. Horrorstruck, Chloe saw through the double glass of the port that the shot man's legs, visible beneath the trailing edge of the Boeing's swept-back wing, were still moving feebly.

Ramon saw it too. The door was reopened. He stood silhouetted against the blaze of sunlight, aiming his Uzi submachine gun downward. He fired a short burst, shocking in its loudness.

Beneath the wing, the legs twitched spasmodically and then lay still. Long scarlet trails of blood webbed the concrete surface of the runway, congealing quickly in the heat.

Dean's face was white. He was on the phone to Quin-

171

nel when the Japanese was killed. "Have them send out an ambulance," he said tightly to Daler. And then, to the CIA man, "Okay, they're starting to play rough. This is where we have to bite the bullet and school ourselves to forget the rules."

"I'll have to report the killing to Mackenzie," Quinnel said. "Your colonel fixed me a direct line with a scrambler."

"As you like." Dean's voice hardened. "But don't forget: I handle this my way. Nothing he says—or his bosses say—can overrule my decisions. That was the deal."

" 'Kay. Keep your cool." Quinnel's flat, emotionless voice was in contrast to the combat leader's crisp, angry delivery. "Be in touch. Call me if anything breaks, huh?"

Daler was standing beside the switchboard. He held a long scroll of teletype paper in his hand. "Passenger list from Pan-Asiatic," he said briefly. "Telex just came in from Tokyo. It's already been communicated to the world press, of course: 'These were the people on the plane believed lost over the sea.' "

Dean nodded and ran his eye down the long list of names. Abruptly he froze. The stiff paper buckled slightly as the knuckles of his clenched hand whitened. He stared. It couldn't be true!

He swallowed. His mouth was dry. He closed his eyes and then gazed again at the list. Surely there must be some mistake? He had misread the teletype. The airline officials had fucked up. They had sent the wrong list. But the damning line was still there, dancing before his disbelieving eyes: "DEAN, PATRICK HUROK (UNACCOMPANIED INFANT): TOKYO-CAIRO."

His own seven-year-old son was on the plane—out there in the insufferable heat, at the end of the runway, in the hands of a group of ruthless killers.

Dean's mind was reeling. How could Patrick *possibly* be on the hijacked Boeing? And then, as his glance fell on the flight number, he knew. It hadn't registered with him before. There was no reason why it should have. But now the number and the date together struck a chord. The flight from Tokyo to Cairo was the one he had originally booked for the boy when they planned to spend a vacation together in Egypt.

But he had cabled Samantha telling her to cancel the ticket.

What the hell could have happened?

There was only one conceivable answer to that question: Samantha had never received the cable.

Dean did not care to think how that could have come about. For an instant there flashed into his mind, as clearly as a slide projected onto a screen, the picture of a man dressed like himself, looking like him, catching a plane to Cairo in the name of Dean. If the CIA had decided that *all* evidence pointing to the fact that Dean had in fact not gone to Egypt must be suppressed . . . ? He put the thought from him: following it through would have made him too angry. In any case, there were other, more urgent problems to deal with.

Samantha.

His ex-wife would believe their son lost somewhere over the South China Sea. After the agony of knowing that the plane he had taken was in the hands of terrorists, she would now have to bear the thought of him lying drowned at the bottom of the ocean, or of his fragile body ripped apart in some midair catastrophe of which she would never know the details.

And there was nothing Dean could do to ease that despair, to alleviate that anguish of the soul. He himself had imposed a total blackout on the news that the Boeing had in truth landed safely in Muong-Thang. If even one person got to know about it outside themselves, he had urged Ngon Thek, it would weaken his hand immeasurably, for the whole world would be on his back trying to railroad him into obtaining the release of the hostages any way he could. It would be entirely against his principles, dealing with kidnappers. And he had brushed aside objections remarking on the distress this would cause relatives of the passengers.

Well, he was one of those relatives now, but he at least knew the 747 had not been lost. Samantha didn't. It was out of the question, nevertheless, that he should even consider getting a message to her saying that Patrick was still alive. He could not make an exception favoring his own family.

And what about those principles now that his own flesh and blood was involved? What price never-pay-a-ransom-demand and too-bad-if-a-hostage-gets-killed when it could mean the death of his son? They had already murdered a teenager and an adult; the next body thrown out of the plane could be Patrick's. Was the tough, intractable line he had taken to prevail with so much that was personal at stake?

White-faced, he looked up from the telex sheet to meet the gaze, half-curious, half-sympathetic, of the four members of his team. It was clear that they had seen the name on the list.

"Okay," Dean said harshly. "My kid's on the plane. So what?"

"So maybe nobody would blame you, you should soften our attitude some on this thing." Wassermann's voice was gentle. Dean appreciated the "our": it lessened his sense of guilt if the others were associating themselves with his hard line.

"Or at least start talking, see if maybe they'd modify their demands a little," said Daler.

"Abe's right," Novotny said. "Ain't nobody aimin' to throw no fuckin' brickbats, whatever you do. Shit, you're the boss, Cap."

Was the tough line to prevail with so much that was personal at stake? Plunged unexpectedly into a private hell, Dean thrust aside the thoughts that were torturing him and decided that it must. "We go ahead and handle the situation the way we planned it," he said.

By four o'clock in the afternoon, conditions inside the Boeing 747 were even distressing the terrorists. The sun hammered down from a sky the color of a bruise, and parts of the fuselage enclosing the flight deck were too hot to touch. Ramon called up the control tower.

"Dean," he said. "I imagine it's Dean, if I'm dealing with the same people who distinguished themselves blocking the assassination attempt? Well, listen, Dean, we're getting impatient. We want some action on our demands. Fast."

"*We have all the time in the world.*" Dean's voice was calm, ignoring the mockery, refusing to be drawn by the jibe. "*You have already been told: your impudent demands are not even being passed on to the governments* concerned. *There is only one course of action open to you: release the passengers and give up.*"

"All right," Ramon shouted. "The shooting begins again. I have been lenient; but now it is time to make my point with more force."

"*In any case, even if negotiations were to start, you must see that nobody could ever get all those opposing governments to agree on such disparate terms. Your so-called demands are totally unreal.*"

"I shall not contact you again," Ramon blustered. "From now on, if you want to talk, you call me. Until you do—and until you do so with some concrete proposals—one person will die each hour. Is that clear? . . . Do you hear me, Dean? . . . Dean: are you listening? . . ."

But there was no reply. Dean had already switched off.

Ramon turned away from the radio to see the man with the Afro standing behind him. "What the hell's all that noise, Mendez?" he asked. An indescribable hubbub was audible from the tourist cabin.

"The sick woman is delirious," Mendez said. "She has gone very pale. I think she may die."

"Give her some help," Ramon said. "Shoot her. Drop the body out like the others." He stood up and stretched. His shirt was dark with sweat. "This goddamned heat! And look—tell Chan to get rid of that teenager's mother. I can't stand that bloody screeching."

The second woman's body was jettisoned from the plane at 1800 hours. Half an hour later, a Cessna jet flew in with Hammer, Mazzari, and a dozen soldiers of fortune they had recruited from Darwin, Singapore, and Rangoon. They found Dean pacing the tower, his face drawn, his expression a mixture of fury and disquiet. His own iron control was equal to the strain, the responsibility of these deaths, but already Daler and the others were beginning to look at him askance. Hardened mercenaries that they were, it was clear that they were nevertheless finding Dean's inflexibility difficult to take. How long, they were thinking, can this lethal poker game go on when the chips are innocent lives? Has anyone the right to gamble when the stakes are human?

In the moral isolation that his decision imposed, Dean knew the way they felt. He knew also that it was on precisely such reservations that the terrorists' own play was based. And he knew, with the kind of arrogance inseparable from strong men courageous enough to make unpopular decisions, that he was right. But—and this was what the others never realized—the cost to himself was high. His was the loneliness of the navy captain who refuses to call off a pursuit to pick up survivors from a torpedoed sister ship, of the officer sending men out on a patrol from which he knows they cannot return; he was the mine superintendent who says, "Too bad about the guys trapped below, we'll have to let the water in."

For Dean, too, there was the additional torment that his own child was among those likely to be sacrificed. But the worst of the worries clawing at his composure was the fact that Patrick's presence on the plane could prove a trump card in Ramon's hand . . . if he knew the card was there.

The combat leader broke out in a cold sweat at the thought. Ramon had only to read through the passenger list, if there was one on the plane; he had only to mention Dean's name in the boy's hearing; Patrick had only to exclaim, "That's my Dad!"

It was tough enough, thinking of the boy in a *generalized* peril along with the other hostages. But what if they found out who he was? Suppose they made a specific threat against him—to place him next on the list and slaughter him in front of his father, perhaps to torture him where the radio could pick up his screams?—for Ramon was capable of anything.

How would Dean's iron control hold up then?

Would he still have the strength to tell the hijackers to go to hell?

The switchboard operator was calling him. Ngon Thek was on the line. "There's been a leak, Colonel Dean," the security minister told him. "I do not know how—from Washington, I think—but I have had the Libyan ambassador, the Saudi ambassador, the Soviet *chargé d'affaires*, and the consulates of Denmark, Belgium, and Cuba hammering at my door. There are, in addition, urgent telex messages from our own representatives in Central America, France, and the United States. All of them are demanding information on the whereabouts of the hijacked airplane and the terms asked by the pirates."

"Holy Christ!" Dean exploded. "Someone in the Agency . . . !"

"They know the plane is here," Ngon Thek continued, "but not, apparently, its precise location. Naturally, a great deal of pressure is being brought—and the man Schenk, the television crews, and several other journalists here have already been in contact."

"You've got to stop them," Dean said. "Close all roads out of town. No foreigners allowed out of the city without a special pass, because of the civil-war situation. No passes issued. Find an excuse to deport Schenk and the TV people. They could be dangerous. Has there been any media cover? Has the story broken on the radio?"

"So far as my department knows, not yet."

"Then we've got to squash these guys before it does. Once we get the place flooded out with goddamn journalists, our hands are tied and we've lost half the battle."

"I will see to it at once, Colonel," Ngon Thek said.

Dean called Quinnel at the Samoa. "What the fuck do you guys think you're playing at?" he raged. "A complete blackout, every single avenue blocked—that was the deal. Now some dumb son of a bitch in your department has opened his mouth and fouled up the whole operation. How long do you think I can hold this tough line with half the world's press on my tail, for Chrissake? To say nothing of all those Brooks Brothers bastards from the dip corps?"

"Hold your hat," Quinnel's calm voice replied. "The leak was at White House level. Mackenzie's as burned up about it as you are. It's no more his fault than yours. And it seems the various embassies informed all promised to sit on the story. Naturally, once they know, they want information. But they agreed: no press tipoff."

"Oh, sure. In a pig's ass they did!" Dean was still furious. "You're asking me to believe that among all those stuffed shirts there isn't one on the payroll of some columnist? . . . that some contact, somewhere, isn't going to be given a hint that maybe . . . *if* they wanted to know more about the mysterious disappearance of that plane . . . *if* they cared to make inquiries, oh so discreetly, not a hundred miles from the capital of Muong-Thang . . . they might even learn something to their advantage? Do me a bloody favor, Quinnel!"

He banged down the receiver. Novotny was standing in front of him. "Message from Colonel Shitface, Cap. It seems there's been too many complaints about the radio jamming. Not only in the city, but from Bangkok, Saigon, Phnom Penh, and even Tavoy too. They can't do it from the Radio Thang transmitter anymore. He's sending out a coupla trucks with specialized equipment that'll block the incoming signals the way you want but localize the interference within a few miles of the field here. Okay?"

Dean sighed. "I guess so."

"Only thing—he's had to quit the overall jamming right away. Pressure from above. And there'll be around a half-hour without any interference at all, until the trucks get here and set up. He said to tell you."

"Okay," Dean said wearily. "I guess we might as well use the gap and listen in ourselves, learn just how far the leak has gone. See if you can raise a news bulletin someplace, Emil."

Novotny found the tail end of the 1930-hours world roundup transmitted from Rangoon. The newscaster was recapping on the main headlines. Riots in Bombay on account of the cotton shortfall: government planning was blamed. Famine in Central Africa, floods in Canada, an earth tremor in Albania. Having caused widespread damage to the islands of Ko Phangan and Ko Samui, off the Isthmus of Kra, Typhoon Terry was now rampaging northward across the Gulf of Siam. British soldiers had fought a pitched battle with an IRA commando in Northern Ireland. Rumania had beaten Paraguay 9–0 in the qualifying round of World Cup soccer.

There was no mention of Pan-Asiatic Airlines Boeing 747 or of hijackers. "Thank God," Dean said. "That gives us breathing space for a few more hours. Now there's just one other hole that I have to block. Abe, I hate to do this, but I think we'd better have Brother Mettner out of the way until this is all over. I don't want to throw him out of the country like the others, because we did promise him an exclusive, and he has helped some. But I'd feel happier if he wasn't around for a while."

"So what do you want me to do?" Wassermann asked.

"Get in touch with Chakrawongse. Ask him to fake some charge . . . political, not criminal. Anything that gives him the opportunity to hold the guy on suspicion. Right?"

"End of a beautiful friendship," said Wassermann, reaching for a phone. "Give me a line, operator, will you?"

Dean turned at last to Hammer, Mazzari, and the tough-looking bunch of men they had recruited. There were Australians, Dutch, Germans, Burmese, and expatriate Britons among them. Each man wore camouflage combat fatigues with plastic concussion grenades slung from the belt. They were armed with Ingram MAC-11 silenced machine pistols—the 8¾-inch, 56-ounce, 1200-rpm miracle weapons so popular with the Green Berets during the Vietnam war.

"I can't give you guys a specific briefing right now," Dean said. "But we'll get you out there, hidden in the scrub beyond the far end of the runway, before dawn. I'll have one more frequency freed so we can keep in radio contact . . . and you'll take your orders from Hammer here and Mazzari when and if we decide to rush the plane. The actual plan of attack, you'll probably have to play by ear," he said to Hammer.

"Do you have some idea, then, the way it'll work out?" the hard-bitten little Ulsterman asked.

Dean grinned. It was the first time he'd smiled in forty-eight hours. "I have the beginnings of a hunch," he said. "But before I know if it'll work out, I have to make it to the city and put in a gang of paperwork with the characters at one of the specialty sections of the radio station."

"Sounds fruitful, old fruit," said Mazzari. "How about cutting in the hired help on the workings of intuition? An inside view of the jolly old epiphany? What section did you have in mind, squire?"

"Two, old boy. Actually," Dean mimicked. He stopped, staring out through the tinted window at the darkened field. There were vehicle lights moving along the perimeter track, and a flood brightening the huge tail of the Boeing far off in the night. "What the hell's that?" he asked.

"Security boys running out the food trolleys," said Daler.

"Christ," Dean said, "they're eating better than we are!"

Wassermann was talking volubly on the phone. "Yes, sir. That's right. Tall, thin guy. Staying at the Hotel Samoa, Room 27. Any way you like . . . Sure, he'll create problems! He'll yell blue murder and the freedom of the press; he'll pull the U.S. embassy and the Rights of Man and the World Newspaper Council on you. But pay him no mind, Colonel. Pay him no mind."

"Goddamn radio's jammed again," Ramon swore. "It was free there for a while, but I can't raise a single fucking station now. Just fish frying all over the world! At least it shows they're working."

"Does this worry you?" Chan asked.

The South American shook his head. "It means they're stalling for time," he said, "and that's what we want."

At the rear of the tourist cabin, Patrick Dean switched off the cassette player and yawned. "Gee, I'm hungry!" he complained to Chloe Constantine. "Why don't they give us something to eat?"

"I wish I knew," the girl replied. "The plane must be bursting with food. There's two other girls as well as me, and two stewards too. It would be so easy . . ." She broke off and shook her head.

"It's kind of smelly in here," he said. "You know, stinky. It's a good thing I had those candy bars, but I could sure use a hot dog right now."

"You must try to get some sleep," Chloe said. "It's long after dark outside."

"These people are making too much of a row. I think I'll give my transistor another whirl. Do you think we'll ever be allowed outside again?"

"Of course we will."

"I wish it would be soon. A boy I know in school has a father works for the FBI. If he was here, he would know what to do. Hey, I'm tired of these silly old kids' stories. I think I'll junk the tapes for now and try the radio again."

19 Jason Mettner

It was just by chance that I happened to listen in on Dean's orders for me to be put in the cooler. Well . . . chance and legwork, if you like.

You know how it is when you're a special correspondent in hostile country. You don't? Well, let me tell you: it's hell. Nobody wants to tell *you* anything; the official news releases are as limp as a used condom; the police are looking for an excuse to run you out of town; and everyone connected with anything has been told that you're strictly bad news. Okay, so what do you do? You hang around Harry's Bar and put your liver at peril and hope to hell some jerk will drink even more than you and spill you a lead.

Harry's Bar? There's one in every goddamn world capital I ever heard of. It's one of the laws of physics. Without it, American tourists would never get to first base (*Ask For Sank Roo Dan-oh,* it says on the Harry's Bar ads in Paris taxicabs). In Am-Phallang, it's Charlie's Bar, but that's because of the Chinese influence. The principle's the same.

So I'm in Charlie's Bar, licking my wounds and wondering why the hell, in Dean's book, Jason Mettner II is just a torn-out page. Not a word since he drove me back from Phra Pradeng; not a merc in sight at any of the town's water holes; a strongarm "No entry!" from the guards at the palace gates. And as for making an approach to that Boeing, you might as well be selling left-wing literature in Argentina.

For these reasons, I'm feeling like an irritable wet nurse ("What's the matter, Master Marc? Cat run off with your tongue?") when I run into the Reuters stringer based on Muong-Thang. For your information, guys from the news agencies have a tough time of it when they're posted abroad. Foreign correspondents are briefed to follow up a single story, often with several weeks in which to do it. But the agency men are expected to file on *every* damned story in their territory. And fast. This is bad enough for the UP and AP operatives, but the Reuter guys are badly paid as well. And as for getting an expense sheet past the accounting department at 85 Fleet Street, London East Central Four . . . don't ask!

Anyway, there's this character hovering near the bar, hoping someone will be charitable enough to buy him a drink—a little dark guy with specs and a clipped mustache, around fifty-five years old, sweating it out until the pension's due. Name of Sidney Nailor. And if Nailor never rated a Pulitzer, won a Journalist of the Year award, or figured in the world-scoop league, he did know the country: he'd been there since it was Siam, for God's sake, practically since they invented the wheel.

"Hey, Sid! What cooks?" I asked. He expects Americans to talk that way.

I must explain that this character is quite a character. For starters, he always wears a topcoat that reaches almost to his ankles, even in the hot weather before the monsoon. Fellows in the Press Club in Bangkok swear that it's the only garment he possesses, that underneath it he's bare as an elm in winter. Nailor himself confides that it's a useful barrier against the cold if you're in a plane flying at high altitude. Someone should tell him, one day, about pressurized planes.

Second of all, he has this amazing knowledge of Shakespeare. He must know practically the whole of the First Folio by heart, because his entire conversation—plus comments on the action around him—is composed of couplets and fragments of speeches that are sometimes uncannily apt. He approached me as I stood at the bar. "Why looks your Grace so heavily today?" he murmured. "Thou art so fat-witted with drinking of old sack, and unbuttoning thee after supper, and sleeping upon benches after noon, that thou hast forgotten to demand that truly which thou wouldst truly know."

I turned and stared at him. *"Henry IV, Part One,"* I said automatically, "with a prologue line from *Henry V.* This fellow's wise enough to play the fool . . . and to do that well craves a kind of wit."

182

He picked up the *Twelfth Night* tag at once. "This," he said meaningfully, "is a practice as full of labor as a wise man's art. Mine's a rye-and-dry, laddie, and what do you want to know?"

I laid a ten-spot on the bar. "I want to get a line on Marc Dean," I said. "The guy who headed the strongarm squad booked to look after our departed monarch. All gates appear to be closed. I hear he looks kindly upon a certain Golden Dawn, who might point me in the right direction. I believe she comes in here sometimes?"

"Ay, marry," he said. The bill disappeared. "But not in the afternoons. You want to try the Fragrant Blossoms or the Harvest Moon."

I ordered our drinks from Charlie—a huge Russian with a tiny head and no neck. Most of his customers looked like superannuated students, Trotskyites, or subeditors waiting for a chance to fracture someone's syntax. A gaunt woman in a black silk dress peppered with cigarette ash careened into the bar. Her painted mouth was a little to one side of the real one, and she was smoking a French Gitane through a heavy veil attached to a pillbox hat. Eileen Allardyce, woman's editor of one of the glossies, sent out to do a piece on Liberty and the Indochinese Woman—Was Kidnapped King a Chauvinist?

"Lo, here she comes! This is her very guise," Nailor said tipsily. "Which times, she chanteth snatches of old tunes, as one incapable of her own distress."

"Piss off, Sid," the woman said. "Unless you're going to break new ground and buy me a drink."

"I tell you there's something screwy goin' on outside the city," a nasal voice said somewhere behind me. "Every road to the north and west is lousy with fuckin' control points—and if you make it to the northeast and then try to cut across, the bastard gooks stop you just the same."

I didn't need any writing on the wall to tell me who that was. Loudmouth Schenk, wonder boy of the Middle West. I didn't turn around.

"Perhaps the comrades have made a spectacular advance," another voice said. I figured it for British. Probably the *Times* man from Rangoon. "Maybe they're using the White Elephant of Phra Pradeng as an advance landing strip!"

183

"It'd be easier than the pocket fucking handkerchief they use for an airport here," a third man put in. "Charlie—two pints and a gin-and-lime, please."

"I'll have the proprietor pull strings in Washington and get me a chopper to overfly the area," Schenk said. "No son-of-a-bitch gook security patrols are goin' to tell *me* where the *Globe* can go. Hey, wait a minute, though! Maybe you got something, limey, at that! It's just possible . . ."

"What had you in mind, old man?" the Brit inquired.

"Oh . . . just a hunch. Come to think of it, it was a lousy idea anyway. Forget it," Schenk said hurriedly. I could see the thought processes in a speech balloon above his head. Kidnap? Security? Airfield? *Hijack!* But don't let these creeps in on it.

"Security people! Shits, all of them! Assholes!" the woman's editor said. "Give us a light, duckie, will you?" She lifted her veil, stuck a fresh cigarette in her mouth and lurched our way. She leaned toward the Reuters man.

Nailor struck a match. As he held the wavering flame out in the direction of her cigarette, the veil fell forward and dropped between them. There was a sudden blaze of fire. The Brit—a fresh-faced young guy in a bush shirt and Bermudas—laid his own cigarette and its holder in an ashtray on the bar. He reached for a pint tankard and emptied the stuff that Charlie called beer carefully over the burning hat, extinguishing the flames.

"Hey, that's my drink!" Schenk yelled.

"Let's get out of here," I hissed at Nailor.

But he had already started his number: "See, now her cheek is pale, but by and by/ "It flashed forth fire, as lightning from the sky . . ."

"For Christ's sake," I said. "Come *on*! I'll buy you another drink at the Harvest Moon."

But he flung off my hand and stood with outstretched arms, shouting: "She burns with bashful shame; he with his tears/ "Doth quench the maiden burning of her cheeks . . ."

Eileen Allardyce stood swaying over a puddle of beer, the sodden cigarette drooping from her lower lip. "Must be a hole in the paper," she grumbled. "The bloody thing won't draw."

Just a normal, everyday slice of life among the Press

184

Club boys and girls when they're hot on the heels of a story.

There were two of Chakrawongse's MP's outside the door. "The man Schenk is the most important," one of them said in Thai. "The one with the loud voice. But the Britishers, the woman, and the television crews must be rounded up and put on the plane too."

I dragged Nailor away from there. I bought him another drink at the Harvest Moon. The girl I was looking for wasn't there. She wasn't at the Fragrant Blossoms either, but Nailor drank again. Finally he took me to an apartment house where he said she lived. We were at the end of the passageway leading to her door when said door opened and a tall, thin, rumpled guy came out and headed for the elevators. It was Quinnel, the CIA character who had the next room to mine at the Samoa.

"What hempen homespuns have we here?" Nailor quoted. "So near the cradle of the faery queen?"

"Just another Agency man," I said. "You're too old to play Puck."

The fairy queen's hair was damp. She looked as if she'd just taken a shower. She also looked like something over a million dollars, plus fifteen percent to take care of inflation. Talking of which, she was wearing a dark blue kimono with a scarlet serpent twined around it. Seeing where the snake's head was, I figured the one in the Garden of Eden for crazy, messing with some old apple.

"Gentleman's anxious to get in touch with Mr. Dean," the Reuters man explained. "Thought you might be able to help, you know."

"I just want to know what's going on," I said.

"Oh, I could have told you that," he said. "I come to answer thy best pleasure; to fly, to swim, to dive into the fire, to ride on the curled clouds: to thy strong bidding task Ariel and all his quality."

I stared at him. "Ariel?" I said. "*Aerial!* You knew?"

"Most of the local folk do; only the foreign journalists remain in the dark." He laid a finger alongside his nose in a gesture that was almost Dickensian. "Safely in harbor is the king's ship . . . but supposing that they saw the king's ship wrecked and his great person perish?"

"*The Tempest,*" I said, "and most apposite, as the monsoon's about to start."

The girl, it seemed, could get me past the roadblocks if we went by boat: she lived officially in a canal village only about six hours' walk from the airfield, and they would let her pass. Nailor got ready to leave us. Like most stringers, he was probably local correspondent also for *The Farmers' Weekly, The Hairdressers' Journal, Weightlifting for All,* and *A Practical Guide to Rickshaw Maintenance.* At the door, he turned around and said wistfully, "I prithee, remember the porter."

"As soon as I've filed my exclusive, Macbeth," I promised him, "I'll let you have some crumbs." Eyewitness crumbs yet!

I lay beneath a thwart for most of the voyage, but when they saw who she was, the guards at all the bridges just waved the girl through. At the conclusion of the safari, we crossed the airfield perimeter between the end of the runway and one of the army trucks. It was dark and they were taking food aboard the hijacked plane. Nobody noticed us.

Before we got to the terminal buildings, an executive jet landed and decanted a dozen or more soldiers on the floodlit apron. We followed them into the empty arrival hall. There were a couple of customs officers there. One was picking his teeth and the other was smoking a black cheroot. Their conversation was therefore indistinct. So far as I could make out, one said that with this heat, the monsoon couldn't fail to break within the next forty-eight hours; the other (him with the cheroot) was of the opinion that Rumania wouldn't have a hope in hell against Belgium in the next round of the World Cup. The soldiers walked past them, and so did we. Mazzari and the little Ulsterman, Hammer, were with them. I figured this for a sign that it wasn't just the monsoon that was about to break. And if there was going to be action, Mettner wanted a ringside seat.

The newsstand was closed, but I left my million-dollar secret sitting beside it. Who needed those girlie magazines with her around? She looked like a centerfold with clothes on anyway.

I sidled up the stairs and paused—thank God!—long enough outside the control room door to hear the words:

"I hate to do this, but I think we'd better have Brother

Mettner out of the way . . ." And then later: *"That's right Tall, thin guy. Staying at the Hotel Samoa, Room 27 . . ."*

I don't know how far back they've been keeping records of the best time for a descent of the eastern staircase of the terminal building at Phra Pradeng airport, but I'll lay even money that I bettered it that night by a good ten seconds and earned a mention in Ripley. "I have to get out of here, fast," I told honeybunch. "Back to the city and then a return ticket here at dead of night, okay?"

She intimated that the plan met with her approval, and we left. Through a side door leading to the kitchens.

I had, you see, been visited by An Idea. All I needed to make it work was to be back at the hotel . . . and have my Swiss army knife in my hand. You want to know why? I'll tell you.

The upstairs passageway at the Samoa terminates in a short T-junction. The crosspiece of the T houses four doors. A linen closet and the emergency exit (at the two ends); two rooms, numbers 27 and 28, facing the corridor.

The Swiss army knife houses some sixteen implements additional to its two blades. Among them are a bottle opener, a toothpick, a nail file, an instrument for removing stones from horses' hooves—and, for all I know, a picklock, a tire-pressure gauge, and a tool for dismantling television aerials. The one that interested me was a small screwdriver.

My thinking was as follows. The security forces had been told to arrest me. Specifically, they had been told to take in a tall, thin guy staying in Room 27 at the Samoa. They had been warned that he would kick up hell.

Point two: I did not wish to be arrested.

Point three: Quinnel was a tall, thin guy, staying at the Samoa. He would certainly kick up hell if he was arrested. The only thing was, he was in Room 28 and not Room 27.

You're with me?

Okay. I'm standing outside these two doors, Swiss army knife, open at the right place, in hand. There's taped Indonesian music—bells that jingle-jangle-jingle—in all the rooms. I hear movement in Room 28, so Quinnel's there. I already unscrewed the white plastic figures spelling out the number of my room; it doesn't take but a couple of minutes to remove his and screw mine on his door in their place. Then it's back into my room with the door open while I complete the substitution.

So the room numbers are switched. And it doesn't show, because the rooms are in a section on their own and don't form part of a sequence of numbers.

Pretty soon I hear the tramp of feet, and then the Muong-Thang equivalent of the "Open up—police!" routine.

That guy Wassermann was on the ball. Quinnel yelled blue murder all right; he pulled the U.S. embassy and the Rights of Man; he didn't mention the freedom of the press or the World Newspaper Council, it's true, but he came on strong with diplomatic privilege and American aid instead. They paid him no mind, as per instructions, and took him away just the same.

Soon afterward, I heard the phone ring in his room. I went in and lifted the receiver. It was a special instrument, chunkier and with a heavier base than mine. A scrambler, perhaps?

"Yeah?" I said guardedly.

"Quinnel? This is Mackenzie," said a far-off voice.

I grunted.

"Look, I don't give a damn what you agreed with this man Dean: the deal's off; he's got to bargain now. Can you hear me?"

"Yep."

"There's four dead already. We can't afford any more. Now that those pricks in Washington have leaked the story, we'll have the whole world on our backs. We have to negotiate, to stall for time, to try to find some compromise before the terrorists knock off someone *important*. Are you with me?"

"Yep."

"So tell Dean to soften his line at once. This comes from Washington, from the White House itself. Because of the leak, and the pressures it's brought, we have to rethink our approach. This time the deal has to be with the kidnappers and not with Dean. Will you tell him that right away?"

"Nope," I said quietly. I replaced the receiver.

Fucking politicians. Teenage girls, invalids, Japanese businessmen, distressed mothers—you can rub out as many as you want. Who cares? But at the thought of someone *important* getting knocked off—someone who could affect a trade balance, an oil delivery, or a vote at the UN—then principles go out the window and we get down on our knees with cap in hand!

I slammed the door of Quinnel's room, ignored the insistent ringing of the phone, and went back next door.

I didn't tell you what happened to the scarlet serpent before we went out to the airfield. It's family viewing time, after all. But I was reminded of it—fairly forcibly—before we hit the canal for our second visit to Phra Pradeng that night.

There she was, naked as a starfish, spread out for inspection on my bed. Golden Dawn.

As Papa Hemingway said, the sun also rises.

20 Marc Dean

Dean was stupefied when he heard the voice. It was soon after daybreak. Haggard and unshaven after a night of torment and self-doubt, he was staring out the control-tower window at the white mist surrounding the giant Boeing. Almost perfunctorily he held one of the UHF headset cans to his ear.

"*I'm* hungry! *Why don't they give us some food?*" the voice said plaintively. "*Why won't they let us eat?*"

And then, a woman's soothing tones, "*Hush, dear. We must be very patient. Perhaps this morning they'll give us something. They sure have plenty in that galley by now!*"

Dean gaped. The first voice—unmistakably—had been that of his son, Patrick. But how the *devil* . . . ?

Never mind how. The combat leader's mind was suddenly racing. The hunch, the germ of an idea he'd spoken of the previous night, had been no more than that—but with an ally aboard the plane, it could be transformed from a dream to reality; it would be a hundred times more likely to succeed. *If* the ally was reliable. *If* the ally was able to fulfill certain conditions. Would a seven-year-old boy be up to it? Could he be counted upon? Might it not lay him open to reprisals, put him in even more danger? Dean shook his head. It had to be tried; it couldn't make things much worse.

He settled the cans over his ears. He leaned forward and flipped a switch. "Patrick!" he said urgently, quietly. "This is your dad. I don't know how come I can hear your voice. Answer me yes or no: are any of the pirates near you?"

There was a long silence. And then, in a small voice, "*No.*"

"Are you on the flight deck, by the plane's radio?"
"*N-no.*"

"Then how is it that I can hear you? What are you speaking into?"

"I've got my transistor. The one you gave me. You fixed it so the tape mike also—"

"Yes, yes. I remember. Where are you? Who's with you?"

"Sitting in my seat with the hostess lady. She's nice. Where are you, Dad?" For the first time the immature voice quavered. *"Have you c-c-come t-to rescue us?"*

"I hope so. I'm here on the airfield, in the control tower. Now, listen, son: you have to be very clever and very brave, and you can help me beat the bandits."

"Like the boy in the story where Daredevil Dan—?"

"Sure. Just like that. Listen, how is it that they let you loose with a radio transmitter?"

"They don't know about the radio. I'm allowed to play the tapes you made, the children's stories. It keeps me quiet," Patrick announced. *"The fierce black lady said it's all right."*

"Okay. Now let's see . . ." Dean stared out at the distant jetliner, concentrating. The sky was overcast. No breath of wind stirred the white surface of the mist. The atmosphere was already hot and clammy. He could scarcely believe that the silver shape rising from the pale vapor hid the fragile body of his son. He tried not to think of the freckled skin, the tousled hair, the vulnerable tilt of neck and shoulders. "I have to sign off for a while," he said. "I have inquiries to make. Now, when I call you back, I'll have instructions for you. You must somehow pass them on to the pilot . . . Are you allowed to go up to the flight deck?"

"No. We have to stay in our seats, except when we—"

"Okay. Then you must explain to your hostess lady and ask her to do it for you. Is she allowed to move around?"

"Yes, she is. You will call back, won't you?"

"Try to stop me! In case anyone overhears, I'll give you the instructions in such a way . . . as if I was telling you a story. Then you can say it's another tape. Do you understand?"

"I think so."

"They'll be instructions for the pilot, so I'll make it sound like one of the space-age tapes. I'll be Daredevil

Dan and you'll be Wonderboy. Think you can manage that?"

"I explain Dan's instructions to Chloe, and she takes them to the pilot. Is that right?"

"Attaboy!" said Dean with a heartiness he was far from feeling. "Captain Future, blasting off on Space Patrol. Close the hatches and prime the first-stage reactors."

"Aye, aye, sir . . . There's somebody coming. I must go." The transmission ceased abruptly.

Dean roused the switchboard operator from his camp bed. He called Colonel Chakrawongse and asked him to come out to the field. He called the meteorological department of the Muong-Thang radio and TV station and spent twenty minutes listening and taking notes. He called Quinnel's room at the Samoa several times but got no reply.

Soon after nine o'clock, despite his statement to the contrary the previous day, Ramon spoke to the tower on the radio.

He was tired of waiting, he said. His demands and those of his companions must be met. He was therefore presenting an ultimatum: there was a bomb on the plane; if he had heard nothing concrete by 1100 hours, then they would consider their cause lost, the bomb would be exploded, and the Boeing and all aboard her would be blown to hell.

Go ahead, Dean told him. Blow yourselves up and save us the trouble. But his throat was dry when he turned away from the radio. Fear clawed at his guts, for he knew that both Ramon and Chan were capable of carrying out such a threat, even if it meant their own inevitable deaths. It was now no more than a question of time. Would his crazy gamble pay off before the ultimatum expired?

Before ten, a gust of hot wind blew away the last shreds of mist beneath the lowering sky. Concealed in the scrub, the eighteen mercenaries sweated in their battle fatigues and awaited a radio signal from Dean. Half a mile away, Jason Mettner lay on top of a bank bordering an irrigation ditch and trained his field glasses on the ring of military vehicles surrounding the 747. In the distance, half a dozen white-jacketed men pushing trolleys filed out from the side of the terminal building.

There was fighting thirty-five miles to the northeast. A rebel spearhead, penetrating deep into the country from a base on the far side of the Khmer border, had been halted on the left bank of the river by a motorized battalion of the Muong-Thang forces supported by the American armor featured in the march-past only a few days before. One of the invading patrols was resting up at the Phra Kao monastery, the olive drab of their camouflage gear incongruous beneath the flaming reds of the blossoms overhanging the clearing.

At the side of the dirt road beyond the bamboo bridge, a white Mercedes coupé parked under the trees. The driver, a short dark man, escorted his passenger across to the island. Halfway to the pottery they were met by Mr. Theng, the import-export expert. The three of them continued to the main building, where they were received in the refectory by Jean-Paul Albi and a uniformed officer. Mr. Theng performed the introductions. "Allow me to present Monsieur the Professor Albi and Major Bandungthen of the Liberation Army," he said. And then, with a sweeping gesture toward the passenger from the Mercedes, "His Excellency, Ngon Thek."

In the cabins of the hijacked Boeing at Phra Pradeng, the complaints of more than 250 people who had been given nothing but water to drink for more than two days were becoming deafening. The voice from the transistor speaker, where Patrick Dean was slumped in his seat beside Chloe Constantine, was scarcely audible over the uproar.

". . . so Daredevil Dan," Dean's voice intoned, "said to Wonderboy, 'You must go to the captain of the spaceship and tell him to make certain alterations to the control surfaces. Now, this is very important,' Dan insisted. 'Do you remember, Boy, what the Flick-flick, the Flack-flock, and the Roar-stop are?' "

"Yes, Dad," the child breathed into the microphone.

" 'Good,' said Daredevil Dan. Then . . . uh . . . then Dan said, 'You must tell the captain to open all of them up to the full.' And he added a piece of vital information about the weather. . . ."

The singsong storytelling voice droned on. Two minutes later, a much harsher one said, "What the hell is this?"

Chloe caught her breath and the young boy blanched. Ramon was standing in the gangway scowling at them. "It's j-j-just . . . I mean I'm allowed . . . the s-s-s-space-age tapes," Patrick stammered.

The terrorist held out his hand for the cassette player, but at that moment the black girl passed. "It's okay," she said. "Just some bourgeois crap . . . kids' stories his old man put on tape." Ramon grunted and continued toward the flight deck.

"You have to tell the pilot to actuate the rudders, air brakes, elevators, flaps, and trimming tabs in a certain way," Patrick said importantly when Dean's message was through. "Now, here's what you have to explain. . . ."

Soon afterward, the girl got permission to take a little water up to the captain and his copilot, who had been forced to remain seated before the controls throughout the whole interminable wait since the plane had landed. She stayed there five or six minutes, talking in a low voice and staring out the windshield at the sullen storm front climbing the sky above the flat, empty landscape.

Chan heard the whine of the electric auxiliaries while he was in the first-class cabin administering another hypodermic injection to the still-semiconscious King Kao Dinh. He bounded up to the flight deck, closely followed by Ramon and Mendez, his pistol in his hand.

"Freeing the control surfaces," the pilot replied calmly to their shouted inquiries. "If you ever plan to get this ship off the ground again, they have to be in one hundred percent working order, don't they? Unless they get a little air circulating around them," he lied, "the whole god-damn thing risks becoming inoperative. A climate like this, the mechanism could rust solid."

Faced with the layman's incomprehension and igno-rance of engineering technicalities, the hijackers could only allow the maneuver to go ahead. They watched ailerons and tabs flick this way and that. They saw the dun surface of the runway appear below as the huge flaps separated themselves from the trailing edge of the wings and canted downward. They observed the massive air brakes rising vertically from the polished silver wing sur-face. At the rear of the great plane, invisible to them,

194

tail-section control surfaces moved to maximum deflection.

A gust of wind plucked at the fuselage as Ramon seated himself before the radio transmitter, shivering the Boeing on its wheels. He picked up the headset. There was still fifteen minutes to go before his ultimatum expired. He must keep up the suspense. The other side must be maintained in a state of continuous anxiety, so that the apparent cave-in, when it came, would appear as an overwhelming relief and a release from unbearable tension—which would, or should, make them that much more likely to accede to his real demands when he made them. He would call Dean and remind him that time was running out.

Dean, to his astonishment, was already talking when he tuned in to their frequency.

"And Daredevil Dan said to Wonderboy, 'There's only one more thing you have to pass on to the gallant space crew: they must fasten their seat belts real tight, son, when blast-off is due.' Okay?"

The hijack leader stared at the dials and switches in front of him. Kids' stories? In *Dean's* voice? Coming through on the radio? *Son?*

He was racing down the aisle toward the rear seat where the kid was sitting with the hostess bitch. Yes, he was right, by the Blessed Virgin! The same voice, spouting the same shit, coming from that transistor speaker? "Daddy's *tapes*, is it?" he roared furiously. "Well, we'll see what Daddy thinks when he knows who's the next little fucker to die!" He lunged toward the terrified child.

It was at that precise moment that Dean's gamble paid off.

Typhoon Terry's remorseless advance had been watched and then carefully plotted by Dean, with the help of the local radio-meteo service. Because of the radio jamming, the terrorists were ignorant of the tempest's existence. It hit the Muong-Thang coast at 1041 hours that morning, snapping the masts of sailboats moored in the harbor, bending trees almost double in the park around the Buddhist temple, ripping roofs from the waterfront shacks lining the canals. The tidal wave that came with it swept up the waterways. Wooden piles and stilts splintered. The riverside homes cascaded into the stream. Bridges collapsed.

Within minutes the city was a dead place. Fleeing the howling tornado that was sending huge seas crashing over the promenades, the inhabitants abandoned cars, buses, bicycles, tri-shaws, and sought shelter behind locked shutters until the first shock wave had passed.

Dean called up Hammer and Mazzari on the second free frequency at 1042. The radio-meteo people just managed to get in the call to alert him before the telephone wires were snatched away. "If my calculations are anything like correct," Dean said, "if I'm not too far out on weight and mass, and the wind direction's true, you should find you can target-in around 450 to 550 yards north-northeast of the present position. Get going now: you don't need to hide out anymore; nothing they can do will alter anything."

Mazzari's vast frame rose upright among the scrub. The wind that had been gusting fitfully had died away, leaving a flat calm heavy with menace, a torrid atmosphere so charged that the damp heat appeared almost physically to press in upon the temples. The sky overhead was the color of a ripe plum. "All right, chaps," the big African yelled, "this is it! Follow Hammer and me and prepare for the emergency drill the moment she stops rolling!"

With the nut-faced little Ulsterman he sprinted along the airfield perimeter, past the runway and the stalled jetliner, past the military vehicles whose crews had been instructed to stay clear of any action, toward a spot a quarter of a mile away, where the asphalt boundary track curved back toward the entrance. They ran openly, their weapons visible, followed closely by Schneider, Daler, Novotny, Wassermann, and the twelve new arrivals.

Five minutes later, at 1047, as Ramon reached for Dean's young son in the tourist cabin of the airplane, the typhoon hit Phra Pradeng.

The warning was minimal. A sudden low moan among the dried branches of the scrub, an abrupt darkening of the sky as the grasses leaned over, and then the shrieking gale was upon them.

The effect on the Boeing was spectacular. The ship was already very light on fuel. Freed of that extra weight, with

196

the control surfaces arranged in the way specified by Dean and passed on by his son and Chloe Constantine, it stood three-quarters-on to the storm. Elevators, ailerons, rudders, were fixed to throw the plane—had it been airborne and a great deal smaller—into a roll. With these surfaces set, and the flaps and air brakes arranged to give maximum interruption to the airflow, the impact of a strong wind was bound to be impressive.

The 747 staggered as the first gust screeched past ... and then, when the full fury of the 150mph tornado struck, the great jetliner rose up on one wingtip and cartwheeled once, twice, three times across the field, finally coming to rest upside down on the perimeter track within one hundred yards of the mercenaries. Before they could reach the wreck, rain lanced down from the sky like steel rods.

Dean was in a jeep, speeding across the field toward the Boeing, when the typhoon arrived. The windshield pillars snapped, showering him with fragments of safety glass, the soft top was whirled away, and the sturdy little utility was blown over onto its side. He scrambled out, bent double against the hurricane-force wind, and sprinted for the runway, his Colt Commando clutched against his chest, his eyes squinted against the lashing of the rain.

The field was littered with fragments of the giant plane that had broken off as it caromed toward its final resting place. A wingtip, part of the tail section, an air brake, the landing gear with the wheels still attached, lay scattered between the runway and the perimeter track, though the inverted fuselage seemed relatively undamaged.

Mazzari and Hammer were already attacking the flight-deck blister where it rested on the asphalt, the smashing of their machetes into plexiglass and dural inaudible over the howl of wind and the tattoo of rain on the stressed-skin body.

The other mercs were feverishly reaching up to batter at the ports on each side of the jetliner. Speed, Dean had told them, was everything: unless the hijackers were overcome before the shock of the typhoon's arrival had faded, they could start a wholesale slaughter of hostages that could be catastrophic. Novotny, the explosives expert, had fixed very small charges of plastic that would blow the door-locking bolts without harming anyone inside the plane. Two of these went off as Dean approached the tail. On the far side, an emergency exit, bravely unlatched by Chloe Constantine an instant before the Boeing was struck, had burst open under the impact.

Dean hauled himself up by means of a crumpled rudder and crouched down on the slippery belly of the plane, hunched against the furious wind as he fired a short burst from the Colt Commando at the hatch through which the food consignments had been delivered. At the same time, Mazzari and Hammer smashed their way through into the flight deck.

Inside the capsized plane there was chaos.

Some of the passengers—and the crew members, who had been warned by Patrick and Chloe—had found time to fasten their seat belts and now hung upside down in the harness. But the majority had been taken completely by surprise. Hurled from one end of the cabin to the other, they lay in tangled heaps along what had been the arched ceiling, surrounded by an indescribable clutter of bottles, books, purses, compacts, and other articles thrown from the hand baggage in the course of the plane's erratic somersaults.

Some of the hijackers had been similarly confounded. Their startled cries and calls to their companions mingled with the shouts and sobs and screams of panic from the passengers.

Ramon had been thrown against a bulkhead and half-stunned during the Boeing's first cartwheel. The Uzi submachine gun spun from his grasp and slid away beneath a seat. But he still had the Walther automatic. He staggered upright halfway down the aisle between the first-class compartment and the seat where Chloe and Patrick were sitting. He had not yet realized that the plane was under attack: the sounds of the storm and the indescribable din created by the frightened passengers effectively drowned the noise of hammering. The whole fuselage was groaning and shuddering under the manic assault of the wind. It was only when Novotny's charges exploded that he realized there was something more than a meteorological freak to deal with. "We're under attack!" he shouted over the pandemonium. "Repel boarders! Fire at anyone!"

Mazzari and Hammer were in the pilot's cabin. Dean

had briefed his team: "You're looking for a Central American, a Chinese, a Puerto Rican with an Afro, three Arabs, and a black girl. Shoot to kill. These people are totally ruthless; there's no question of inviting them to surrender." There was nevertheless the problem of identifying the terrorists among the mass of passengers. It was not until he heard Ramon yell and saw him lurch upright with the gun that Hammer reacted and prepared to fire his own. Even then, he was obliged to aim high because there were men and women struggling behind the bandit.

Hammer's snap shot at shoulder or head missed its target, and he was then forced to duck back, because Ramon fired in his turn. The reports were deafening. There was a fresh outburst of screams. The two channels between the three rows of lockers in what had been the Boeing's ceiling offered no cover from one end of the giant cabin to the other. In panic, the passengers who had just levered themselves upright flung themselves flat again or fought to reach the far end of the cabin.

One of the Arabs had lost his gun. He was pulled down by half a dozen of the braver hostages, but the feet and fists ceased their pummeling when a second Arab fired his burp gun point-blank at the nearest attacker. The passenger rolled away with blood pumping between the fingers of a hand clasped to his side. The third Arab had hurled himself at one of the doors blown open by Novotny. Thrusting his head, shoulders, and an arm through the gap, he blazed away at the group of mercs below. One of the Australians dropped like a stone and lay with outstretched arms. Another man reeled away clutching his thigh. Then Daler, braced against the gale on the belly of the plane above the buckled door, fired the whole thirty-round magazine of his MAC-11 in the astonishing one and a half seconds that the 1200rpm machine pistol could make. The Arab's head was literally torn from his body; he slumped dead in the opening, with the lashing rain washing long streams of blood down the curved side of the fuselage.

At that moment, two of the mercs on the other side of the plane lobbed concussion grenades through the emergency door that Chloe had opened.

The plastic projectiles, which stunned without doing any physical harm, exploded almost simultaneously. The noise in the two cabins ceased instantly as passengers and hijackers alike relapsed into unconsciousness.

Suddenly the shriek of wind and the drumming of rain were loud again, loud as the hollow tramp of the mercenaries' feet on the outside of the Boeing's hull. But there was still movement inside. Hammer, who had edged into the first-class cabin for another shot at Ramon, was a victim of the grenades, but Mazzari, lower down on the flight deck, escaped the full effect of the detonations. He was shaking his head groggily, on hands and knees in the rounded blister over the pilot's seats, when he looked up and saw, ten feet away at the entrance to the galley, the malevolent face of the black girl from the Caribbean. "Hey, black boy, nigger," she called, "how come you fight on the side of the pigs?" Her finger tightened over the trigger of the automatic in her hand.

"Principles, old girl!" Mazzari shouted, sighting his own Browning. The two reports sounded as one. Mazzari was knocked sideways, spun away, and dropped to the ceiling of the blister, below the heads of the crew members still strapped in their seats. But his shot had been the more accurate of the two. Between the black girl's eyes, a third opening bloomed horribly, spouting crimson as she collapsed.

Behind her body, the squat and sinister figure of Chan emerged from one of the first-class toilets and loomed menacingly through the haze of cordite smoke. The gun in his raised arm was pointing at the helpless Mazzari.

Dean dropped through the tail hatchway and took in the situation at a glance. It was a difficult shot, past the unconscious body of his son supported in its harness, angled down through the haze along the whole length of the cabin to the flight-deck entrance. He fired from the hip; there was no time to aim. And luck, or the involuntary reflexes of experience, or perhaps just the good fortune of the righteous, was with him. The volley of 9mm slugs stitched a pattern of red diagonally across the back of the killer's jacket, slamming him forward to slump across Mazzari in the blister.

Over the roar of the typhoon, Dean called his team to come in.

Three hundred yards away, Jason Mettner fought his way, reeling, to his feet on the lip of the bank where he had been sheltering. He was drenched through and through, his clothes were plastered to his body, his hair was blown into his eyes, and his teeth were chattering. Worst of all, it had been physically impossible to keep a cigarette in his mouth for the past fifteen minutes.

But he had the ringside seat he had craved.

He was unable to stand against the lunatic force of the wind. Crouched down on the lee side of the mound, he fingered the zoom lever and maneuvered the hood of his Hasselblad to keep the torrential rain off the lens.

The mercs had vanished inside the body of the wrecked Boeing, but suddenly a single figure dropped through the shattered windshield and started running frantically away from the plane.

Ramon.

He hadn't a chance in hell. Mettner could see that with the benefit of distance. The hijacker ran like the wind . . . and he ran with the wind, so that he was half-sprinting, half-blown along, hurled forward like a leaf in a squall. But one of the military vehicles surrounding the jetliner's original position at the end of the runway was moving after him.

The distance between the fleeing man and the scrub beyond the field that would bring him safety was diminishing fast. But the distance between the armored vehicle and its quarry was diminishing more quickly still.

Dean appeared in the Boeing's tail hatchway. He was shouting and waving his arms. But whether he was encouraging the security men or warning them off, it was impossible to say.

The muzzle projecting from the vehicle's turret belched flame—not, Mettner saw with a thrill of horror, the vivid flash of a gunshot but the long, boiling tongue of fire erupting from a flamethrower. It was almost beautiful— Mettner's camera clicked—the licking tongue stretching and unfurling like one of those curled squeakers that blows out flat on New Year's Eve and at children's parties. The range was still too great for it to touch the running man, but he must have felt its hot breath on his heels, for he gave a terrified look over his shoulder and increased his pace still more.

The armored vehicle accelerated. The turret moved.

Once more the long, wicked tongue of flame boiled out.

This time the range was right. The tip of the tongue, advancing fast and fiercely, licked Ramon's back. At once he became a human catherine wheel, cartwheeling, blazing, rolling on the wet ground in a bouncing ball of fire. It was a trick of the wind, but Mettner imagined he heard him screaming. And then the flame snapped back into the gun muzzle, the rain lanced down, and the armored truck braked by a black cinder steaming in the wind.

The camera clicked and clicked.

In the Boeing, Marc Dean dropped back through the hatchway—and discovered almost at once the solution to the mystery of the starving hostages. The galleys were packed full. But not with the containers and shallow trays that should have been brought out in the trolleys wheeled by the restaurant personnel. The shelves were stuffed with hundreds and hundreds of plastic sacks, each weighing about one pound. Many of the sacks had fallen when the 747 crashed upside down. Some of them had burst open, spilling their contents.

A crystalline white powder, slightly bitter to the taste.

Epilogue Jason Mettner

"It had to be Ngon Thek, of course," Dean told me later. "As soon as I saw those little sacks, and realized they'd been brought out to the plane instead of food, and remembered that the guys bringing them were special security operatives . . . well, he had to be in on it."

"And the stuff in the sacks, of course . . . ?"

"Was horse, the big H, heroin. Prime grade. The purest, most-refined product. They wanted to get rid of it before the market was saturated and next year's crop on the way. Pottery jars with false bottoms weren't shifting the stuff quickly enough, so they had to find some way of transporting it in bulk. Only, Kao Dinh was leaning very heavily on the drug scene: you may recall, when we were on that assassination kick, he agreed that every available man should be switched to the hunt . . . *except* the antidrug squad and customs officers. Even when his life was at stake, he was determined to keep the pressure up."

"Yeah," I said. "Okay. But this whole plane-hijack scene: I don't see . . . I mean, I can't figure out why the hell . . . ?"

"The same kind of thinking as our assassination-kidnap deal," he told me. "You know: wily Orientals."

I sighed. I fed another Chesterfield into my mouth and set fire to it. "All right," I said. "Tell about the wily Orientals. Pour it on."

We were sitting over a vat of planter's punch in the Fragrant Blossoms. It was hotter than Memphis in June, and the rain savaging the leaves outside sounded like the applause after a concert by the Vienna Philharmonic. "What," he asked me, "would you say is the one condition under which stuff loaded onto a plane is exempt from customs inspection?" And then—he never did rate journalists' IQ's very high—he answered the question himself.

203

"When the ship's in a hijack situation and it's landed to take on fuel or food to feed the hostages."

"Only this time they didn't get the food," I said. We get around to the point in the end.

It was nine hours since the Boeing had been bowled over by Typhoon Terry, though it seemed more like nine days. Dean had lost one man (the Australian) killed and two wounded. Mazzari's was only a flesh wound in the upper arm; the guy with the slug in his thigh had been hospitalized. Ramon, Chan, the black girl, and one of the Arabs were dead. Mendez and the two surviving Arabs had been handed over to the tender mercies of Colonel Chakrawongse and the Muong-Thang judiciary. The guy zapped with the Arab's burp gun was the only passenger casualty, and he would survive too.

"In the first case," Dean said, "they fooled us into blocking a murder attempt when in fact their aim was a snatch. In the second, their idea again was to channel our thinking in one direction while they worked in another. We were so traumatized by the deaths of the hostages and the ridiculous demands they were supposed to be in aid of that we never thought to check out the food shipments delivered to the plane."

"Just a minute," I said. " 'Supposed to be in aid of'? Are you saying . . . ?"

"You don't catch on too quickly, do you?" he said kindly. *Those demands were never meant to be met.* They were deliberately made contradictory, too extreme, impossible to fulfill. The demands—and the cold-blooded murder of the hostages—had one purpose only: to make us stall long enough for them to ship their dope aboard. They couldn't believably ask for food more than three times a day, so, with the amount they had to shift, we had to be made to stall for some time. The last thing they wanted was for us to talk terms."

"And when the consignment was all aboard?" I asked.

"Mendez sang before they took him away. The plan was for Ramon to allow himself to be—apparently—talked out of his hard line. As a big-deal concession, he would then release all the hostages—on condition that the plane was refueled and he was allowed to fly off to wherever they aimed to sell the stuff."

"Neat but not gaudy," I allowed. "Why snatch the king?"

"We were told at the beginning," Dean said, "that there were two really strong men here: Ngon Thek and the monarch. Take away Thek, as leader of the conspirators, and that leaves Kao Dinh. I guess they were afraid that he might tumble to the fact that the hijack was a phony and order a check by the customs on *everything*—food deliveries or whatever. Having him on the plane was kind of a bonus, an extra VIP whose health we could worry about while we fucked around wondering how the hell to handle the situation."

"Colonel Chakrawongse doesn't strike me as a weakling," I said.

"Certainly not. But he was in a subordinate position. And remember, he knew nothing of Ngon Thek's treachery: the guy was his boss, dammit."

I murdered another Chesterfield. I said, "Accepting that there's always a motive in the fact that your famous white powder spells out H as in Loot, there remain three questions: Why? Why? And again, why?"

"You smoke too much," he said.

"I know," I said. "It may endanger my health. It says so on the pack and in the ads. The surgeon general himself says so. Why the *hell* would folks go to this length, mount such an elaborate double bluff, simply to shift a consignment of horse? And who are 'folks,' anyway?"

"I think there's no question about their identity," Dean said. "I mean, clearly it's the rebels and their backers. They went to that amount of trouble because they need to sell the whole consignment at once, not in dribs and drabs. And they need to sell it all at once because they require a large sum to buy modern hardware that will match the U.S. armor displayed at that march-past. Next question?"

"This guy Thek was a big noise. Home-security boss, number two to the king, plenty of bread. Why would he risk all that? For what?"

"He probably met the opposition characters when he was a guerrilla himself, before independence. My guess is that he was suborned with offers of even more loot, an even more important post—maybe number one, president of a puppet state, when the comrades took over." Dean

205

shook his head. "He certainly took off with them. Chakrawongse heard this afternoon. Kao Dinh's troops fought off a rebel penetration up near the old monastery . . . and it seems that Ngon Thek, Albi, and the mysterious Mr. Theng retreated across the border with the invaders. No point hanging around when the game's lost."

"Probably another of your man Furneux's ferrying contracts," I said. "Third and last question: "Why did they call you in? It was Thek himself who came stateside to hire you, wasn't it?"

He nodded. "Sure. I think it was obvious that, with all the assassination threats, and pressure from the U.S. narcotics people, the king was going to take *some* action. Thek probably figured the best defense was attack: call in some dumb foreigner, give him a few clues to follow up, and the king will think everything's under control. The same thinking they used for the snatch and the hijack. It was easy enough for him to keep track of our movements and block them if necessary: we were *consulting* with the guy, for God's sake!"

"How *is* the royal personage, by the way?" I asked.

He grinned. "Resting. They knocked him on the head during the original snatch, and then kept him under sedation. Usual amnesiac syndrome. He doesn't remember a damned thing after he stepped forward on that rostrum to take the salute at the march-past!"

"Shit," I said, "I was hoping to get a regal eyewitnesser out of him: Inside the Hijack Jet. My Life with the Killer crew. Now I'll have to make do with your son and the stewardess."

The grin widened. "There aren't enough pages in your paper," he said, "to take all the stuff Patrick has to tell you!"

I left the two of them to their love-in and went back to the Samoa. Checking first that Quinnel wasn't around, I started typing. Hell, the exclusive I had already was a world beat! I began tapping out:

Byline Jason Mettner II our special correspondent in Indochina fullpoint Am hyphen Phallang open bracket Muong hyphen Thang close bracket comma Tuesday fullpoint dash Hamlet found something rotten in the state of Denmark semicolon he should have been in this wartorn Southeast Asian principality this week exclamark As with William Blake's sick rose comma the rottenness started from within comma at the center . . .

When I had quarried out three thousand scholarly words, I cabled the story Press Collect to *Worldwide*. I had already sold my photos to *Paris-Match* for (as they say) a tidy sum, and I was feeling good. Then the echo of the *Hamlet* quote reminded me: I'd promised to wise up poor old Sidney Nailor. I found him in Charlie's Bar, staring glumly at a half-pint glass of beer. "Sicklied o'er with the pale cast of thought, by gum!" I greeted him. "Where got'st thou that goose look, Sid?"

"It's all very well for you to joke, old man," he said, "but you should have seen the bloody rocket I got from head office this morning." I ordered a couple of drinks and he fished a crumpled cable form from the pocket of that topcoat. It was about 140 degrees in there and the moisture was running down the walls. He held out the paper. I read: *"Where kingsnatch planejack coverage also typhoon querymark rely you upgetting exass filing fullest soonest = Reuter."*

"And that's only the followup," he confessed gloomily. "Mine eyes smell onions; I shall weep anon."

"All yet seems well," I told him, "and, if it end so meet, the bitter past, more welcome is the sweet."

He pushed aside the beer and sipped the Scotch I'd bought him. His eyes brightened. "You mean . . . you'll give us the lowdown?"

"I promised, didn't I?"

I told him the whole story, including the whys and wherefores I'd choked out of Dean, omitting only certain personal details unsuitable for a national news agency. When I'd finished, he said, "Very decent of you, old chap, I must say. Being able to file all that will get me out of a hole, I don't mind telling you. For saying so there's gold: mine own escape unfoldeth to my hope, whereto thy speech serves for authority."

"Swell. Now, there's one question you can answer for me . . ."

"The only thing is . . ." He was looking dubious.

"Supposing they had set the bomb off when they attacked the plane? The office will want to know—"

"There was no bomb," I interrupted. And then—I figured I might as well push it onto him—"You don't catch on too quickly, do you? The whole thing was just a gigantic bluff—except of course for the people they did kill. But that was to support the bluff."

He frowned. "But suppose they had—?"

"They wouldn't have," I said firmly. And then, to get him off his story and onto mine, I tempted him with another *Twelfth Night* tag. "Knowst thou this country?"

Back came the automatic reply, "Ay, sir, well: for I was bred and born not three hours' travel from this very place. If you take a plane, that is: the guv'nor was a tea planter in Malaya. Why do you ask?"

"This broad," I said. "Golden Dawn. You're practically a local. I mean, what about her? Dean figured her at first for an operative on Ngon Thek's payroll; then he thought she might be an agent for Thai intelligence, put in to find out what ticks. Now he just doesn't know. Yet she *is* the niece of that old bastard at the pottery. She was pretty close to Dean, yet we saw Quinnel coming out of her apartment. I myself . . ." I coughed. "What about her?" I repeated.

Nailor nearly smiled. "I thought everybody knew *that*," he said. "My guess is that the conspirators deliberately put her next to Dean, I mean like introduced them, simply because they knew what would happen—and they knew it would confuse the trail."

"You mean . . . ?"

"She's no agent, old man. And there's nothing secret about her either. Even I . . ." He coughed in his turn. "She puts it about, is all. She has hot pants. She's nympho. She's crazy about cock. You know?"

I sighed. "I know," I said.

LOOKING FORWARD

The following is the opening section
from the next novel in the exciting
MARC DEAN—MERCENARY series from Signet.

THE BLACK
GOLD BRIEFING

Oil in Troubled Waters

It seemed always to be happening to Marc Dean. It was not that he had any particular objection to the mixture of business with pleasure, but simply that each time he devoted his talents to the pursuit of pleasure, there appeared to be a business opportunity at the end of the chase. And Marc Dean's business was danger.

Fortunately he took a great deal of pleasure in his business anyway, for there was danger in every seductive curve of the raven-haired Lebanese girl he met at the sidewalk cafe in Paris's Champs Elysees that evening in early summer.

He didn't see that at once, but he saw that she was trouble. It was implicit in the curl of the lip, the arrogant flare of the nostril, and the bold dark stare of those challenging eyes. A thoroughbred, Dean thought to himself, pulling out a chair at a vacant table to one side and a little behind her. Temperamental. High-spirited. Needs to be kept on a tight rein—but hellishly rewarding once the tapes are up and the going is good!

Within less than a half-hour he was forced mentally to rephrase that male-chauvinist evaluation, but for the moment he was content to sip a tall glass of Alsatian beer and enjoy looking at her.

It was an agreeable task. She was tall and slender—very tall indeed for a young woman whose aristocratic nose, tawny skin, and bruised eyes testified to origins at the eastern end of the Mediterranean (Dean discovered later that she was in fact only three inches short of his own husky six feet). Her hair, which tumbled with expensive abandon over her bare shoulders, was of that particular soft and lustrous black that nevertheless shows no highlights. The jade-green, one-strap summer dress that she wore was cut with such stunning simplicity that Dean knew it must have come from one of the top couture houses in the Place Vendome and had probably cost about as much as a six-month-old Cadillac. A sable wrap was flung carelessly over the back of her chair and the expression on her face mingled pride and awareness of her own beauty with a faint and quizzical disdain. Plus the haughty challenge that Dean could never resist.

He wondered at once what would be the best way to approach her. She was sitting alone, drinking coffee with brandy. It was a little after eight o'clock, at the hour when dusk thickens the air like a sediment, when the heat and fragrance of the day still hang over the bookstalls along the quais of the Seine, when the yellow eyes of Porsches and Alfa Romeos so expertly driven by the call girls of the capital seek out their prey along the Avenue Georges V and the Rue de la Boetie. It was early for a woman alone to be taking an after-dinner *digestif;* if she was waiting for someone to take her to dinner, it was a little late for a cocktail—and anyway, he'd be crazy to keep a girl looking like that waiting. It was, on the other hand, an odd place, at that time, to find any girl sitting on her own unless she was a hustler. And Dean would have bet the shirt off his back that this was no pro. The shirt came from Sulka, too.

It was while he was trying to decide on some opening that would be at least one degree up on the corniest thing you ever heard that she turned around and looked him in the eye. "You've been staring at the right-hand, rear-three-quarter view for long enough," she said. "Don't you think it would be braver to look at the front?"

Dean started to his feet, astonished. For once in his life he found himself at a loss for words. "I'm sorry . . . Mademoiselle . . . Excuse me . . ." he stammered.

She glanced at him appraisingly—180 pounds of lean muscle, tough as whipcord; the short, crisp, pale hair; a determined chin and a wide, firm mouth that could be both cruel and tender. "Sit down," she said. Her voice was musical, quite deep, with a slight accent that he could not place. He sat.

A waiter bustled up, tray in hand. It was early; less than half the sidewalk tables were occupied. *"M'sieu? Madame?"*

"Encore un cafe express, et une fine champagne, Baron Otard," the girl said.

"Bring me another beer," said Dean.

Before the waiter left, she opened her purse—it was black crocodile—and picked up the ticket from beneath her brandy glass. Dean reached for his billfold, but she stopped him with an imperious gesture. "You may buy me a drink," she said, "but I pay for the one I already had." She took a bill from the purse and handed it to the waiter.

She snapped the purse shut—but not before he had seen the tiny nickel-plated gun with hand-carved ivory butt plates that was lodged in a special pocket alongside the comb and mirror and lipstick and gold cigarette case inside. The girl grew more intriguing every minute, he thought. What the hell would an eighteen-carat, race-bred, handcrafted baby like that be doing with a pistol?

She knew he had seen it. She was direct enough not to pretend otherwise and smart enough to read his thoughts. "I had it made for me at Togliatti's in Milan," she said. "Ordinarily they don't do handguns, but my father put money into the company in the fifties. It's a twenty-two Long, Berretta action, twelve-shot automatic. Lightweight, but dangerous if you know exactly where to put the slugs."

"Expensive, too, I guess," Dean said dryly.

"You should know, Colonel Dean," the girl said.

He stared, amazed again. "You know my name?"

"I am not in the habit of accepting drinks from strangers." Once more the supercilious droop of those slumbrous eyelids.

Suddenly Dean grinned, the tanned flesh at the corners of his eyes crinkling, the rakish, devil-may-care expression all at once boyish and eager. "All right," he said. "I'll buy it!" He was free; he had money in the bank; he was just back from an exhausting mission in Southeast Asia; and he was in need of relaxation. What better way to spend a summer evening than explore the mystery of a beautiful girl who clearly knew more about him than he did about her? "If you were waiting for me, you must be pretty smart: I only decided to drop by here at the last minute—a spur-of-the-moment choice as I was walking past—yet you seemed already to be installed when I sat down!"

"It is a matter of training," she said indifferently. "You are a soldier of fortune, Colonel Dean."

It was a statement, not a question. "I prefer the term combat leader," Dean said. "There is a difference between an ordinary mercenary, a soldier who fights for money, and a commander whose skills are for hire—a man who plans, organizes, equips, and directs the battles such a mercenary fights." He smiled. "In the latter case, the fortune is more ample. And it is to this second category that I belong." *What the hell kind of training* (he thought) *does a girl like this have when she can operate as adroitly as a world-class tag?*

"Use whichever term pleases you," the girl said. "I am familiar with your record. It is impressive." She paused while the waiter set down their fresh drinks. Inside the brasserie, a French family seated around a long table were tucking napkins in at the neck before they attacked a huge stack of seafood on a bed of cracked ice. "The opportunity to add another success to that record," the girl continued, "could result from our meeting tonight."

If only you meant my record with women, Dean thought with a glance at her svelte figure, *baby, I'd be with you all the way!*

But who the hell was this girl, anyway? She wasn't the fanatic student-intellectual type customarily recruited by the PLO. An agent working for the Mossad, the Israeli secret service, would never have a generous-enough expense account to wear clothes like that. He said, "Sounds the kind of subject that would go well with dinner."

She nodded. "It has been arranged that we dine together." She raised one hand. Diamonds and emeralds sparkled on the fingers. A waiter materialized as rapidly as a demon king in a pantomime. "But first I want another drink."

"I am not in the habit of drinking with ladies to whom I have not been introduced," Dean said primly.

For the first time she smiled. Very even, very white teeth. Beneath the exquisite makeup, the skin was taut and resilient. Dean placed her age between twenty-eight and thirty. She said, "Claudine Zaheddin," holding a lean, elegant hand across the table. Feeling faintly ridiculous, Dean raised it to his lips. It was a left hand. There were no rings on the third finger. The clasp was firm and dry. *"Enchante, Mademoiselle Zaheddin,"* he murmured. "From . . . Egypt?"

"From Tarabulus, in the Lebanon. That, at any rate, is where I am based at the moment." She sank the third brandy very quickly and rose to her feet.

"It's Friday night," Dean said. "Maybe I should call some restaurant first and reserve a table?"

"They are keeping one for us *chez* Drouand, in the Rue St. Augustin," she told him. Dean raised an eyebrow and went to call a cab. He was further mystified to discover, when they arrived at the famous family restaurant in the narrow street near the opera, that the table had been booked in his name.

He scarcely noticed the food and wine—which were admirable—as he concentrated all his attention on the tantalizing features of the girl facing him across the lemon-yellow linen tablecloth. *Daughter of a wealthy Egyptian expatriate hoping to restore the monarchy? A Persian princess who resented the sack of her country by the ayatollahs? Yet another Libyan prepared to sink money in a scheme to oust the mad dictator Qaddafi?* The name, perhaps the features too, were unmistakably Arab, yet Dean didn't think she was any of those things. But he wasn't going to kid himself that such an elaborately prepared meeting was on account of his beautiful blue eyes.

Claudine Zaheddin nevertheless spent the entire ninety minutes of their dinner giving a spirited impersonation of a girl on a date who found her escort both attractive and stimulating. *Okay,* Dean thought, *she's called the tune so far; this is her number—I'll go along with it and see what breaks.*

They talked of books and movies and the theater; they discussed economics and the social changes resulting from a world recession; they enthused over baroque music in general and the harpsichord sonatas of Scarlatti, Couperin, and Vivaldi (of which Dean was a passionate admirer and no mean performer) in particular. And during the whole hour and a half, under the spell of those large, dark, magnetic eyes, he learned nothing personal about her at all. It was only as they drank their coffee that she broached the subject of her own background.

"What do you know of Shahrud?" she asked suddenly.

"Shahrud?" Dean echoed, slightly taken aback—they

had been talking about the growing strength of the ecology movement. "I know that it's one of the United Arab emirates on the Persian Gulf. I know that the ruler, one of the world's richest men, I believe, was recently deposed in some kind of bloodless coup. I think the place is run now by the usual military junta. Why do you ask?"

"The ruler is my uncle, the Emir Shawaz Suleiman ben-Gazan."

"Oh," said Dean. "I'm sorry. That must be . . . worrying." He could not at the moment think of any more helpful comment to make.

"The revolution would be of minor importance," she said, "except for one thing. Please ask the waiter to bring me another Armagnac."

Dean raised a peremptory finger. "And the one thing?"

"Shahrud is one of the tiniest of the emirates. Until now, it has been only an insignificant producer of oil—but a hitherto unsuspected geological fault has revealed the existence of a geosyncline stretching far out under the sea that cradles an oil field big enough to dwarf Abu Dhabi and Bahrain combined."

Dean pursed his lips in a soundless whistle. "I guess that modulates 'minor' to 'major,'" he said, "for all the developed nations as well as for your family. Was the discovery made before the coup?"

"Just before—although that wasn't the main reason for it."

Suddenly Dean became very wary. It didn't, he reflected, require an Einstein to deduce that they were now approaching the main reason for the meeting she had engineered.

So far, nothing had been suggested. When the bid, whatever it was, came, he must be doubly on his guard; he must in no way allow himself to be influenced by the fact that he found her irresistibly bedworthy. He was a soldier by profession, but she too had a gun; like other members of what Bernard Shaw had called "the monstrous regiment of women," she had other weapons as well. *Who was it coined that phrase, the female of the species is more deadly than the male?*

But even as he prepared himself to resist any feminine wiles, she surprised him again. She dropped the subject of her country as abruptly as she had introduced it. "I

214

think it is time we left here," she said—and then, as he turned to call a waiter: "The check has already been taken care of."

More mystified still, Dean helped her on with her sable wrap. The only thing he had learned for sure was that Claudine Zaheddin had a remarkable capacity for liquor. He had seen her down three brandies on the Champs Elysees; she had swallowed a fourth before they ate; although Dean had schooled himself to drink sparingly, they had finished two bottles of wine with their meal—and she had then consumed a couple of Armagnacs with the coffee. Yet the outward indications were minimal: a slight misting of the eyes, perhaps a barely perceptible slurring of the consonants when she spoke. Her walk was perfectly steady, so the soft pressure he felt when she leaned momentarily back against him while he settled the wrap around her shoulders must have been deliberate.

"Now I would like us to go somewhere private," she said.

"I . . . uh . . . my apartment's not too far," Dean ventured. "Just off the Place Clichy. Five minutes in a cab."

"Your apartment in the Rue Cavalotti has a floor area of only seventy-five square meters," she said. "I like to pace about when I talk; I need space to move around in. We'll go to my place."

He laughed aloud. "Mademoiselle Zaheddin," he said, "as a New York friend and colleague of mine would say, you take the fucking biscuit already!"

"My place" proved to be a duplex at the top of a black-glass building on the Quai Louis Bleriot, at the far end of the snob sixteenth arrondissement. The building was so exclusive—and so burglar-conscious—that neither the apartment doors nor the individual stories were numbered, and buttons in the elevators were blank.

The huge living room and the stairway curving up to the sleeping quarters were carpeted in wall-to-wall wolfskin. "It is a little vulgar," Claudine said, "but—que voulez-vous?—the decorations were done for my uncle." She paused at the foot of the stairway. "I will be with you very soon. Fix yourself a drink, and make mine a brandy-and-soda."

While she was on the upper floor, Dean wandered around the sixty-foot room. The walls were covered in a silver-and-gold metallic paper that he knew cost more than a hundred dollars a foot. The furniture was modern Italian, all chromium and black hide and custom-built, honey-colored wood elements. Punctuating the indirect lighting, spots picked out a tiny Corot landscape and a Bernard Buffet canvas of a Breton fishing port that took up one whole wall of a dining alcove.

On a lower level, fifty or sixty different brands of liquor packed a cabinet beside a beaten copper hood that crowned an open hearth. Dean poured the drinks and stood gazing out the wide windows at the lights of traffic crawling along the ring road on the far side of the river.

When Claudine returned, she came downstairs so quietly that he did not at first realize she was back. Looking up suddenly, he saw her standing at the top of the three steps leading down to the fireplace. Her hair was gathered on the nape of her neck by a large black bow, and she had changed into a floor-length housecoat in some metallic material that shimmered softly in the low-key lighting. "Is that my drink you're holding, or yours?" she asked.

"Yours," Dean said, holding out the glass.

She undulated down the three steps and stood very close to him. He could feel her winy breath warm on his face. "Why don't we sit down?" She indicated a white leather settee built in a semicircle at one side of the empty hearth. "Your good health, Colonel!"—subsiding elegantly onto the cushions. "Do you know, there's one thing I *don't* know about you: your first name."

"Marcus Matthew. Marc to my friends." Dean's mouth was suddenly dry. He saw that the robe had no zipper and no buttons: it was fastened simply by a belt of the same material pulled tight and tied at the waist.

"Perhaps I shall be one of the friends . . . Marc?" She looked up at him quizzically, challengingly, over the rim of her glass. Again there was that very slight thickening, the barely noticeable slurring of the words indicating the load of liquor she was carrying.

"I see no problem . . . Claudine." He sat beside her and raised his glass. It was his turn to be challenging. "Well?"

She sighed. And then began talking as though nothing had interrupted her discourse on the emirate of Shahrud at the restaurant. "Naturally our small country has now assumed international importance. The limited amount of oil drilled on the landward side of this geological fault was always, in my uncle's day, sent overland to join the pipeline terminating at the port of Masqat, in Oman. The advantage of this was that Masqat gives directly onto the Indian Ocean . . . and we thus avoided the possible complications of a voyage around the Hormuz peninsula and into the gulf. Especially after the war between Iran and Iraq started."

"You talk like a company secretary!" Dean teased.

"I hope I do not look like one." She drained her glass and lay sensuously back against the leather cushions. With a sudden tightening of the throat, he saw from the soft shifting of flesh that she was naked beneath the stiff material of the robe.

"Not really," he said, "you look—"

"The military junta running the country now," she interrupted, "have threatened to change this system because of the new oil field that has been discovered. Umar al-Maziq, the colonel who heads the junta, is French-trained. But he feels it might be more advantageous to cut out the tankers taking oil to the West and pipe it direct from off-shore rigs to Russia. It would be a relatively simple route: across the gulf and up the fiftyth parallel, then through the Iranian mountains to the Caspian Sea, where it could join supplies from Soviet Turkestan sailing for the refineries at Baku."

It was warm in the big room. The liquor he had taken was beginning to affect Dean. *The hell with it,* he thought, *what kind of scenario is this chick setting up? What does she take me for? The big seduction routine must either be (a) because she's nympho and it's nothing to do with whatever proposition she has to offer; or (b) because she hopes to use it to influence me to accept that offer. In either case, if there's any seducing to be done . . . well, I'm the guy who'll be calling the play.*

He drained his own glass, set it carefully down on a marble occasional table, and leaned toward her. He laid a hand on her knee. "I have to tell you," he said thickly, "that you are just about the most exquisite, maddening, sexy, provocative lady I've met in the last thirty years—which is to say since I came out of short pants."

The robe fell away from her leg, exposing the inside of

a thigh as smooth as the marble of the occasional table. And as cool, he found, moving his hand. Claudine said, "To many countries, such an alteration in the balance of oil power would be inadmissible. Greece, Turkey, Israel, Pakistan, Britain, France, and even Egypt are among them. So is the United States. But none of them will dare to do anything about it."

She held out her glass. Like a sleepwalking man, Dean refilled it and his own, his eyes on the loose knot tying the belt at her waist.

"Even a secret counterrevolution," she said, "would be too dangerous if, like Cuba, it was financed from outside. The Soviet Union is already in Afghanistan. Umar al-Maziq is basically a Muslim nationalist like Khomeini, but he would not hesitate to ask for Russian help, which is freely offered to all revolutionaries, if he felt threatened by any kind of outside interference. And a Soviet presence in the emirates would—or at any rate could—extend through Saudi Arabia to Egypt and Qaddafi's Libya, landing the whole eastern half of the Mediterranean like a fish in the Communist net, and threatening Europe from the south. Yet if the new regime is not overthrown somehow, the results could be equally disastrous."

Dean drank and replaced his glass on the table. "There's something about your mouth . . ." he said.

"It is obvious, therefore, that a countercoup must be made—but it must be made from inside the country, so there will be no excuse for foreign interference, Eastern or Western." Claudine leaned farther back on the settee and closed her eyes as Dean's hand felt the warmth of her body through the robe where it hugged the pliant curve of her waist. She said, "Forces do exist in Shahrud which could pull off such a maneuver with one hundred percent chances of success. Our puritanical colonel is not popular with a great number of the people—especially those newly rich through the oil discovery. My cousin Hassan would be the natural choice as leader of such an uprising. Unfortunately, Hassan is in prison."

"That's tough," Dean said. His fingers were at the knot fastening the belt. "Honey, if only you knew how much I want—"

"All those who could organize and lead such a movement are in prison, the same prison. Umar al-Maziq has shut up his political adversaries in an old Arab fortress on the coast."

"My God, you have the most fantastic body!" The two ends of the belt had fallen apart. The edges of the robe gapped open. He was gazing at a subtle curve of belly, lightly tanned and as smooth as alabaster, at the shadowed triangle of silky black hair between her thighs.

"You! Oh, you!" She clasped her hands around the back of his head, her interlaced fingers pulling him down until his lips closed on the satin skin. "What we want you to do is get them out."

Dean's hands crept up her sides until he could cup the soft, taut weight of her breasts. The nipples were hard against his thumbs. Abruptly she pushed him away and rose to her feet, allowing the robe to slip from her shoulders to the floor.

Naked, she stared down at him. Her body was, as Dean had said, magnificent. "I think we would be more comfortable upstairs," she said. "There would be no need for you to take part in the actual coup. The released prisoners, together with sympathizers still at liberty, will provide a strong enough force to take over. All we wish you to do is organize a small raiding party that can fight its way into the fortress and set them free."

In the bedroom, inside a glass case on a plinth, was a priceless ritual vase excavated from the ruins of the city of Ourouk, in Mesopotamia. The face of a pagan goddess on one side of the vessel, carved three thousand years before the birth of Christ, regarded the huge divan with fathomless ambiguity.

She was—Dean thought, waking as the dawn light filtered through the drapes—no more enigmatic than the splendid creature sprawled sleeping beside him.

Later, when Claudine herself opened her eyes and rolled toward him, she put a hand up to touch his face and murmured, "You will do it, won't you?"

"Do it?"

"Organize an assault on the prison in Shahrud."

"Shall you be there when the raid is planned?" he asked.

She yawned, stretching like a cat and rubbing her eyes with the back of her hand. "Oh, yes," she sighed. "I shall be there."

"Of course I'll do it," said Dean.

Great Fiction From SIGNET

(0451)

- [ ] **THE RUNNING MAN by Richard Bachman.**
(115082—$2.50)*
- [ ] **SLEEPING BEAUTY by L.L. Greene.** (115481—$2.50)*
- [ ] **WIFE FOUND SLAIN by Caroline Crane.** (116143—$2.50)*
- [ ] **DEVIL'S EMBRACE by Catherine Coulter.** (118537—$2.95)*
- [ ] **MINOTAUR by Benjamin Tammuz.** (115821—$1.50)*
- [ ] **THE CURE by Len Goldberg.** (115090—$2.50)*
- [ ] **KINGDOM OF SUMMER by Gillian Bradshaw.**
(115503—$2.75)*
- [ ] **NEW BLOOD by Richard Salem.** (116515—$2.50)†
- [ ] **ROOFTOPS by Tom Lewis.** (117352—$2.95)*
- [ ] **GAMES OF CHANCE by Peter Delacourte.** (115104—$2.95)*
- [ ] **POSITION OF ULTIMATE TRUST by William Beechcroft.**
(115511—$2.50)*
- [ ] **LIONHEART! by Martha Rofheart.** (116178—$3.50)*
- [ ] **EYE OF THE MIND by Lynn Biederstadt.** (117360—$2.95)*
- [ ] **MY LADY HOYDEN by Jane Sheridan.** (115112—$2.95)*
- [ ] **TAURUS by George Wells.** (115538—$2.50)*
- [ ] **MIDAS by Piers Kelaart.** (116186—$2.50)†

*Prices slightly higher in Canada
†Not available in Canada

Buy them at your local bookstore or use this convenient coupon for ordering.

THE NEW AMERICAN LIBRARY, INC.,
P.O. Box 999, Bergenfield, New Jersey 07621

Please send me the books I have checked above. I am enclosing $_____
(please add $1.00 to this order to cover postage and handling). Send check
or money order—no cash or C.O.D.'s. Prices and numbers are subject to change
without notice.

Name_____

Address_____

City _____ State _____ Zip Code _____
Allow 4-6 weeks for delivery.
This offer is subject to withdrawal without notice.